FIVE STEPS AHEAD

Samantha Baca

Dark Shadows Series

Five Steps Ahead
Ten Seconds Too Late
Against The Clock

Contents

Contents

One

Hannah

Drip. Drip. Drip. The sound of leaking water filled the empty room that smelled of mildew from the dampness in the air. My head hung against my chest as I tried to lift it, the weight of it unbearable. Slowly I forced my head backwards and took a moment to rest as I opened my eyes and looked around. The room was dimly lit with concrete floors and windowless concrete walls with nothing around me other than the wooden chair I had been bound to with rope. I tried to pull at the restraints as the thick rope bit at my skin without giving.

I listened for the sound of the dripping water but couldn't hear it anymore. Did that mean that someone was there with me? My body trembled as I strained to hear any sounds that might tell me where I was or who was there. As I slowly tilted my head forward my eye caught a glimpse of something shimmering on the floor from the dim light that barely hung from the ceiling. I leaned forward as far as the rope would allow as I tried to see what it was. As my head dipped forward toward the ground, I heard the familiar dripping sound once more as I felt something wet trickle down my face. Beneath my chair was a puddle of blood. My blood.

Two

Hannah
21 Days Ago

"Do you want another cup of coffee, Han?" My mother peered at me over the top of the coffee carafe she held up as she awaited my answer.

"I'm good, thanks, mom." I shuffled the papers together that I had been working on for my final project and shoved them in the binder with the other items that I needed to complete before the weekend was over. I sighed as I unplugged my laptop and stuffed it in my backpack along with the binder before zipping it shut.

"Are you off already? I feel like you just got here." Disappointment crossed her face as she noticed my belongings packed up as I tucked my chair back under the wobbly kitchen table that she refused to get rid of. It had been in our family long before I was born and it was needless to say that it was literally on its last leg.

"I have to meet up with my group for our final presentation next week, then I need to finish the three term papers I have due. There's a lot to get done. I'm sorry, mom." I gently reached over and touched her arm before sliding on my backpack and bouncing it against my back as I tried to shift the contents inside to balance the weight. Once situated, I pulled my beanie on and adjusted it so my hair wouldn't be a mess later when I took it off. My hair was thick and full, and always a magnet for attracting static cling, especially with beanies, but it was too cold outside not to wear one.

"You work yourself so hard, I just don't want you to burn yourself out." She sighed as she smiled up at me, sympathy reflecting from her emerald green eyes that I was blessed to get from her. "I'm proud of your drive and ambition, I really am. My baby girl is going to do big things with her life."

I smiled back at her warm smile and leaned in to kiss her cheek. It killed me that I couldn't spend more time with her, even though we both knew that it would happen when I decided to go to school in the city. One of the hardest decisions I ever had to make in the 19 years I had been alive was leaving home right after my father died, and abandoning my mother so I could go to the college that I prayed for years to get accepted to.

The train ride back to the city was relatively quiet as people moved around me over the duration of the 2 hours it took before it reached my stop. I listened as the automated voice announced the next stop and put my notebook and pen back in my backpack as I stood up to get off on the next exit. I was thankful to have had the time on the train to work on one of my term papers but still felt overwhelmed with how much work I needed to get done over the next three weeks.

The ground was snow packed from the recent storm that had moved in while I was at my mom's and I was thankful that it cushioned the slippery ice beneath. Trekking through

New York City in the winter was a skill that I hadn't fully developed just yet and never understood the women who would breeze past me in bad weather without losing their footing. Granted I had always been a clumsy person so I couldn't blame it ALL on the weather.

I walked the few blocks to the coffee shop where I was meeting my group and slipped inside the door as a couple was heading out. The wind had started to pick up and I was anxious to get inside and let my body warm up for a few minutes before I had to dive into another school project. I'd learned that the majority of the professors preferred group projects which was a big change compared to high school. I wasn't a fan of working in groups and hated that I was socially awkward. But then again, wasn't your freshman year in college supposed to be all about social awkwardness?

The coffee shop was busy with people at every table and a line that wound its way to the door. I pulled off the brown knit beanie and let my silky brown hair fall down to the center of my back. A wave from the back of the room caught my eye as I made my way to the back table where my group was already sitting. I smiled as I made my way over and stopped in the corner to pull off my backpack and jacket before sitting down to join them.

"Hey, Hannah." Amber pulled a seat around from behind her for me to sit.

"Thanks." I smiled as I slid into the hard metal chair and scooted myself up to the table. Our group was small, only five of us, which helped keep my anxiety down. Amber and

I had all of the same classes together, which I was thankful for, so we spent a lot of time together. I looked around the table, noticing that we were still waiting for Joel. I sighed a breath of relief that I wasn't the last one who had kept everyone waiting.

"How was your mom?" Amber asked quietly as the other two from our group talked about a project they were working on for another class.

"She's good. It was nice to see her but this weekend just felt like it went by so fast. I don't feel like I even saw her much while I was there, we were both so busy." I rubbed my hands together while I worked to warm myself up from the brutal cold I had just been in.

"Is she still working at the diner?"

"Yeah. And now she started a second job working at a coffee shop in the morning. She's literally working 10-12 hours a day between both jobs. I wish I could help her with the bills but I can barely afford things here." My chest rose and fell with the heaviness of the burden that I knew my mom had taken on after my dad died. He didn't have life insurance and they were barely getting by when he first got sick. Things just kept getting worse as the months went on with medical bills piling up and my mom having to miss work to be with my dad.

My heart pulled in my chest and I blinked rapidly to force away the tears that threatened to spill over. I missed my dad more than I could have ever imagined I would have. When we found out that he was terminally ill we tried to brace ourselves for what it really meant but no one told me that I would have to learn to live with a heart that was missing a huge piece of it.

Amber offered a sympathetic smile as she patted my hand. Joel made his way over to the table as he squeezed in between the tables and spun a chair around backward before plopping himself into it. He grinned as he tugged off the Yankees beanie that was plastered to his head. He was always late and honestly, I was surprised that he had even bothered to show up.

The hours went by quickly and I glanced up to look around the coffee shop as I noticed it was almost 7:00. I still had a ton of studying to do and had this overwhelming feeling that I would always be behind in this class after struggling through it all semester. Amber looked over and studied my face as I sorted through the notes I had taken and highlighted a few things that I would need to study before the final exam.

"You okay?" Her voice was gentle as she nodded to the notepad that was almost covered in yellow highlighter.

"Yeah, I'm just trying to wrap my head around everything for the final exam. Professor Wright pulled me aside last week and warned me that I needed to do well on the final exam or I might not pass the class." I let out a heavy sigh as I remembered our conversation as I was leaving class.

"Do you have a quick minute, Hannah?"

"Sure."

"I'll make this quick and to the point. I know that it's your first year in college and things feel different than high school, but things move quickly here and it's very easy to go under before you even realize you're in trouble. My advice is to find a study group or a mentor on campus and get the help that you need so you do well in my class. Right now, I don't see you passing unless you really push yourself to learn the material."

"You'll do just fine, Hannah. You're a smart girl." Amber smiled reassuringly. I wasn't the type of person who had ever been in a study group but I had decided to take his advice and luckily, Amber invited me to join the one that she was in. There was so much more work involved and it made me wonder if I was actually putting in the right amount of effort on my own once I saw how much effort these study sessions required.

I shook my head to try to clear away some of the frustration and get in the right mind set for the somewhat blind date I had agreed to meet here after we were done. I didn't date often and I would usually prefer to go home and freshen up and get ready before a date but with my busy schedule these days there just wasn't any time for that. Amber had talked me into getting on Single2Mingle which was supposed to be a more modern dating website that focused on building a relationship from a friendship. I hadn't been in the city very long before the school semester started so I hadn't made any friends. Amber thought the app would be great for helping me make friends and possibly find a hook up or two.

Amber's eyes locked onto mine as I scanned the room for the guy I was supposed to be meeting. I watched as she wiggled her eyebrows and subtly nodded behind me. Slowly I turned my head as I looked over my shoulder to see a guy sitting at a table a few feet away from us. His head was down as he looked at his phone, his sandy blonde hair falling across his forehead. I couldn't see his face but the black leather jacket fit his body in a way that I could see the definition of his muscles beneath it. A wave of giddiness flowed through me as I waited for him to look up so I could see if I recognized his face.

I felt my phone buzz on the table and looked down to find a message alert on the screen. Excitement coursed through me as I hoped it was my date telling me he was there and to look behind me. I still hadn't gotten a look at the guy's face but part of me hoped it was him.

Disappointment hit me as I read the message that he was running late. I looked at Amber and shook my head no. She gave a half smile as she packed her things into her backpack and stood to leave as she waited for someone to pass by so she could get out. The rest of the group had started to pack up their things and were leaving as well as I rifled through my purse to find my makeup bag. Since he was running late, I had a few minutes to try to freshen up.

I quickly applied a light peach colored lip gloss and added a quick touch of powder to freshen up my makeup. My finger ran under my eyelashes as I attempted to wipe away a rogue eyelash when I felt dark brown eyes watching me in the mirror. My eyes made contact with his and for a moment I got lost in his look. There was a pull that I had never felt before and part of me wanted to go over and talk to him and forget about the date that I was actually waiting for.

"Hannah?" A deep male voice startled me as I jumped in my seat and slammed the compact shut. My hand went to my chest as I looked up at the guy standing in front of me. Tall, husky build, wavy jet-black hair, and a letterman jacket that barely fit the width of his body. He looked exactly like his online picture.

"That's me." I stood up to shake his hand as he pulled me into a bear hug and almost knocked the breath out of me.

"Of course it is, beautiful green eyes and brown hair, with a sexy little body- just like in your profile picture," he whispered in my ear, still holding me in a tight grip.

Out of the corner of my eye I saw the guy behind us lower his head as he tried to stifle a laugh. I waited until he let me out of his embrace before sitting back down and waiting for him to take his seat. He stood behind a chair with his hands on the back of it as he looked at me expectedly.

"Everything okay?" I asked as I looked at him with confusion. He created a nervousness inside of me that I couldn't put my finger on. Maybe it was his over the top aggressive greeting or the fact that he was reluctant to sit down like a normal person.

"Yeah, aren't we going to go get coffee?" He nodded to the line that still wrapped around the tables and was now outside the door.

"Um, yeah, we can do that. I just don't want to lose this table since it's so busy in here." I watched as he looked around, completely oblivious to the number of people there until I mentioned it.

"Oh. Wow. Yeah, one of us should stay and hold the table then I guess." He waited as he watched me to see if I was going to offer to go get the coffee for us. Now I wasn't one of those women who believed that men had to pay for everything and do everything for women, but I did expect a LITTLE bit of romance. A small gesture of some sort. For Pete's sake, it was a $4 coffee, not a steak and lobster dinner. I waited in my seat as I thought about ways to end the date so we didn't have to decide who was going to go get the coffee when I saw him shrug his shoulders and look at me.

"Alright, I'll go stand in the line. Do you want just regular coffee or do you want something fancy?"

"Regular coffee is fine, thank you." I replied through somewhat clenched teeth. This was the worst start of a date I had ever been on and I was kicking myself for listening to Amber when she encouraged me to give him a chance.

"Cool, I'll just tell them I'm with my grandma. They always give old people free coffee." He patted the back of the chair as he walked off and stood at the back of the line.

I slumped back in my chair and tapped my fingers along the table as I contemplated ways to escape without being noticed which was downright impossible given there was only the one entrance at the front, where he was standing, and the emergency exit in the back which would sound off an alarm if I opened the door. I could just see the headline now:

College student flees coffee shop using emergency exit to get away from cheap date!

The line moved quickly as I continued to think of ways to get out of this awful date when I felt someone watching me. Out of the corner of my eye I could swear that the guy behind me was still watching me but as I slowly turned my head in his direction his eyes were glued to his phone while he slowly lifted his coffee cup to his lips. I must be desperate if I thought he was watching me when he was really just there to drink his coffee and look at whatever held his attention on his phone.

A few minutes passed by as Chet made his way back to the table with our drinks. If ever there was anyone clumsier than me, it had to be Chet. He stumbled over the leg of a chair as he tried to maneuver through the packed maze and sat the drinks down on the table with so much force that the coffee in my cup sloshed around and spilled from the closed to-go lid.

"So, Chet, tell me something about yourself." I popped the top off of the coffee and wiped the cup down with a napkin. Deep breaths, I reminded myself as I flicked the sweetener packets he had brought with him before tearing them open and pouring them in as I waited for an answer.

"What do you want to know?" He wrapped his mouth around the plastic straw and pulled a large drink of his frozen coffee through before reaching up and grabbing his head.

"Ahhhh…brain freeze!"

I had to try to control myself as I fought to roll my eyes for fear that they would get stuck in the back of my head. I continued to stir my coffee while I waited for him to recover from the trauma he was suffering at the hands of a $15 drink that was mostly ice. A few minutes passed by with him grunting and holding his head and with each minute my interest in continuing the date faded.

"Woah. Talk about a headache. That one is gonna linger for a bit." He pushed the drink to the side as if its presence offended him.

"Okay, something about myself…ummm…I don't know? What do you want to know? "His face wore the same pouty look that I had seen every time someone asked a child what they learned in school that day. This was definitely not turning out to be a good date.

"Do you have any hobbies? Any extracurricular activities?" I tried to feign interest as I brought the cup to my lips and took a sip of the hot fluid that was already ten times better than this date.

"I don't really do much. School. Play football. Hook up with girls." He smiled after he said the last sentence and looked at me. "A LOT of girls, if you know what I mean."

I couldn't tell if my eyes actually got stuck in the back of my head or if they just felt like they were. How had I ended up on this date? Why hadn't I said no? Then I remembered that I agreed to it because there weren't any other guys wanting to meet me and I had started to feel a little desperate. I looked away, disgusted with myself for still sitting here with this idiot, when I saw him open the dating app on his phone and swipe right. Seriously? He was accepting another date while sitting in front of me? I took a deep breath as I drank the last of my coffee and sat it down on the table.

"Wow. That's great. Really great." I slid my cell phone across the table and tucked it into my pocket. "I'll be right back, I'm going to use the restroom." I stood up before he could say anything and discreetly picked up my backpack as I made my way through the few tables at the back and made my way into the bathroom. It was small but had 3 stalls and two sinks along the vanity with a full-length mirror. Suddenly I didn't feel well and bent over as I splashed my face with cold water.

The room started spinning as my body fought to stay standing. I tried to hold on to the counter as my mind scrambled to make sense of what was happening. I was fine until a few minutes ago. Until I drank the coffee. Panic filled me as I tried to figure out what to do before it was too late. I tried to will myself to reach down and dig my cell phone out of my pocket but I knew that if I let go of the counter, I would fall. My legs felt like they were weighted down and unable to move. Quickly it spread through the rest of my body until I had no choice but to let go as everything turned black around me.

Three

Max

20 Days Ago

"Ma, I don't have time to track her down right now. I'm at work." I ran my hand through my hair in frustration as I stood over my desk, listening to my mom carry on about my youngest sister. "I get it, she's mad and she left. She'll be back, you know that."

I shifted my weight as my mom started rambling on in Italian about Elena and their fight over Elena's new boyfriend that my mom already despised. It wasn't anything new. Elena was the baby of the family and dad always let her get away with everything, much to the frustration of my mom. After seven children, six of them girls, my dad found it was better not to fight about much when it came to Italian American women. Couldn't say that I blamed him.

"Ma, listen, I really have to go. I'll come by later and check on things. Okay?" I grabbed my cell phone off the desk to see Elena's name on the screen. "No ma, I can't just put a warrant out for his arrest because you don't like the guy." I slid my finger over the button to answer my cell phone as I tried to end the call with my mom. "Yeah, okay, I'll see you tonight. Love you too, ma."

I let out a deep breath as I lifted the phone to my ear, waiting to hear my sister's high pitched shriek that she always had when she was upset.

"Hey Leni." I started to pull the phone from my ear in anticipation when I noticed how quiet it was on the other line. A shiver ran down my spine as my gut told me something was wrong.

"Help me." Her voice was a soft whisper but there was no doubt that it was Elena.

"What's wrong?" I sat in my chair and pulled myself into the desk as I unlocked my computer and pulled up the cell phone tracking screen. I could hear faint movements in the background as she stayed silent.

"Leni, where are you?" I asked quietly to make sure whoever she was with didn't hear me.

"I don't know. It's dark. And cold." Her voice was so quiet that each word almost broke off before she could get it out.

"Try to look around and see if anything looks familiar or if you see anything that you can tell me about." I coaxed her as I entered her phone number in the tracking system and waited as it tried to locate it.

"Who's there with you?" I probed as I stared at the spinning circle as the system continued to try to locate her. My years in law enforcement taught me that if it didn't pop up within a few seconds, it wasn't going to pop up. My mom hated that I went into law enforcement at the tender age of 21 and even 8 years later, she didn't hate it any less.

"I think I'm by myself now." I could hear the fear in her voice and every part of me wished I could figure out where she was and go and save her. "I'm scared Max."

"It's gonna be okay. We're gonna work through this together." I reached for a pen and the notepad on the corner of my desk so I could take down as many notes as possible when I saw the pop-up window confirm no trace was found on her phone. My anger started to rise as quickly as my anxiety as I tried to get out of my own head and think through things like the detective I was supposed to be.

"Are you able to walk around?"

"Yeah."

"Okay, that's good. Do you see any windows? Any light coming through from outside?"

"There aren't any windows. Just a light hanging from the ceiling." Her voice was still low and I wondered if she thought someone was there.

"Keep walking, tell me what you see as you walk."

"There's nothing, Max. It's concrete walls and a concrete floor."

My mind tried desperately to remember when my mom had said that Elena took off so I could try to figure out how much time had passed and narrow down a possible location. It sounded like she was in an abandoned warehouse but there were a ton in our neighborhood so that didn't help much.

"Do you see any-"

"Shhhh!"

I froze as I tried to listen to what was happening as she urgently shushed me before the phone went eerily quiet. Something had startled her and freaked her out and I needed to know what it was. I waited patiently with my ear pressed as hard as possible to the phone.

"No! No! Please! Don't!" I could hear commotion as Elena begged in the background and my stomach clenched as I listened to her. My jaw tightened while my knuckles turned white as my grip on the phone increased. There was a loud sound that I couldn't make out followed by footsteps. I prayed that it was Elena coming back to the phone and that she had fought off whoever was there. I held my breath as I waited for her voice when I heard someone pick up the phone.

"Wrong number." A low voice growled into the phone before it was disconnected.

"Son of a bitch!" I slammed my phone down on my desk as those around me looked up, startled. My body was on edge as adrenaline forced its way through me. I ran a hand down my face over the scruff of my jaw as I tried to calm myself down. There was no way I could just sit there when my baby sister was missing and in trouble. I grabbed my things before I checked out for the day with my team and made my way to my mom's. I hoped she had the answers that I was looking for.

I had been at my parents' house for an hour and felt frustrated that it had taken so long for everyone to sit down and just listen so I didn't have to keep repeating myself. By now all 5 of my sisters and my parents were sitting at the table as they listened to what I had been trying to tell them.

"That's all that I know, so if you have any information about where she's been, who she's been hanging out with or talking to, or what time she left last night - now is the time to tell me." I looked around the dining room table. Time was ticking and I needed them to focus before we lost more valuable time. Every second mattered at this point.

My mom sat at the table with her hands folded in front of her while my dad gently rubbed her shoulders. I knew this was hard for her and that the amount of guilt she had from their fight was blocking her ability to remember anything that had happened before then. There was mumbling around me as my sisters talked quietly in small groups, working to get the information that I had asked for. There were plans to meet up with neighbors and check in with her friends to see if anyone had talked to her but I knew that still wasn't going to get me the information that I needed.

I continued to watch my phone for any calls or messages from Elena but it had been silent ever since our call had been disconnected. My department had started working on the case and still hadn't been able to get an exact location on her cell phone. I knew they were working every angle they had but it didn't help the helpless feeling that continued to eat at me. My head was pounding from the stress of the day, the intensity getting worse from the constant noise in the room. I needed to get away from everything for a few minutes and just clear my head. Allow my instincts to take over. I wandered through the house as everyone stayed focused on their conversations in the kitchen and made my way up to Elena's room.

My parents' house was small for the number of people that lived in it over the years. Growing up we always shared bedrooms until I reached the preteen years and my dad insisted that I needed my own space. They had converted the attic into a room for me and the 6 girls split the two bedrooms while my parents slept in the smaller room of the 3-bedroom house. Over the years as my sisters grew up and started their own lives, they moved out and everyone would shift accordingly. Elena and the 2 younger girls were the last 3 to still live at home and Elena had decided to take the attic so she could have her own space once she started her freshman year of college.

I climbed the ladder that led to the attic and looked around the small space that had once been my sacred space. Clothes were tossed about the back of the chair that sat in front of the makeshift desk holding her laptop. There was a pile of papers and notepads to the left and an empty coffee mug to the right of the computer. Other than that, it was pretty clean. I sat on the edge of the bed as I quickly flicked through the papers, hoping to find something that might be helpful.

Notes from her psychology classes and a to do list for her upcoming finals made up the pile as I sat them back down where I found them. I let out a frustrated sigh as I picked up her laptop and opened it, surprised that she didn't have it set up to require a password to get into it. I had nagged her for years about making sure she had a password to make sure no one could get in, and for once I was thankful that she hadn't listened.

The screen glowed brightly at me as I looked at the login page to her school email account. She had logged out of it but hadn't closed the window. I looked around and found a few other open windows as well, all of them school related with search results related to psychology. I was about to close the laptop when I looked down and saw a chat text box in the bottom right corner of the screen.

I moved the mouse over and clicked on the button to enlarge it to full screen as I scrolled up to the top of the messages. Along the top was a banner for an online dating website, a new one that I wasn't familiar with. I personally hadn't used any online dating websites but I knew that a few of my sisters had used them. I leaned back against the wall as I pulled out my phone to get a few pictures of the screen in case I needed it later for the investigation.

My sister's user name was shown as EROM31802 with a picture of her from her senior trip to DC last year as her profile picture. There was a lengthy conversation between her and a user named 5StepsAhead that started last night around 10:30. There wasn't a profile picture for the other account so I assumed it was a guy, though I didn't know why she would be talking to a guy that didn't have a profile picture. Had I not taught her anything?

I scrolled through the messages after taking down the information I needed and felt disappointed when there wasn't much in the conversation that was helpful. A lot of basic questions about how school was going and if they were ready for winter break. Maybe this was someone from one of her classes? But why would she be talking to them on a dating website? Why not email or text? From the tone of the messages it didn't seem like she knew this person very well, but I could be wrong. I was almost to the end when I saw a message from Elena, complaining about the fight with my mom. 5StepsAhead had been quick to respond to her, offering comfort as he confirmed she didn't deserve to be controlled by anyone anymore, she was a strong independent woman. Elena responded with a winking emoji followed by a few heart emojis as the guy continued to compliment her. My heart started to race as I continued to read their conversation and dropped once I read the last few messages.

5StepsAhead: Why don't I meet you for a cup of coffee so we can talk? Maybe I can cheer you up?

EROM31802: I don't know, it's getting kind of late. I don't know if anything is still open.

5StepsAhead: There's a coffeehouse right there on the corner of Union and Second street. They stay open 24 hours. I can meet you there in 15 minutes.

EROM31802: Okay, I'm on my way.

I took a picture of the screen with the date and time stamp that showed 10:47 last night and forwarded it to my partner as I closed the laptop and put it back where I found it. She had left to meet someone from an online dating app and I had no idea if she actually knew this person already or not. I wouldn't imagine that she was the kind of person to go meet a random stranger that late at night but Elena was always the most unpredictable out of all of my sisters. I sighed as I left her room the way I found it and was about to make my way back to the office to work through the new information I found when I got a call to head to the hospital to talk to a college student who had been given a date rape drug at a coffee house last night. I was about to protest and tell them to find someone else to do it when I heard the tone in my partners voice as she added that the victim had met the guy through an online dating website. My stomach churned as I made my way to the hospital to see if there was any connection to my sister.

<u>F</u>our

Hannah

20 Days Ago

I woke up to a pounding headache as I looked around to find the machine that was making the god-awful beeping noise. My mind was foggy as I had no idea why I was in the hospital. I looked down and found an IV in my wrist and a hospital band with my information on it. Why was I in the hospital? How did I get here? I felt my anxiety rise as I started to freak out. My breathing quickened as I struggled to take a deep breath which caused another alarm to start beeping.

A few minutes later a nurse walked in and smiled as she went to the cluster of machines next to me and looked at the screens.

"How are you feeling? Any pain?" Her voice was calm though there was concern in her eyes as she looked me over.

"Why am I in here?" My voice was shaky as I held onto the side bed rail and looked up at her.
"You were brought in last night. You passed out in the bathroom of a coffee shop and a woman found you and called 911."

I stayed silent as I tried to figure out why she was giving me the look she was giving me. It felt like she was waiting for me to confess to something but I had no idea what. I didn't remember much after meeting Chet last night but I did remember getting up and going to the bathroom because the date was going so poorly.

"Is there anyone that I can call for you?" She pressed a few buttons on the monitors as she made notes on a small piece of paper she had pulled out of the pocket of her scrubs.

"My friend, Amber. Her phone number is in my cell phone." I looked around and realized that I had no idea where my personal belongings had gone and whether I even had a cell phone anymore. The nurse walked over to a closet and opened the door to pull out my backpack and the clothes I had been wearing last night. She sat both piles on the foot of the bed as I patted the pockets of my jeans for the cell phone. I was relieved when I felt something hard and reached in and pulled out my phone.

"I can go ahead and call her." I offered as I held up my phone.

"Sounds good." She gathered my belongings and put them back into the closet before walking out and closing the door.

I pulled up Amber's name in my contacts and was about to press send when I heard a knock on the door. The door opened and I had to blink twice, not trusting my eyes when I saw the most drop dead gorgeous man walk in. The olive colored skin. The strong jaw line that framed his perfect face and full lips. The golden brown eyes that studied me as if I was an animal in the wild. He looked like he could be a model, rocking the tousled hair look and making jeans and a gray T-shirt look beyond sexy. My heart skipped a beat as he came closer.

"I'm Max, NYPD." He approached the side of my bed with caution as he lifted his shirt for me to see the badge that was attached to his belt. A sliver of well-defined muscles greeted me as I smiled back at him.

"How are you feeling this morning, Hannah?" He pulled out the stool that had been slid under the sink and sat on it as he studied me. I felt nervous that I still didn't remember what had happened last night and now all of a sudden I had NYPD visiting me in the hospital.

"I have a terrible headache and I'm still not sure what's going on or why I'm here."

"Well, hopefully we can help each other figure that out." He let out a deep breath as he looked down at the file he held in front of him. "Can you tell me what you do remember about yesterday?"

"I can try. Where do you want me to start?"

"Let's start with the morning. Then just walk me through your day. People you saw. People you spoke to. Anyone that you had contact with."

"I started the day at my mom's house. She lives in Hudson. I took the train back into town around 1 and got back a little after 3. I met with a group from school at Java Jazz

Coffee Shop around 3:30 and then met a date around 7:15 at the same coffee shop. We didn't spend that much time together, maybe 30-45 minutes? Then I excused myself to use the restroom and I don't remember anything after that." My hands trembled as I felt embarrassed that I didn't know what happened after that. My eyes looked up from under my eyelashes as I watched him write down what I had told him.

"Can you tell me about the guy you were meeting?" His tone was soft, like the tone you used when you had bad news to give someone.

"His name was Chet. I met him through an online dating app. We didn't talk much so I didn't know much about him other than he went to NYU, like me."

"What dating app was it?"

"It's called Single2Mingle."

"Would you be able to pull up his online dating profile for me?"

"Sure." I reached for my phone that was sitting in my lap and unlocked it. Once I had his profile pulled up, I handed the phone to Max and watched as he wrote down some more information.

"I apologize, but why exactly are you here?" I asked, hoping it didn't sound as rude as I was worried it did after I had already said it. He smiled as he closed the file and clicked his pen before sliding it into his back pocket.

"After you were brought in unresponsive last night, they did some blood work to try to figure out what happened. The blood work showed you had Rohypnol in your system." He looked at me with one eyebrow raised as the blood drained from my face.

"Oh no…no no no no. I don't do drugs! I can barely afford ramen noodles!" I held my hands up in defense as I realized that they thought I came in passed out last night because I was on drugs. And now NYPD was there, ready to take me in for drug use. I lowered my hands and shook my head as I started to cry.

"Hannah, I'm not sure that you understand." His voice was sympathetic as I looked at him through blurry tears.

"You think I'm a drug addict." I sobbed as I tried to get my words out. "And now…now you're here to arrest me." I lowered my head into my hands as I cried harder.

"You're not under arrest." He took a deep breath as he rolled the stool closer to the bed and folded his hands on top of the file folder.

"I'm not?" My face was red and splotchy as I looked around for a tissue to wipe my nose with before snot ran down my face. Between the two of us, I was not the attractive one at this point.

"You're not." He smiled a tight smile. "I'm here because we have a missing person case that also deals with someone who she met through the same online dating website."

"A missing person? Did they meet up with Chet also?" Confusion was setting in as none of this was making any sense.

"We don't know yet. But given that you had a date rape drug in your system while on a date with someone you met from the same website, we want to look into every possibility."

"Date rape drug?" My eyes grew big as I now understood what he was getting at. No wonder I couldn't remember what had happened.

"It's usually slipped into a drink. The victim rarely knows it's there until it's too late and already in their system. Can you tell me what all you had to drink last night and if Chet had access to your drink?"

"Coffee. I had already been there with my study group but had been drinking from my water bottle. He offered coffee and had been the one to wait in line and get it."

"Were you able to see him the entire time?"

"I wasn't watching." I let out a breath of frustration. Not with the questions but with myself for being so stupid. "Did he have access to your drink?"

"Yes."

"Are you willing to file a police report and give us a statement about what happened?"

"Yes."

A nurse walked in as he stood up and scooted the stool back under the sink.

"Thank you for your time today. An officer will be by shortly to have you complete the paperwork and to take your statement, but if you need anything in the meantime, here's my card. If you remember anything that might be helpful- call my cell." He extended a business card to me as I reached up and took it.

My mind was still trying to process everything that had just happened. The missing girl. The date rape drug. Things could have been so much worse than they were so I tried to stay focused on the fact that nothing else could possibly go wrong. Just as I was about to pick up my phone to call Amber, I saw a voicemail alert on my phone. I didn't feel it vibrate and the number on the call log showed as restricted.

I pressed the play button as I held the phone to my ear and listened.

Hannah, this is Claire at Ferguson and Wales. We've been waiting for you to show up for work today, however since you still have not arrived and it is 3 hours past your start time, we are accepting your no call no show resignation. Please call me to set up a time to come in to collect your personal belongings and final check.

My stomach dropped as I listened to the voicemail again. Okay, so I was wrong. Things could get a lot worse.

Five

Max
17 Days Ago

The bar was quiet for a Thursday evening as I waited for
Trevor to meet me. He had been my best friend since we
were in elementary school and felt like the brother I never
had. When I first told him that Elena was missing 3 days
ago, he hit the ground running and stopped everything
he was doing to help me find her. I hadn't slept since her
disappearance, and there had been no leads, which made it
worse. There didn't seem to be a link between the guy she
met online and the one that Hannah had met. Frustration
continued to eat away at me.

The door opened and the afternoon sunlight filtered
through the dingy dive bar as Trevor gave a quick nod to
acknowledge Jon, the bartender, before making his way
to the high-top table where I was sitting. This was our go
to spot and we had been coming here so long that Jon no
longer bothered asking what we were drinking, he just
brought our usual and kept them coming until we nodded
that we were finished.

"What's up, man?" Trevor gave a quick pat to my back
before sliding out of his black leather jacket and hanging
it on the back of his chair as he sat down. He had perfect

features that drove women crazy and made me think he should be featured on the cover of some cheesy romance novel. His eyes scanned the room as he smiled at me and ran a hand through his already tousled hair as some blonde in the corner lowered her head and blushed.

I gave him the same look I had been giving him for years when I would catch him flirting with a girl who was barely legal.

"What?" He laughed as he leaned back for Jon to sit his beer in front of him. "I can't help it if she finds me attractive." His smile spread across his face as he looked past me to make eye contact with her.

"One of these days you're gonna be calling me to come bail you out of jail and I'm gonna say- I told you so!" I laughed as he took a drink of his beer, pretending he didn't hear what I said.

"So any news on Leni?" His eyes met mine and I could see the anguish mirrored in his that I felt in mine.

"Nothing. They're coming up empty with every lead. Since I can't work the case because she's my sister, I feel even more out of the loop. And it doesn't help that my mom is up my ass, calling fifty times a day to see if I've heard anything." I lowered my head as I spun my empty beer bottle around on the worn-out cardboard coaster. I wasn't sure what the purpose was for the coaster given that the table was in worse shape.

"I've been asking around the coffee shop and the other businesses close by. No one remembers anything." He sighed and took another swig. "Anything come from the online dating stuff? Were you guys able to get any information from the profile?"

"Very little. It wasn't the same guy that met up with the other victim. Apparently, a lot of people use this app in that neighborhood and meet up at that coffee shop. We're still looking into it though."

"What about her cell phone? Was Mindy able to track it after all?" There was a desperation in his voice that I could relate to. It was the same desperation that had clung to me like a wet T-shirt for the past 3 days. Mindy was my partner and had taken the lead on this case for me. We had been working together for the last 2 years and she had met my family several times, attending a few of my sisters' high school graduations so this felt personal to her as well.

"The last place they were able to accurately trace the call was a few blocks north of the coffee shop. There are a lot of businesses in that area and Elena described a vacant warehouse type of building, which there aren't any in that area. So, we still have no idea how far away she is from where her phone was tracked to." I ran my hand down the thick scruff of my jaw from the beard that had voluntarily decided to sprout when I didn't make time to shave this week.

I felt my phone vibrate on the table and looked down, praying that it was Elena or at least an update on her. I unlocked the screen to find a text message from an unknown number.

Unknown: Hi, Detective Romano, this is Hannah. We met at the hospital. I wanted to see if you had a few minutes to talk? I think someone might be stalking me. Strange things have been happening since I got home from the hospital and I don't know how else to explain it.

I felt Trevor's eyes on me as I reread the text again. I shook my head no quickly to confirm that it wasn't about Elena as my fingers started to reply.

Max: Hannah, are you safe where you are? I'm on my way to meet you, confirm the address where you'll be and I'll head your way now.

I waited as I saw the dots bounce across the screen as she typed. A message popped up confirming that she was safe and that she was in her apartment. I looked over the address and knew where it was.

"Hey, I gotta go. The girl from the hospital thinks someone might be stalking her so I need to go check it out." I slid a twenty dollar bill onto the table and tucked it under my beer as Trevor finished his drink.

"Want me to go with you?"

"Sure, let's get going. She's a couple blocks away, I told her I was on my way." We walked toward the exit and waved at Jon on our way out. The sun had started to set which made the temperature outside feel twenty degrees colder than it actually was. I pulled my black beanie down further on my head as I shoved my hands into my overcoat for warmth. Trevor and I walked in silence the short distance to

Hannah's apartment. As we stood outside her door I thought about sending her a message to let her know that Trevor was with me but then decided it wasn't official police business so it shouldn't be an issue.

A few seconds later her door swung open and her eyes were wide, a fear on her face that I didn't remember seeing at the hospital. The tension from her jolted me to move my hand to my gun, unsure of what the real threat was.

"Hannah, are you okay?" I asked cautiously as I tried to peer around her to look into the apartment for any sign of a threat.

"Um, yeah. I think so?" Her voice was low as her dark green eyes scanned the empty hallway behind us. I met Trevor's eyes as he subtly shrugged, as he quickly scanned the hallway, not seeing anything odd on the way up to her apartment either.

"Do you mind if we come in?" I kept my voice calm and looked directly at her as I tried to get her to make eye contact. Once she did, I saw the tension in her shoulders ease some as she stepped back and held the door open for us.

"This is my friend Trevor," I nodded behind me as we stepped into the small space of her studio apartment. "We were meeting for a drink when I got your text. I hope you don't mind him coming along."

"Not at all," she mumbled as she closed the door and stood by the kitchen counter. I didn't know what had happened before we got there but whatever it was had her spooked.

"Are you sure everything is okay?" I probed. "Your message said that you thought someone might be stalking you?"

"Yeah. It's been a few days and things have just been weird since I got home from the hospital." She sighed as she looked over at us as we stayed standing by the door. "You can sit if you want to." She nodded to the couch that lined the wall with a window behind it.

To the right of the couch was a bed and a dresser, to the left was the kitchen with a small island that had 2 barstools. There was no room for a kitchen table or chairs, the full-size refrigerator taking up the majority of the room in the small kitchen. I looked around, taking it all in and found a door along the wall that was closed. My guess was that it was the bathroom, a very small one at that.

"Can you tell me about what has been happening?" I pulled a pen and a small notepad from the inside pocket of my coat and sat on the couch as Trevor sat next to me.

"It started out as little things. Things that were just odd but could have been from me being too tired or stressed with finals. When I first got back from the hospital, I had put my backpack on the floor by the door, it's where I always put it. After I took a shower, I came in here and it was on the floor by the couch. The next day, on Tuesday, I went to my work to give them a doctor's note from the hospital to try to get my job back and when I got back, the window was open. That's when I started to get freaked out. I NEVER open that window. For one- it's really old and I worry that it would break if I did open it. And two, it's like 18 degrees outside- there's no reason to open it." She took a deep breath as she walked to a barstool and sat down. Her hair was pulled up into a messy knot on her head, a few short strands of brown hair falling loosely around her face. It reminded me of Elena and how she wore her long brown hair in a similar knot on her head as well. My chest hurt at the thought so I tried to redirect my thoughts and focus on the information she was giving me.

"After I closed the window, I looked through the apartment and obviously didn't find anyone. I mean, it's pretty small- where would anyone hide?" She expanded her arms out as she showed the size of the room. "I'm on the top floor, it's not like anyone is coming and going on the fire escape without drawing attention from the apartments below. So, I checked the locks again, made sure the door and window were secured, and took a shower. After my shower I realized that I needed to do laundry so I gathered everything up and went to the laundry mat down the block. I came home and put away my clean laundry before I left to meet my group for a study session. When I got back, there was a black lacy bra and matching thong laying on my bed." Her eyes looked past us at the bed as I watched the color drain from her face.

"Does anyone besides you have a key to the apartment?" I asked as I finished writing down the last note about the lingerie.

"No, just my mom. But she lives 2 hours away and wouldn't have any reason to do any of this."

"Is there anything else that has happened since Tuesday?"

"Yesterday I had my first day back at work and when I got

home the door was unlocked. Not open. Just unlocked. I looked around and nothing was missing so I don't think someone broke in to steal from me. I checked the apartment again and didn't find anyone. I ended up pushing the coffee table against the door so I would hear it if anyone tried to open it last night while I slept."

Her eyes looked tired and now I could see why. I hadn't been able to sleep knowing that my sister was missing and she wasn't getting any sleep because someone seemed to be getting in her apartment and messing with her head.

"And then today..." Her voice trailed off as she looked at the counter beside her. "There was this note under my door when I got home from work this evening. That's when I decided to text you."

She picked up a white envelope and handed it to me. I sat the notepad and pen on the coffee table in front me as I took the envelope and pulled out a single piece of paper that had been ripped out of a textbook. It was clear it had been ripped by the jagged lines and the uneven shape. In black marker were the words:

You should be careful who you meet online.

I lowered the note and looked over at Hannah as I laid the note on the coffee table for Trevor to read. He knew better than to touch it as it was now evidence.

"Do you know who would have sent this to you?" I asked as I nodded at the letter. She shook her head no as she got down from the barstool and walked over to her backpack. I watched as she sat it on the island and pulled a textbook out. She walked over to us and opened it to a page that had been torn and was missing a chunk in the same exact shape as the note sitting on the coffee table in front of me.

"No, but they tore the page out of my textbook." She sighed heavily. "I hadn't even made it to that yet. Bastard."

I had to bite the inside of my cheek to keep from laughing as I saw the faint smile pull at the corners of her mouth. I was happy to see that she hadn't completely lost her sense of humor but wouldn't blame her if she had. All of this was creepy as hell. Something about her smile pulled me in and made me want to see more of it.

"I can write you a note for your professor if needed, we will need to take this into evidence." I offered a gentle smile as she laid the textbook on the table in front of me and took her seat on the barstool again.

"The really creepy thing, the one that bothers me the most, is what had happened right before you got here." Her eyes met mine and I waited anxiously for her to go on. I arched an eyebrow as she subtly nodded her head and continued.

"I was using the restroom," she looked over at the closed door, "and as I was about to flush, I heard the front door slam closed." She pulled her lower lip through her teeth nervously as she watched for our reaction. It made sense now why she had acted the way she did when we first got there.

"May I?" I looked toward the bathroom for permission to look inside as she nodded yes. I got up and made my way the short distance to the closed door and pulled it open. It was a small space, as I had guessed from the width that her door sunk in from the outside wall. There was a small shower to the left, a toilet in the middle, and a sink with very small counter space on the right. I took a step inside and pulled back the shower curtain to confirm there was no one there, granted she had already said she heard someone leave, not come in.

I backed out of the bathroom and closed the door as I had found it as I heard Trevor and Hannah talking about online dating. I picked up my notepad and made a few additional notes while I listened to their conversation. Trevor had this natural ability to ask the right questions to get people to really open up and it had always frustrated me that he never wanted to go into law enforcement with me. He would have been great at it. Instead he managed a local gym and was a personal trainer, which he was also great at as well.

"Have you met any other guys from the dating website?" Trevor asked Hannah as I looked up to wait for her answer.

"Not on this one, no. I had just started this one recently and didn't put a ton of effort into it because I've been so busy with school and work. I used a couple of other apps before this but it's been a few months since I've been on a date with any of them." She looked over at me as her cheeks flushed and I wondered why she would be embarrassed about admitting that in front of me. It's not like I was one to talk. I couldn't even remember the last date I had been on.

"If you can, make a list of everyone that you've recently had contact with, on all apps. Any message requests, and hook up requests- anyone who you may have declined to respond to. Once you have that list, we can look it over and see if we can narrow down who this might be." Trevor explained as he looked at me with a smug smirk.

"I can probably do that for you now. Chet is really the only guy I've talked to in over 4 months. That was part of the reason I said yes. I wasn't getting any other requests so I figured I shouldn't be picky and just give him a chance. Maybe he's mad because he thought I walked out on our date after I passed out in the bathroom and never came back?" She looked between us as if one of us would have the answer.

"It definitely could be him. Guys do stupid stuff when they take a blow to the ego. We'll pick him up and see what we can find out." I clicked my pen and slid it into the inside pocket of my coat along with the notepad and Hannah's note. "Do you feel safe to stay here tonight or do you have somewhere else you can stay?"

"I actually asked my friend Amber to come stay with me. She still lives at home and needs a break so she's going to stay for a few days."

"Sounds like a good plan. Remember to call me if anything happens, I live close by and can get here quickly." I smiled warmly as Trevor stood up and we walked to the door.

"Thank you, I will." She held the door open as we stepped into the hallway and smiled again. "Will I get an update on what happens with Chet?"

"As soon as I have more information, I'll touch base with you to get you an update."

"Thank you, I really do appreciate your help. It was nice to meet you, Trevor."

"You too." He smiled as he turned away, lowering his head so I couldn't see his face as we heard the door shut behind us. I listened closely to make sure I heard the locks before we walked down the hallway to the stairs.

"What's that look for?" I asked as we started down the stairs, shoulder to shoulder.

"You know she's barely legal, right?"

His smirk got under my skin as I knew what he was getting at. Was she hot? Fuck yeah. Was I interested? Probably. Was I going to act on anything? Not while my baby sister was still missing and some psychopath was stalking Hannah. It was definitely going to make it harder to work on her case when I felt such a strong electricity between us.

"You read it wrong. I'm not interested in her. I'm just doing my job." I side eyed him as we continued down another flight of stairs.

"Is that so?" He chuckled. "I've never known you to go to someone's house when you're not on the clock to help with something that a service aide could do."

"She had my card, I told her to use it. I'm still technically working her case with the date rape drug."

"Yeah and she sure used it alright. She could hardly keep her eyes off of you and you know it."

"Whatever."

Was that true? Was she interested in me as well? I felt myself getting excited at the thought and quickly shook it away.

"Is that why you had to keep adjusting yourself while we were sitting on the couch? Or was it cause I'm just so desirable, you couldn't help yourself?" He bumped his shoulder against mine as we reached the final stair and opened the door into the cold chill of winter.

I rolled my eyes at him as I had nothing to say to that. Did she physically impact me while I sat so close to her? More than I would ever be willing to admit. We walked the short distance to the subway and said goodbye as he headed home and I headed to the office to update the information I had from Hannah and to put in the request to bring Chet in for questioning.

<u>Six</u>

Hannah
16 Days Ago

"How did you sleep?" I asked Amber as she slowly sat up on the couch and stretched her arms up over her head.

"Good for the most part." She rolled her head a few times as she stretched some more and I knew the old worn-out couch had left her feeling stiff like it had done to me the few times I had fallen asleep on it.

"I told you, you should've slept in my bed with me. There was more than enough room." I walked into the kitchen and filled the coffee pot with water, desperate for that first sip to wake me up. We had been up late last night talking but even after we fell asleep I was restless the majority of the night, feeling like someone was watching me.

I tried to push everything out of my mind and just focus on finishing my last few classes but I couldn't shake the idea that someone was actively going through stuff in my apartment. At first I thought I was just crazy, then I thought maybe I had a random homeless person who had figured out how to get in, but after I got the note yesterday I knew it was Chet.

It was my own fault for not finding out more about the guy before agreeing to go on a date with him, but even then, how was I supposed to know that he would become this obsessed weirdo and stalk me? We definitely didn't click when we first met each other but I didn't pick up the vibe that he thought it was going all that well either. I imagined he thought of me as the girl you take in the bathroom stall for a quickie, not the girl you take home to mother. If I was so disposable then why was he going to these efforts to mess with me and stalk me?

The last few drops of coffee trickled into the pot before I poured two cups and made my way over to sit next to Amber on the couch. The snow had started to come down hard this morning which left a chill by the window. We sipped our coffee in silence as we watched the snow fall peacefully outside.

"Did you sleep better last night?" Amber asked as she took a sip of coffee and sat her cup down on the coffee table.

"A little, but I was still restless. I had this really uneasy feeling that someone was watching me." A shiver ran through me as I remembered being extremely anxious and freaking myself out throughout the night.

"It was me. I was watching you," Amber joked as she wiggled her eyebrows at me. I rolled my eyes as I tried to keep from laughing so I didn't spew coffee at her.

"So that's why you didn't want to share the bed? I get it, you're one of those girls who likes to watch people. What's that called? A voyeur?" I winked as I saw the flush in her cheeks from my teasing.

"You know it!" She giggled as she pulled her legs up underneath her and turned to face me head on. "But seriously though, I kinda had that same feeling, like someone was in the room, watching us." Her tone was serious, all joking gone as she watched for my reaction.

I didn't know what to say. I didn't want to think that someone had gotten in again last night, while both Amber and I were in the room. How would they have even gotten in? Before I played around with the idea that maybe I was such a heavy sleeper that I didn't hear them, but last night I heard every time Amber got up to get a drink of water or to use the bathroom. Maybe it was just our minds playing tricks on us and forcing us to believe that someone had been watching us because we were so fixated on everything that had been happening.

"I'm sorry, I know that having me stay here was supposed to be helpful and make you feel safer. I wasn't trying to freak you out." She reached over and touched my leg gently. "I shouldn't have said anything."

"No, it's okay. You don't need to be sorry." I looked around the room as I toyed with the idea of calling in sick for work today. It wasn't really that far of a stretch given that I had this constant headache and nausea for almost a week. As much as I didn't want to go in, I knew that I needed to since I had already been fired once this week and barely got my job back. Reluctantly I sighed as I stood up and sat my empty coffee mug on the table by Amber's mug that was still more than half full. Either she was slow at drinking her coffee this morning, or there was so much anxiety pushing through me that I had drank mine in record time.

"I'm gonna jump in the shower and get ready for work. There's food in the kitchen if you want to help yourself to breakfast."

"Thanks, I'll see what I can find to cook for us before you go."

I smiled as I walked over and pulled out clothes to wear from my dresser and headed into the bathroom. I closed the door but didn't lock it in case Amber needed anything, which sounded silly and overly paranoid.

Once the water warmed up, I took a quick shower and let myself enjoy the hot water as it ran down my face for a few minutes at the end. The pipes squealed as I turned the water off with one hand while reaching behind the shower curtain to grab my towel from the hook where I always kept it with the other. My fingers scraped along the bare wall as I kept patting, trying to find the towel. Cold metal found my fingers as I felt the empty hook. I pulled the shower curtain back, expecting to find the towel in a puddle on the floor but it wasn't there. I looked around the small space of the bathroom and found it neatly folded and piled on top of my clothes on the bathroom sink.

My stomach sunk as I pulled the shower curtain around me in an effort to cover myself while I stepped forward and reached over to lock the bathroom door. My fingers trembled as I fumbled with the lock before turning it successfully. I let the shower curtain fall as I quickly grabbed the towel from underneath my clothes and wrapped it around me. A nagging feeling inside told me that something was wrong. I had put my clothes in the same spot

I put them every time I took a shower, how did they end up on top of the towel that was hanging by the shower when I first got in?

I quickly dried myself and slipped on the yoga pants and sweatshirt I had been wearing earlier as I struggled to hear what was going on in the apartment. Everything sounded quiet, no sounds of Amber being attacked which was where my mind was currently going.

I kicked the towel to the side as I slowly unlocked the bathroom door and stepped into the open space of the apartment. The room was eerily quiet. The front door looked like it was still shut and I could smell food cooking on the stove but there was no sign of Amber. I slowly took a few steps toward the kitchen as I smelled the food starting to burn when out of the corner of my eye I saw something dripping off the coffee table.

My eyes followed the trail of coffee that was slowly trickling from the puddle on the table into the new puddle that had started on the floor, the coffee mug laying on its side by the coaster it had been sitting on. A shiver ripped through my body as my eyes slowly moved up, the sheer curtains blowing gently from the outside breeze that was sending an icy chill through the room. I stepped around the puddle of coffee and kneeled on the couch as I pulled the curtains back and looked out the open window. Amber's body laid lifeless on a fresh blanket of snow as the blood pooled around her. I covered my mouth as I began to scream, the sound muffled by the pounding in my head as my heart threatened to explode.

Seven

Max

16 Days Ago

"Hannah, can you walk me through what happened this morning?" I sat on the edge of the coffee table and looked at her as she watched the forensics team move around us, collecting as much evidence as they could. The call came in from a neighbor reporting a suspicious person running from the back alley, no one knew at the time that it was actually a murder. Hannah remained shut down and didn't respond to any of my questions. I wasn't sure that she even knew I was there. Her eyes were red and puffy as she held a trembling hand up to her mouth and rocked back and forth on the couch. My instincts shouted to grab her and hold her, to comfort her and make her feel better, but I knew I couldn't. I looked around for the detective who was taking over this portion of the investigation and waved him over.

"Are you done with her?" I asked as I nodded at Hannah.

"Just about. We may have more questions for her but we won't really know any more until forensics finishes up." He tugged at the brim of his hat and looked sympathetically at Hannah.

"Well, if it's all the same to you, I'd like to get her out of here." I pulled a business card from inside my overcoat pocket and handed it to him. "She'll be in my custody if you need anything else. My cell is on 24/7."

"You got it, Detective." He slid the card in his back pocket as his attention was drawn away by another officer calling him.

I looked around to see what she might need since she wouldn't be able to come back to the apartment for a while. I grabbed her cell phone from the coffee table and tucked it in my pocket as I made my way to the door and grabbed her backpack. She was still rocking back and forth on the couch so I didn't bother asking permission before opening her bag and looking inside. The front pocket had her keys and a small canister of mace. The middle pocket had a phone charger and a couple of protein bars, a beanie, some gloves, and her metro card. The back pocket had her books and notebooks for school. I zipped it up and walked to the bed as I looked around for a suitcase or duffel bag for her clothes.

I gently tossed her backpack on the bed as I leaned down and felt around under the bed. I was relieved when I saw a small suitcase tucked in the corner under the bed by the nightstand. I pulled it out and shook it a few times to clear the dust from it before standing it upright and unzipping it. I had no idea what clothes to pack for her and it felt slightly inappropriate to be going through her personal belongings but she wasn't in any position to pack her stuff herself so I didn't really have a choice. There was a likelihood that her apartment would be off limits for a few days to a week while they continued to work the crime scene below. The murder was one thing but with the added report of having someone stalking her, they would be sure to scour every inch of her apartment.

I pulled open the first drawer of her dresser and breathed a silent sigh of relief when I found pajamas and sweats. I grabbed a few pair of sweatpants and tucked them into the suitcase along with the NYU sweatshirt she was wearing last night when I saw her. I quickly went through the rest of the drawers, working my way down one side then up the other. I knew the last drawer had her most personal belongings and my palm started to sweat as I looked over at her before pulling it open. Inside were rows of neatly folded bras and panties, arranged by color. I tried not to overthink anything as I grabbed random garments and forced myself not to picture her wearing any of them. I was about to grab a handful of panties when I felt a piece of paper under my fingertips. I reached down and pulled out a small folded note that was tucked inside a pair of black lace boy short panties.

Thought of you when I bought these, can't wait to see you in them.

My eyes darted over to Hannah as I held the note in my hand. I looked back down at the note and found that it was written in black marker, matching the note she had shown me last night. The writing was block like in style, each letter crisp and clean. It almost looked like it was typed out and printed, the penmanship consistent and fluid. There were a few spots that there was a slight bleed from the ink and my guess was that they had used a fine point permanent marker. I slid the note into my pocket as I zipped the suitcase shut and walked over to the detective I had been talking to as I nodded my head for him to step to the side.

"I need these ran through forensics ASAP." I said quiet enough for only him to hear as I handed him the pair of underwear. His eyebrow arched as he looked at the sexy pair of underwear in his gloved hand.

"I've been working this case and we believe she's being stalked by a guy that she met from an online dating site. She was found in a bathroom, passed out, Rohypnol in her system when she was admitted to the hospital. She's been finding notes and I just found one tucked inside of those." I looked down at his hand as he reached for an evidence bag and dropped them inside.

"I'll let you know as soon as we have something."

"Thanks, I appreciate it." I turned and walked the short distance to gather the suitcase and backpack from the bed as I made my way over to Hannah.

"Hey, let's get you out of here, okay?" I smiled warmly as I reached my hand out to her to help her up. Her eyes met mine, filled with tears, as she grabbed my hand and allowed me to help her up. I was relieved that she was able to acknowledge that I was there, but the sadness in her eyes nearly broke my heart. I had seen sadness plenty of times in my career but had always been able to keep people at an arm's distance so it didn't impact me. This was different. This felt more personal. Maybe it was because my sister was still missing and no one had heard from her in days, or maybe it was because I could see the goodness and the purity in Hannah's eyes and someone like her didn't deserve to have to go through this.

My apartment was only a few blocks away and thankfully the weather had cleared most of the traffic which made it a quick trip. Once we were inside, I sat her belongings down on the bistro table that was tucked in the corner, behind the couch. The living room and kitchen were basically one fluid room with nothing separating them other than a small island that jetted off of the counter by the sink that sat below the small window. There was a stove next to the fridge that shared the same wall as the bedroom and bathroom on the other side. I had been in this apartment since I first left home at 17 and at one time, had shared it with Trevor. Before I graduated and became an officer, rent was impossible to pay on my own.

I watched as Hannah lingered in the doorway, not at all aware that she was somewhere else. I needed her to talk to me and walk me through what had happened but I knew that as long as she was in shock, I wasn't going to be able to get anything out of her. I gently led her to the couch with my hand on her lower back and helped her to sit. My phone vibrated against the thick denim of my jeans as I walked into the kitchen to get her a glass of water. I reached in and pulled it out, sliding the button to answer it.
"Romano," I said as I held the glass under the water dispenser in the fridge and filled it.

"Detective Romano, this is officer Stamos. We were able to locate the suspect you asked us to bring in, Chet Johnson." Her voice didn't sound too pleasant and I wondered if she was just trying to be professional or if that was just her natural, unenthusiastic personality.

"Okay, great. Can you please let my partner know? She'll be in to question him. Just keep him in holding until then."

"I'm sorry, I can't do that."

I sat the glass down on the kitchen counter as I watched Hannah look absently at the tv across from her.

"And why the hell not?" There had better be a damn good reason why I was being told that we couldn't hold this asshole for questioning when he was now a murder suspect. I would talk to whoever I needed to talk to if it meant we talked to this guy now.

"Because, he's dead. With all due respect, sir, we found his body an hour ago."

What the fuck? I ran a hand down my face and closed my eyes as I shook my head.

"Cause of death?"

"It's still to be determined but it appears to have been blunt force trauma. There are several bruises as well as puncture wounds. Possible strangulation. We don't really know yet."

"You know all of this and he barely died an hour ago?" I questioned; it didn't add up. How did he sneak into Hannah's apartment, murder her best friend, then was beaten to death himself less than a few hours later?

"Sorry, we found his body an hour ago. He appears to have died several days ago. I would guess close to 5 or 6 days based on the decomposition."

"Get him to the morgue and I want an update as soon as possible. Have them rush the autopsy. I want a cause of death and time of death as soon as possible."

"Yes sir."

I hung up the phone and slammed it down on the counter as I looked up at Hannah. She didn't even flinch from the sound. Sitting in front of me was a woman who was in more danger than she could even know and it was now my job to try to save her while I continued to look for my missing sister. I opened the cabinet next to me and grabbed the bottle of antacid as I threw a handful in my mouth and started making calls to my team with the update.

Eight

Adam
16 Days Ago

I rolled my eyes as I watched the overweight rent a cop scurry around the dead body as if it was going to change the outcome of the situation. Little did they know he had been dead almost a week so it was a little too late to be worrying about him now. I leaned back against the cold brick wall of the abandoned building behind me and took a deep drag off my cigarette as I watched the shit show continue to unfold.

The problem was that this was all completely avoidable, yet no one was smart enough to see that. I was the kind of guy that went after the things that I wanted. There wasn't anything that I wanted that I couldn't have. Sure, sometimes there was a struggle and some push back. But in the end, I always got what I wanted. Even if I had to get rid of the things that threatened to stand in my way.

I pushed off the brick wall and tossed the cigarette to the ground before stomping it out with the heel of my steel toed boot. It was a short distance to the abandoned building that held the last girl who said no to me. While everyone was still fixated on the dead frat guy, I didn't want to risk them hearing the obnoxious screams that threatened to undo everything that still needed to be done.

Nine
Hannah
16 Days Ago

They say that the first time you experience the death of someone who is close to you, that you learn what death really is. You learn how to go through the grieving process, how to work through each of the 7 stages of grief. That you grow from it. You learn to value and appreciate life more and your relationships with others. What they don't tell you is that each time you see a dead body, it imprints itself on your memory. A permanent reminder of what you've lost.

I didn't know anyone when I first moved to the city. I was scared and alone and desperate to prove to myself that I could do it. That I could live in a big city that would swallow me whole the first opportunity it had. And it almost did. Then I met Amber and things felt easier. More balanced. Calmer. Happier. She became my best friend and I felt like she was the sister I always wished for growing up as an only child.

Her life was beautiful and she was the symbol of happiness. She was popular without being stuck up. Nice without having people walk all over her. Strong and determined. And thanks to me, her life was cut short. She would never have her fairytale romance that she had dreamt about since she was a little girl. She wouldn't have tiny fingers wrapped around hers with little voices calling her mommy. A tear rolled down my cheek, my hand absentmindedly wiped it away, the ache from the raw skin burning at the touch.

Max sat across from me in an oversized leather recliner and rocked gently as his fingers moved quickly across his cell phone. He was trying to work through the details of everything that had happened this morning but I could see the stress etched on his face, the worry beneath his brow, as he became more distracted by whoever he was talking to on his phone.

We had gone over the details several times, each time an attempt for me to remember something else that might be helpful. What more could I say? We were talking on the couch, drinking coffee, then I went to take a shower and someone murdered my best friend and threw her out the window of my apartment as if she was nothing more than the trash that littered the sidewalks below.

My head ached as I shifted my position on the couch and pulled my knees closer to my chest. My cell phone screen lit up with a new email alert and I instinctively reached for it, worried about the lectures I had missed today that would be guaranteed to show up on the final exams in a few weeks. I slid my finger across the screen and pulled up the email from Joel to our group. There was a quick note about sending the lecture notes from the classes we missed and a joke about our late-night partying that must've been the reason to keep us out of class today.

I let out a shaky breath as I wiped another tear away and sat the phone down on the couch beside me. Max's eyes caught mine as he looked up from his phone, noticing the new tears. I shook my head no as I pulled the blanket up closer to my chest and tried to bury myself in it.

My mind raced as I thought about how I was going to tell those in our group about what happened to Amber. Sure, they weren't as close to her as I was but they still spent the past 14 weeks getting to know her. I felt my chest tighten as I thought about everyone that would soon be finding out, a reminder of how I felt when my mom told me that my dad had died. The difference was that we knew it was coming. I was able to try to brace myself for the inevitable. This was the complete opposite. There was no bracing yourself for something like this.

"Everything okay?" Max's voice was low and even as he studied me from across the room, his phone now sitting on the end table next to him.

"Yeah, it was an email from my study group. They were sending the lecture notes from the classes that I missed today."

"You're welcome to use my computer to print them if you want to. I know you have finals coming up and probably need hard copies." His eyes looked tired and I heard the empathy in his voice as he tried to sound reassuring while knowing that finals were the last thing on my mind right now. We were in that awkward moment of not knowing what else to talk about while trying to avoid talking about what was really on our minds.

"Thank you, that would be great." I smiled as I pulled the blanket off of me, eager to get up and do something other than sit on the couch and obsess over Amber. Even though I knew I would be a total wreck, I regretted not going in to work today and worried that their sympathy would only last so long before they let me go again. At least I would have had a distraction from everything that had happened if I would have just gone in. It was too late now.

He walked me down a short hall to the bedroom and pointed to a small wooden table against the wall that housed a computer and printer that barely fit the length of the table. I pulled out the metal folding chair and sat down as I waited for him to finish typing in the password to unlock the computer. As he pressed enter the screen changed and a picture of him surrounded by a handful of girls and two older people greeted me. I looked up at him in question as I hadn't expected a family picture to be his wallpaper.

"I'm the oldest of 7 children, only boy." He smiled as he folded his arms across his chest and leaned back against the wall, one foot crossed over the other.

"Your poor dad," I joked as I studied the picture. The girls were all young looking and aside from a few, all looked like they could be the same age. Each girl had dark hair and dark eyes, but there was one who stuck out to me the most. She looked familiar and I couldn't put my finger on how or where I knew her from. Her eyes were slightly lighter than the others, more of a hazel color than brown. I continued to study the picture when I felt Max's eyes on me.

"That's my baby sister, Elena." He started to smile and I noticed that it faded as quickly as it started. He looked away and I wondered what the story was.

"She looks really familiar." I turned my head slowly back to the screen and studied her features. She was smiling but it was one of those smiles that didn't fully reach the eyes. It was more of a forced smile, one that you give when someone is taking your picture. Not a real smile. There was a look on her face that made me feel uneasy. It almost felt like she was silently asking for help. From what, I had no idea. So many of us have our own personal demons that no one ever knows about.

"She went to NYU and was studying Psychology. Maybe you guys had a class together?"

"Elena? What's her last name?" I pulled my brows together as I tried to remember if the name sounded familiar but I was drawing a blank.

"Romano." He shifted his weight and turned slightly on the wall to look directly at me with his arms still crossed over his chest. The last name sounded familiar but I still couldn't picture her as Elena. The softness of her voice filtered through my mind as I remembered her from my intro to psychology class. She had made a joke on the first day when we did the mandatory self-introductions that she was just like Joey's family on *Friends*- Italian American family with 6 girls and 1 boy.

"Leni? Does she go by Leni?" I asked as I looked up at him and saw a shift in his posture when I mentioned her name.

"It's been her nickname since she was a baby." He smiled sadly as a private thought made its way through his mind. "I gave it to her."

"It's a cute nickname." I smiled. "She's in my Intro to Psychology class." I felt satisfied now that I knew where I recognized her from but something about the way Max reacted to her tugged at my heart. Something was wrong, I could feel it.

"Wait, did you say she *went* to NYU? Did she recently decide to stop going?" I was trying to remember the last time I had seen her in class. The class wasn't that big so it should have been easy to notice if someone was no longer in it but then again, I was hardly ever focused on who was showing up for class unless they were in my group. Max's face fell and a paleness washed over his olive toned skin as he looked down at the floor.

"She's missing." He slowly lifted his eyes to meet mine as his shoulders slumped after having said the words out loud. I brought a hand to my mouth as I took in the information. It all made sense now. His reaction to her picture, the added stress I've seen weighing him down today, the somberness to his tone when we discussed what happened to Amber. My mind struggled to try to process what he had said, too many questions fighting to be asked first.

"How long has she been missing?"

"Since Monday." He ran a hand through his hair and let out a deep breath as he pushed off the wall and sat on the edge of the bed across from me. The room was decent sized for a New York apartment but the confined space between the bed and the desk meant that we were even more in each other's space. I could feel the heat from his body as his leg slightly brushed against mine as he sat down. The smell of his shampoo lingered in the air making it hard to breathe anything other than his scent.

"Technically since Sunday night but I didn't know about it until Monday morning when she called." His eyes filled with tears and I saw his jaw clench as he fought back the emotions he was feeling. "She called me for help and I still haven't been able to find her."

I could hear the anger and frustration in his voice as he sat up taller and squared his shoulders. I didn't have any siblings so I didn't know what it was like to have someone to look after and take care of, but I imagined that him being the older brother meant that he was feeling a huge amount of guilt right now for feeling like he couldn't protect her. He was trying to be strong and not show his emotion but I could see right through the tough guy act. I saw the sensitive, caring man who needed someone to tell him that it would be okay. I wondered if he had anyone who would do that for him.

In the family photo he was in the center with the girls spread out on both sides of him and in front of him with his parents behind him. It portrayed as him being the center of the family, the one who held everything together. I reached forward and placed my hand on his knee, feeling him tense beneath my touch as his eyes wildly looked into mine, unsure of what I was doing.

"I'm really sorry about your sister, Max." I smiled as I maintained eye contact, almost a challenge for him to let down his guard with me. I didn't know him aside from the detective who was helping me with my own problems but something told me that he needed a friend right now as much as I did. Someone to just be there and say that everything would be okay.

I felt his body start to relax beneath my hand as he placed his hand on top of mine. I sucked in a breath and held it as I waited for him to push my hand away but was relieved when he gently squeezed it before holding it. It was surprisingly soft, the warmth of it comforting.

"I'm really sorry about your friend."

The tears started rolling down my face before I could try to stop them. Tears for Amber. Tears for myself. Tears for Max. They fell together in a perfect blend of sadness and loss as I felt him move his hand from mine and gently pull me over to the bed next to him. I sat beside him as he pulled me close to him and held me as I cried. I felt his chest shake and refrained from looking up as I knew that his tears had started to join mine. He needed this embrace as much as I did.

We spent the evening in the living room trying to forget the morning and everything else that was currently plaguing us but found it nearly impossible. His mind was still on trying to find something on his sister and mine was refusing to focus on the notes I had printed that Joel had sent. I tossed my highlighter on the coffee table and leaned back against the couch as I stretched my legs out in front of me. I had been sitting on the floor for hours and my body was starting to protest. I was about to get up when I heard a knock on the door, Max looking at me in question.

"Don't ask me, I don't live here." I joked as he laughed and walked to the door. I could tell that he wasn't expecting anyone which made it even more unsettling that someone was showing up unannounced at his door when his sister was still missing. I've seen plenty of shows where the police show up unannounced to tell you someone died. I lifted myself from the floor and my stomach tightened as I waited for him to open the door.

"I brought beer and pizza," Trevor announced as he walked in holding a pizza box and a 6 pack of beer. His eyes went wide when he saw me, first looking at me then looking at Max with a smirk on his face as he walked in and sat them on the island.

"Hey Hannah, nice to see you again." He side-eyed Max as he looked back at me with a huge grin. "Didn't expect to see you here. Am I interrupting something?"

"Hannah is staying with me for a little bit." Max closed the door and folded his arms over his chest as he looked at Trevor and waited for his response. I watched as Max's jaw tightened as he had some unspoken showdown with Trevor. Trevor looked like he was trying to figure it out but I knew that he was about to lose whatever game he thought they were playing.

"Is that so?" Trevor turned to look at me and I felt Max's gaze turn my way as well.

"Yup. It's true." I pulled at the bottom of my oversized NYU sweatshirt and anxiously chewed my bottom lip as the two of them continued to watch me. There was a thick tension in the air and I waited for someone to give in and say something to break it.

"Someone broke into my apartment again and murdered my best friend, then threw her out the window of my apartment, so I'm kinda staying here for a little bit until it's safe to go back." I shrugged my shoulders and took in a deep breath to replenish the one I had used to get all of that information out in one long winded sentence.

Trevor's eyes shot up as Max's face relaxed before they exchanged a look between them. I plopped myself down on the couch and pulled my legs up underneath me, trying to curl into a tiny ball under my sweatshirt.

"God, Hannah, I had no idea. I'm so sorry." Trevor came and sat on the other end of the couch and gently patted my leg. I had just met him last night and yet he was one of the most sincere and caring people I had met since moving to the city.

"Thank you." I smiled as he continued to pat my leg, thankful for the comfort he was offering. Max grabbed the beer and pizza from the island and sat it on the coffee table as I moved my stuff out of the way. He opened the pizza box and nodded for me to take a slice. I wasn't used to being the center of attention and it definitely felt strange being it with two very attractive men. I reached in and grabbed a slice then retreated back to my corner of the couch as I watched them get their slices. Max got up and went to the kitchen, bringing napkins and a bottle opener back with him. I reached out and took a napkin as I stuffed another bite of pizza in my mouth. I hadn't realized how hungry I was, especially given that I hadn't eaten all day.

Max opened a beer and handed it to Trevor before opening another and extending it to me. I froze and didn't know what to do. I didn't want to be rude and decline his offer but I also didn't want to get caught drinking underage in the presence of law enforcement. I quickly chewed my bite and blotted my mouth with my napkin as I tried to swallow as quickly as possible.

"I um, I can't." I could feel the heat creeping up my neck as I felt the embarrassment wash over me. If we were anywhere else and he was anyone other than the detective that was helping me, I would have accepted the drink in a heartbeat. I felt like such a prissy good girl for having to say no, but I didn't want him to think that I was reckless and irresponsible.

"You don't drink?" Trevor asked sincerely without the judgement I had expected to hear.

"I'm not 21. Yet." My face felt like it was on fire and suddenly I wished I was anywhere but there.

I saw a smirk cross Trevor's face as he took a bite of pizza and watched Max's reaction to the news. Max had to have some idea of how old I was if I was in the same class as his sister, right? I could see the slightest blush on his face as his shoulders tightened and he avoided Trevor's look.

"Hannah, it's fine. You should have a beer with us." He nodded to it as he continued to hold it out to me. My eyes searched his face, waiting for the punch line or for him to deceive me and arrest me once I took the bait. I looked to Trevor who looked at me with a smile that said he knew something that I didn't. He raised his eyebrows as if challenging me to take it as he slowly brought his bottle to his lips and took a sip.

"I promise, I'm not going to arrest you or turn you in for underage drinking." He sat the beer in front of me then took his place on the floor by the recliner again. "I have 6 sisters, the youngest is 18. I know that none of them waited until they were 21 to start drinking. I don't expect that you're waiting either."

Reluctantly I reached forward and grabbed the beer from the table as I smiled at Max who gave me a subtle nod as he took a sip.

"So, just how old are you, Hannah?" Trevor rested the beer bottle on his thigh and settled against the couch, waiting on my answer.

"I just turned 19 a few weeks ago." I took a sip and closed my eyes as the cold liquid made its way down my throat. I hardly ever drank and knew that it wouldn't take much for me to get buzzed. Part of me wanted the beer to take hold and help me forget what had happened but part of me knew that I couldn't allow that to happen.

"Still just a babe," Trevor said as he looked at Max over the top of his beer bottle as he took another drink.

"How old are you?" I looked at him with the smirkiest look

I could manage, unaware of whatever was going on between the two of them.

"How old do you think I am?"

"27? 28?" I tried to do quick math so I didn't sound stupid but I had no clue how old you had to be to make detective. I was hoping my wild guess worked in my favor.

"We're both 29." He pointed a finger back and forth between him and Max, though there was no one else there for me to be confused about who the 'we' might be.

I took another drink as I sunk lower into the couch, allowing the pizza to digest and the beer to take its hold on me.

"Is that too old?" Trevor asked as he watched me.

"Too old? For what? Like life in general?" I was confused on why he would ask me that then I saw the blush on Max's face again and it clicked. I heard Trevor chuckle as he finished his beer and sat it on the table next to the almost empty pizza box.

"Want another?" Max asked him as he reached to grab him another bottle.

"I don't know? Am I too old for another one, Hannah?" His laughter was contagious as I rolled my eyes and watched him take the beer from Max. I didn't bother responding as I knew I had already labeled myself as the geeky little girl who wasn't very bright and didn't bother to take any risks. Of all of the first impressions I could make, this was the one that I screwed up the easiest.

The night went on with us finishing off the pizza and talking over beers. Laughter floated around the room as they told stories about their wild days growing up together and even though my mind constantly stayed focused on what had happened to Amber, I was thankful for a small break to feel something other than grief.

Ten

Max

13 Days Ago

I've had plenty of girlfriends throughout my life yet none
of them have ever made me feel the way I've felt having
Hannah stay with me. It was completely unexpected and
honestly I never imagined that I would be taking her back
to my place after her best friend was murdered, but that was
exactly what had happened.

There was something about Hannah that made me want
to protect her, and not just in a - it's my job- kind of way.
I wanted to protect her as much as I wanted to protect my
own family. Maybe it was because she was the same age
as my baby sister, who was still missing, or maybe it was
because I felt like she was an innocent naive girl that needed
someone to look out for her.

We had talked about Leni and for the first time since she
went missing, I actually broke down and cried. I was so
frustrated and disappointed in myself for letting Hannah
see that side of me but as hard as I fought to hold it in,
she fought even harder for me to let her be there for me.
Someone who was going through a loss of her own, that
same day no less, took the time to hold my hand and
comfort me. I've never known anyone like that in my entire

life. I have always been the one to hold things together and to be there for everyone else, I never knew what it felt like to have someone be there for me.

When I first met Hannah I pegged her as this wild, reckless, college girl who got herself into the same situations as my sister and never saw her as the mature, responsible person she really was. It was almost like she didn't know how to be wild or reckless. Something told me that there was a lot in life that Hannah hadn't yet experienced and that piqued my curiosity in the worst way.

The weekend flew by with Hannah trying to force herself to study and get through the last few term papers she had due while I worked on trying to find new leads on Elena's case. It was driving me crazy that I wasn't allowed to work her case, and even more so when I couldn't get updates from my team.

Trevor had been by a few times to bring food and coffee for us after I failed to realize that I needed to go grocery shopping. Hannah never complained about the food options and half the time I had to remind her that she needed to eat something. I knew that no matter how hard she tried to throw herself into her studies she wasn't able to get out of her own head or to stop thinking about what happened. She would sit on the couch or the floor and be so consumed with whatever she was reading, pushing her reading glasses back up her nose as they would slide off. It was adorable. I found that she had quite a few little quirks about her that made me want to memorize every little thing that she did. I found myself wanting to know more about her and then hating myself for it when I knew that there could never be anything between us. I wasn't a relationship kind of guy and she deserved much more than a random hookup.

The walk across campus was cold as the wind started to pick up, forcing us to walk faster. Over the weekend I had been reassigned to work Hannah's case and nothing else, which meant that I was to keep her in my sights at all times until we caught the person who was stalking her and had murdered her best friend. That meant that not only was she still going to live with me, but she was going to have me escort her to work and school until we felt there wasn't a direct threat against her. I worried that she would feel like she was being treated like a child but she surprised me with how easy going her attitude was with everything. Almost like she liked my company.

Warmth greeted us as I pulled open the heavy door to the old building and held it open for Hannah. The heater was on full blast, warming the hallway that reminded me of high school. There were classrooms lining both sides of the long narrow hallway which felt oddly quiet for the end of the semester. I looked around and found a few classes that were filled with students but most of them were empty.

I followed as she made her way to the only room that had its door propped open. The room was small and set up lecture style with all of the desks facing toward a desk and whiteboard at the front of the room. Hannah lowered her head as she walked in, a few students already in their seats while the professor stood behind his desk. I knew it would be hard for her to show up to classes that she had with Amber, having to answer questions from her classmates about where she was.

The professor took notice of me as I walked in with Hannah, taking my place along the back wall while she took her seat and started pulling out the items she needed from her backpack. He looked to be in his mid-thirties to early forties, muscular build from what I could see from his button-down shirt and fitted jeans. I imagined this was the image girls fantasized about when they thought about hot professor types and a fury of jealousy flowed through me as I wondered if Hannah was one of those girls.

I gave a tight smile as he continued to watch me out of the corner of his eye while he wrote out a list of topics on the whiteboard. A few more students shuffled in and took their seats until there were only a few empty seats left. I watched Hannah chew nervously on the end of her pen while she stared at the empty seat next to her and knew that it had to be Amber's seat. I wanted to go to her and comfort her but now wasn't the time or the place. The professor walked over and squatted down beside Hannah as the rest of the students started to fill their seats. I kept my head down as I tried to avoid being any more of a distraction for her than I already was.

"Good morning, Hannah. I just wanted to check in and see how things were going with the study group?" His voice was low with an empathetic tone to it.

"Good morning. It's going well. I feel like I'm more prepared for the final exam." She let out a shaky breath as she forced a smile. "Or at least I hope I am."

"I'm sure you'll do just fine. Your last assignment reflected the progress you've been making, but maybe try to squeeze in an extra study session or two before the final if it makes you more comfortable."

"Thanks, I'll try to do that." She let out a soft laugh as she tucked a strand of hair behind her ear as he stood up and walked to the front of the class to start the lecture.

I felt my phone vibrate in my pocket as the room grew quiet, heads down as hands worked quickly to write down the notes as he spoke. I unlocked my phone and found a text message from Mindy confirming that she had the autopsy report on Chet as well as some updates from forensics about Hannah's case. There was a back door to the classroom which allowed me to sneak out of the room to call her without disrupting the class. I slowly closed the door, waiting until I heard the click, before sitting down on the bench that lined the wall in between the doors of Hannah's class. I knew Hannah was safe and she wasn't going to be able to leave the room without me seeing her so I didn't have to hover over her right now. I held my phone to my ear and waited for Mindy to answer.

"Hey, how's college treating you?" She joked as she answered the phone, knowing where I would be since Hannah had a full schedule of classes today.

"Good, I think I'm ready to pledge a frat and make really bad decisions," I teased back, thankful to have a lighthearted conversation with Mindy, even though I knew it would be changing in a matter of seconds. She laughed and I could hear the change in her tone when there was nothing else to joke about.

"So, what's the news?" I asked as I looked down the empty hallway.

"The autopsy shows that Chet died a week ago today. Blunt force trauma to the head, several broken ribs, a punctured lung, and a fractured skull. He would have bled out from the head wound if he hadn't been strangled to death first. It was a very violent death and unfortunately they weren't able to recover anything that could be used for DNA testing." She let out a deep breath and I knew that it was about to get worse.

"We also got a trace on Elena's phone and were able to follow it to an empty warehouse a couple blocks away from the coffee shop she had met the online guy at."

My heart started racing, I couldn't believe there was finally a break in the case. I wanted to be ecstatic that we had a location to go off of but Mindy's voice said it all. If there was good news, she would have started with- Max, we found her! But she didn't. She saved the bad news so she could wait just a little bit longer to break my heart.

"Where did they find the body?" I swallowed hard, trying to force the bile back down.

"In a warehouse. The body isn't recognizable, we're still waiting for confirmation. But Max, they found her cell phone next to the body." The last words came out as a whisper. My head dropped as Mindy continued to talk, her words floating in the air around me but never actually making it to me. I sucked in a deep breath as I stood up and walked outside, welcoming the harsh chill in the air as it prickled the back of my neck. My breathing was ragged as I slammed my fist into the brick wall, leaving a trail of blood along the way.

I was too late.

Eleven

Hannah
11 Days Ago

"Is there anything I can help with?" I asked Amber's mom as I followed her into the kitchen with an empty tray of food. It felt weird being there when it was supposed to be a small gathering of Amber's family to remember her, but her parents had insisted that I come and I didn't have the heart to say no. The funeral had been that morning followed by the wake at her parents' house. Both were emotionally draining as I relived that morning over and over. To sit with her family and hear them tell stories about how wonderful she was felt like a dagger was jabbed into my heart over and over as I sat there knowing that her death was my fault. I was the reason that they were sharing stories and crying weeks before Christmas.

"I've got it honey, thank you." She smiled up at me with a smile that never met her eyes. There were bags under them that confirmed she hadn't slept in days mixed with the puffiness from crying. Still, she had a motherly look, one of love, as she came over and placed her hand over mine and smiled at me.

"My Amber sure was lucky to have such a wonderful best friend. I'm so happy she had you in her life, dear."

I wanted to tell her not to say nice things, to take back the adoring look she was giving me and replace it with the hatred she should feel for me because it's what I deserved. My lip trembled and I fought desperately to hold the tears back. This woman didn't deserve to have to comfort me when I was to blame for what happened. My hand trembled beneath hers and I forced myself to look away.

Warm arms pulled me and wrapped me in a hug as she gently rubbed my back. Unable to hold it in any longer a sob escaped my throat as the tears spilled over, staining the navy-blue satin shirt she was wearing. I was embarrassed that I was falling apart in front of her mom but I also felt comforted for the first time since everything had happened in a way that no one else could comfort me. The way only a mother could. I desperately wished to have my own mother there with me, to hold me and tell me everything was going to be alright, but that would mean that I had to tell her what had happened. I couldn't bear to add any additional stress to her life, she was already struggling to keep herself afloat and didn't need anything in addition to worry about. Besides, there wasn't anything she could do anyways. I was still staying with Max and that was the best protection I could have right now.

I felt her hug me tighter as my sobbing continued, a week's worth of stress finally dissipating. Quietly she whispered there, there, over and over, my body responding to her calmness. I slowly pulled back and quickly tried to wipe my tears away with the back of my hand even though it was evident I had been crying. She smiled sympathetically and my heart broke all over again for her.

"I'm so sorry about what happened to Amber," I blurted out before I could think about what I was saying. "It was all my fault, if she wouldn't have come stayed with me, she wouldn't —— she wouldn't——" The words caught in my throat as I struggled to get them out while sobbing again. I felt a hand on my lower back and knew it was Max as my body shook from the weight of my grief.

"Hannah, look at me, dear." Her voice was gentle, her eyes waiting patiently for mine to find hers through the blurriness of the tears. I looked at her and tried to take deep breaths to get my breathing back to normal.

"Hannah, you didn't do any of this. This wasn't your fault. We all know that it wasn't your fault, none of us blame you for what happened to her."

"But..," I stammered as she held up her hand for me to stop.

"No, I repeat, it's not your fault." She pulled out a chair from the small dining table and sat down as she nodded toward the other chair for me to sit in. I pulled it out and sat down, waiting for her to continue.

"Amber went to stay with you because she loved you and she wanted to make sure you were okay. She had told me about what was happening and assured me that she was going to keep you safe. No one could have predicted what would have happened honey, not a single one of us." Her voice got quiet as she finished her sentence, her attention focused elsewhere.

"I was actually on the phone with her right before it happened." She looked up at Max and I felt his weight shift behind me as this was news to both of us. "She had called me when you were in the shower and told me that she felt like someone had been watching you guys. She tried to stay awake to catch them but she never saw anyone. I remember hearing her get the pan out and her telling me that she was going to make breakfast before you left for work, then all of a sudden her voice sounded further away and I could tell she was talking to someone."

"Did you hear what they were saying?" Max asked as he pulled a notepad from his coat pocket and patted his other pocket until he found a pen.

"I couldn't hear it very well but I know that she asked what they were doing there so it seemed like she knew the person. I didn't hear much after that but it sounded like there was struggling and things were kind of muffled. A few seconds later a man's voice came on the line and said 'wrong number' and hung up." She trembled and looked up at Max as he wrote the information down.

"Are you sure that's what they said?" he asked with his brows pulled together, the pen hovering over the notepad.

"Yes, it was definitely 'wrong number'. I remember it because I thought it was odd he would say that when she had called me, even though he probably didn't know who had called who, let alone that I was her mother."

Max's face was pale as he stared down at the notepad before writing the information down. Something had changed in him when she told him about the phone call and I wondered if he was mad that his team didn't think to check her phone records since this seemed to be important information.

"Thank you, ma'am, for the information. I appreciate it. It's very helpful." He put the pen and notepad back into the pocket and looked down at me with a serious expression that I hadn't seen from him before.

"Hannah, I need to get some information back to my team so I need to go in for a bit. Do you want me to have an officer come meet you here and escort you back home when you're ready?"

"No it's okay, I can go with you now." I smiled and reached out to hold Amber's mom's hand as we both stood up. "Thank you for including me today, I really appreciate it and again, I'm very sorry for your loss."

We said our goodbyes to Amber's family then made our way to the station so Max could work on whatever it was he needed to do. He was strangely quiet and it was eating at me that I didn't know what had happened that could be upsetting him this much.

The snow crunched beneath our boots as we walked in silence, the weather surprisingly calm yet freezing as usual. I shoved my hands into my coat pockets in an effort not to reach out and grab his hand that was so close to mine that I could feel the heat of his body through his leather gloves.

"Is everything okay?" I asked as we walked up the steps to his office and waited for him to punch in the code to open the door. He glanced at me as we waited for it to beep, his hand on my lower back, guiding me in once the door opened.

"She said that it was a man's voice and he told her it was the wrong number." He nearly sprinted down the hallway of offices while I quickened my pace to try to keep up.

"Yeah, and?"

"When I was on the phone with Elena, some guy came on the line and said 'wrong number', then hung up on me. It can't be that big of a coincidence, right?" His eyes were wild as they searched mine to tell him he was right.

"I don't think I would call it a coincidence." I wasn't sure where he was going with his train of thought but the fact that there was a connection to his sister who was taken and then murdered and my best friend who was just murdered made my blood run cold. I ran my hands up and down my arms as a shiver ran through me.

"So what does this mean? What's next?" I asked even though I knew it probably sounded stupid.

"I want to look at the information my team has collected on Elena so far and see what other leads they might have had. Then maybe I can start trying to find a connection and we can nail this guy."

I watched as he walked into an office with two desks across from each other, a large whiteboard with a cork board on each side of it took up the wall in between their desks. I looked at the whiteboard and noticed a few things scribbled on it with arrows pointing to additional information and a few pictures taped in between. Max stood in front of the wall as he frantically searched back and forth, running a hand through his hair in frustration.

"What's wrong?" I asked as I stood beside him.

"It's gone." His voice was low and angry.

"What is?"

"Elena's case. All of the information I had gathered for them and sent to them- it's gone. It should be up here as an active case and it's fucking gone!" His voice boomed as I saw his fist clenched, ready to punch something. I flinched at the bandage that was already wrapped around his fist from when he hit the wall when he first got the news about Elena. I reached up and put a hand on his shoulder to try to calm him down and felt him immediately pull away from me. Embarrassed I pulled my hand back down and tucked it in my pocket, stepping further away from him to give him distance while I tried to pretend like I wasn't embarrassed by his rejection of my touch.

"She's not even in the ground yet for fucks sake! How could they do this?" He turned to look at me as he pointed at the wall, anger and disgust written on his face. "The case isn't closed until we have the killer and they're already moving on as if she didn't matter!"

I could see his chest rise and fall with each breath he struggled to take and wished there was something that I could do for him. If I had Trevor's number, I would call him and ask him to come but I didn't. I stood helplessly in the corner as he turned his attention back to the whiteboard. The office was small and sitting on the desk beside me was a framed photo of a pretty blonde woman and a man who had his arms wrapped around her as they shared a kiss. My guess was that it was his partners' desk from what he had told me, though I didn't know what she looked like. The desk was organized though there were stacks of files lining most of it. Off to the side on the top of two piles of files were two black folders with a post it note on top that read:

Romano
Myers

My heart sank when I saw Amber's last name on the post it note, a reminder that they both had shared the same unfortunate fate. I wondered if the black folders meant that the victims were deceased. Max was at his desk looking through a small pile of papers when I saw him look over at me.

"There are files over here that say Romano and Myers, are those what you're looking for?" I asked as I nodded at the edge of the desk where they sat.

Max stalked across the room as his eyes darted around to find the files in the piles that I was referring to then stopped dead in his tracks when he saw the black folders. His hand shakily reached out and grabbed them from the pile as he pulled the post it note off.

"What does black mean?" My voice was quiet as I wasn't sure what his mood was at this point.

"It means the case is dead. It'll be filed as a cold case because they weren't able to solve it." His eyes found mine and his shoulders slumped as I took in his words.

"But Amber hasn't even been gone a week, how can they say the case is closed? And you haven't gotten the report back yet on Elena, they haven't even confirmed it was her." I immediately felt the anger and frustration that I had seen on him when he saw the board had been cleared of their cases, meaning no one was going to work on them anymore.

"I know. Let's take these and get out of here." He shoved the files inside his leather coat and zipped it up as we made our way out of the office and back to his apartment.

Twelve

Max
11 Days Ago

I had been a total dick and I hated myself for it. Hannah wasn't someone that I ever wanted to hurt but I saw the look on her face when she tried to comfort me and I pulled away from her touch. There wasn't anything I could do to change what had already been done but I still felt like shit for what happened and didn't know how to bring it up. We had been back at the apartment for a few hours and had started writing out everything we knew so far between Elena's case, Amber's death, and the stalking that had been happening with Hannah. We were looking for any possible connection but at this point we were drawing blanks and I knew we needed to take a break and eat something since we hadn't eaten since the wake this morning.

It was after seven when the Chinese food was delivered and my stomach growled in anticipation of it. We cleared the table and sat on the couch as we ate, neither of us speaking as we shoveled food into our mouths. I felt bad that I had been so distracted that I hadn't bothered to take care of feeding either of us, especially since Hannah had been through so much in one day with the funeral and finding out that they had already closed the case on Amber's murder. I was thankful that Hannah had taken some time to talk with her mom on the phone before the food got there, even though she had mentioned that she still wasn't going to tell her what was going on. She seemed to be a little more relaxed after their conversation which helped me to relax as well.

We finished our meal in silence as a movie played on the tv for background noise. Now was the time to try to talk to Hannah and apologize for earlier but I didn't know what to say or how to say it. Being the coward that I am, I got up and went to the kitchen for the bottle of wine that was still sitting in my fridge that I hadn't bothered to open after my last date went south. I opened the bottle and poured two glasses, bringing it back and setting it on the coffee table as I handed a glass to Hannah. She eyed it suspiciously as she reached out and took it.

"I'm not sure you're really that good of a cop if you keep giving underage girls alcohol." She raised an eyebrow as she took a sip. I watched the way her mouth moved as she drank the wine, the slight lick of her lips as her body relaxed with the first taste.

"Technically I'm a detective. That means I'm just supposed to solve cases, not worry about intoxicated minors." I winked as I took a sip and watched her fight the smile that threatened to take over as she took another sip and focused on the tv.

"I'm really sorry about earlier." I took a deep breath and waited until I had her full attention before continuing. "I wasn't trying to be rude when I pulled away from you."

A slight shade of red crept up her chest and neck as she took another drink, her grip on the stem of the glass firmer as she avoided looking directly at me. Her hair was pulled up into a messy knot on her head again, giving me a perfect view as the blush lingered on her fair skin.

"It's not a big deal." She shrugged her shoulders and shook her head as she turned back to face the tv. I hated that she felt this way about it and I hated even more that I was starting to feel something for her and wanted to feel her touch again.

"Hannah, it is a big deal. I didn't mean to hurt your feelings."

"You didn't."

"I think I did."

"You must be wrong." Another long sip of wine as she continued to avoid looking at me, her glass almost empty. The way she purposely avoided me reminded me of Elena and her fiery temper.

"Then why won't you look at me?" I probed as I sat my glass down.

"I'm watching this movie."

"Yeah? What's it about?" I smirked knowing that she hadn't been watching it and by the look on her face right now, she had no idea what movie it was.

"It's about this guy who works at a hotel and his family gets to live there." She turned toward me, her jaw jutted out with the most adorable, sassy look on her face. I chuckled much to her irritation.

"Is that so?" I asked as I turned slightly against the couch to face her.

"Yes, he was given the hotel to look after during the quiet season and he's living there with his family. He's going to teach his son about managing a hotel."

"Have you seen it before?" I already knew the answer but asked anyways.

"Obviously, it's like a classic." She rolled her eyes for dramatic effect as she finished the last sip of wine and sat the glass on the coffee table. Against better judgement I leaned forward and refilled both glasses as she leaned back and pulled her knees up to her chest.

"Does it have a happy ending?" My smile spread across my face and there wasn't a damn thing I could do to stop it.

"It sure does." Her matter of a fact attitude made it even more hilarious that she was trying to bluff about knowing the movie.

"Should I be worried that you think it's a happy ending when he goes crazy and tries to kill his family?" I raised my eyebrows as her head whipped toward me with shock on her face.

"That doesn't happen," she scoffed while eyeing me suspiciously.

"Watch and see." I pointed to the tv and watched her reaction as the famous *Here's Johnny* scene played out, her eyes wide with horror that she was caught. She looked over at me as she chewed her bottom lip back and forth between her teeth.

"Well, who's to define what a happy ending should look like anyways?"

"Is that your psychology approach to being wrong?"

"Shut up!" She reached over and pushed my chest playfully as I caught her hand and pulled her into me. Her breathing hitched as her mouth was inches from mine, the smell of the wine sweet on her breath. Slowly I ran my hand behind her head and waited, unsure of whether to kiss her. Everything inside of me wanted it but I knew that I shouldn't go for it. She was too young and more importantly, I was supposed to be protecting her, not making out with her.

Her eyes closed and her lips parted slightly as she let my hand hold her close to me.

"Hannah..." I breathed, fighting everything that told me this was a really bad idea. "I don't want to take advantage of you." I swallowed hard as I tried to force myself to let go of her. She was just a baby and who knew if she would still want to kiss me if she wasn't buzzed from the wine and emotionally vulnerable with everything going on. I owed it to her to do the right thing. Her eyes fluttered open as she pulled back a little and tilted her head to look at me.

"Why would you feel like you were taking advantage of me?" Confusion etched her face along with the disappointment I had seen earlier.

"Because you've been drinking and you've been through a lot recently. A lot today." I ran a hand down my face, the stubble on my jawline prickly beneath my fingers. "I don't want to take advantage of the situation."

"Max, I'm not some young, stupid kid. I'm fully capable of making my own decisions and knowing what I want."

"What do you want?"

"You."

Her voice was direct as she looked me in the eye. There was something different in her that I had never seen before. A passion that I was curious to explore combined with a maturity that I had been doubtful of. I watched as she turned and straddled me, taking my face in her hands before leaning down and gently kissing me. Her lips were soft against mine, the taste of wine mixing with the taste of her. I closed my eyes and allowed myself to enjoy the moment, knowing it would be over before I was ready for it to end.

Her fingers made their way through my hair as she deepened the kiss, her tongue gently making its way into my mouth. I felt her body shift as she sank lower against me and leaned in, her breasts pressed firmly against my chest. Her kiss became more urgent as she slowly rocked her hips against me and for a moment, I felt what it might feel like if she were riding me. I tried to push the thought out of my head while trying to keep my erection from protruding through my jeans. As if knowing my dilemma, I watched as she pulled back and broke the kiss, biting her lip as she pushed herself down lower, directly on top of my throbbing dick. She reached down and started to lift her sweater up when I gripped her wrists to stop her. She pulled back as if I had slapped her and studied my face as she tried to figure out what had happened.

"We can't do this Hannah." I blew out a breath and leaned my head back against the couch, her sexy body still straddling me.

"Why not?" There was an irritation to her voice as she scowled down at me.

"Because, it's not right. Because I'm way older than you. Because I'm supposed to be protecting you. Because I just can't take advantage of you, Hannah." I worked my jaw back and forth in frustration. "There's too much at stake here and I don't want you to get hurt."

"Okay." She pursed her lips as she rolled off of me and stood up beside me. She looked around before spotting her backpack and walked over to grab it.

"What are you doing?" I asked as she slung the bag over her shoulder and stuffed her cell phone into her pocket. She grabbed her coat from the recliner and hung it over her arm as she walked to the door. I jumped up and stood in front of it before she could open it.

"I'm leaving," she snapped and I could tell that she was pissed. I didn't blame her, I knew I shouldn't have let things get that far, but I also couldn't let her leave.

"Hannah, I know you're mad and I'm sorry. I didn't mean to lead you on and I'm not trying to make you feel unwanted or rejected. Please stay," I pleaded as I begged her to stay.

"Look, I've stayed long enough. Nothing else has happened, I think it's time I go." She blew out a breath and looked past me to the door. "If you don't mind?" She looked pointedly at me until I moved from the door and let her pass.

"Hannah. Please?"

I closed my eyes as the door slammed shut knowing that it wouldn't do any good to follow her at this point. I picked up my phone and called Mindy. Regardless of how pissed I was with how they were handling my sister's case, I still needed her to get someone to watch over Hannah since we hadn't figured out who was stalking her. It was going to be a long night.

Thirteen

Hannah

8 Days Ago

I hadn't spoken to Max since Wednesday after I left his apartment, all calls forwarded to voicemail and text messages had been ignored. The minute I walked out his door I was instantly filled with regret. Regret for allowing myself to think he was interested in me and making a move on him. Regret for allowing myself to think that a real friendship was developing between us and that I could feel safe with him. And most importantly, regret for leaving and going back to my apartment where I was reminded of Amber and felt the most vulnerable. I didn't know anyone else in the city well enough to ask to stay with them and I hadn't worked as many hours this week so I couldn't afford a hotel room. The only choices were to stay with Max and be constantly reminded of his rejection or to stay by myself and pray that the rookie looking cop posted outside my door was enough to keep me safe.

I hadn't noticed anything unusual in my apartment since I had come back and every time I left to go to class or work, there was an officer waiting outside my door. It was oddly reassuring that I wasn't really alone but unsettling that my every move was being watched. The sun peaked through the sheer curtains, casting a warm glow across the hard wood floors as the sun made a rare appearance. Today was supposed to be a break from the weather which was nice except that it didn't really matter for me since it was Saturday and I didn't have anywhere to go.

I pushed the blankets back and sat up, stretching to relieve some of the pain I had from sleeping on Max's couch. Sitting on the coffee table were piles of text books and notebooks with a handful of highlighters and pens next to them, waiting for me to dive in and start studying for finals. I took a deep breath and let it out, dread flooding through me as I thought about trying to study. I hadn't been able to study for over a week and today didn't feel like it was going to be any different. Reluctantly I slid my feet down into my slippers and got out of bed. I grabbed a hair tie from my nightstand and twisted my hair into a bun on the top of my head.

My feet padded lightly across the floor as I made my way to the coffee pot when I noticed something under the door. I slowly walked over and bent down, a dark red liquid slowly pooling in from the hallway. My body tensed as I stood up and looked around, the bathroom door still closed. Slowly I walked over and pulled it open, turning to look inside. Holding a breath, I grabbed the shower curtain and yanked it to the side, my heartbeat pulsing in my ear. I brought a hand to my chest and leaned against the wall as I dropped the curtain, relieved no one was behind it.

As I made my way back into the room, I swiped my cell phone from my night stand and unlocked it. I didn't know who I should call since I didn't know what was actually happening. Was my mind playing tricks on me and making me think something bad had happened? Was I just seeing things that weren't really there? Maybe the cop, I still couldn't remember his name, had spilled a soda and that's what was coming in?

I slowly walked back to the door and looked down at the puddle that had grown dramatically bigger in the few minutes I had been gone. The liquid was too thick to be soda. Deep down in my gut I knew that it was blood. Problem was, I didn't know whose blood it was. I tried to stand on my toes and peek through the peephole without touching the blood which was rather hard given that it had pooled under the door. Taking another deep breath, I slowly moved to the side and opened the door. A loud thud rang through my apartment as the cop who had been sitting in the chair outside my apartment fell into the room and landed lifelessly on the floor.

I brought a hand to my mouth to stifle a scream as I jumped back, tears flooding my eyes. My fingers rapidly found Max's name in my contacts and pressed send. I waited for him to answer as I stood trembling over the dead cop, each second feeling like an hour had passed. After the sixth ring the call went to voicemail and my frustration started to build. I felt open and vulnerable as the person who was assigned to protect me laid dead in my apartment. And my guess was that it had just happened or someone would have freaked out and there would have been commotion in the hallway. I hung up and pressed the button to call again, shifting my weight from side to side while chewing my fingernail.

"Hannah, I'm so glad you called me back." His voice sounded groggy like he had just woken up.

"He's dead! Max, he's dead!" I nearly shouted into the phone as my panic continued to rise, my eyes constantly searching the hallway for any signs of movement. What if whoever did this was still outside?

"Who's dead?" His tone was sharp and more focused as I heard movement on the other end.

"The cop, the one outside my apartment. He's dead and he's in my apartment. And he's dead, Max. Dead!" I knew I was borderline hysterical and he could hear it in my voice but as I continued to stare at the dead body everything around me felt like it was closing in.

"I'm on my way."

I could hear the sound of his keys followed by the sound of a door slamming and heavy footsteps.

"Stay on the phone with me, okay Hannah?"

"Okay," I whispered as I clutched the phone to my ear and paced back and forth. The pool of blood had gotten even larger and I had to take a few steps back to avoid stepping in it. As I walked backwards, I felt the smooth wood of the coffee table as I bumped into it, almost knocking myself over. I sighed as I turned to focus on getting myself to the couch without tripping over something else when I looked down and found a note on the couch cushion.

"Oh my God," I mumbled, forgetting that Max was still on the phone.

"What's wrong Hannah?" He sounded winded as if he was running and trying to talk at the same time.

"There's a note on my couch."

"What does it say?"

"Some people shouldn't sleep on the job."

"What?"

"That's all it says- 'some people shouldn't sleep on the job.' There's nothing else."

"Okay, I'll be there in just a second. I'm down at the front door now." I heard a click as he hung up and continued to stare at the note in my hand.

A few minutes later Max's head appeared in my doorway as he spoke into his cell phone, his eyes landing on me as soon as he stepped inside.

"Are you okay?" He reached down and rolled the body over, feeling for a pulse while he studied me. I could see the tension in his body as he stood up and ran a hand down his face as he took in what had happened. I didn't know if he knew the cop but I had to imagine that it was hard to see one of your own down regardless. A few minutes later I heard heavy footsteps coming down the hall followed by cops making their way into the apartment and talking to Max. I leaned back against the couch and closed my eyes, trying to remember a happy time in my life that didn't involve death or fear.

Eventually Max was able to break away while the other officers took over the scene. He sat beside me in silence as I continued to sit with my head resting against the couch, my eyes clenched shut.

"I know that you don't want to stay with me anymore, and I respect that, but you won't be able to stay here for a while since it's an active crime scene." His voice was gentle but I could hear pain behind his words as they lingered on the topic I had refused to talk to him about since I left that night. "Is there anyone that I can call for you that you can stay with?"

"I don't have anyone. Amber was my only friend and she's dead." I opened my eyes and turned to look at him as tears filled my eyes. "Honestly, I would go back home to stay with my mom if I didn't have finals next week, but I'm kinda scared that I have some sort of curse on me that people who come within a 50-yard radius of me end up dying. You might want to move further away." I closed my eyes and leaned my head back again feeling defeated by life in general.

"Would you consider staying with me again? Please?" I felt his hand reach out and hold mine, the warmth comforting. "I don't think that's a good idea."

"Why not?"

I looked at him and raised an eyebrow, my expression doing the talking for me.

"Hannah, you haven't given me a chance to explain what happened."

"I know what happened," I snapped, cutting him off before he could offer some overly recited explanation about how it wasn't me, it's him. I hated that I was acting this way with him but honestly, it felt better to keep him as far away as possible. If he was far away then I wouldn't feel the pain each time he rejected me.

"No, Hannah, you don't. And quite frankly, you're being real immature by refusing to listen."

My eyes flew open as I stared at him, disbelief that he had the nerve to call me immature. I saw a smirk start to cross his face as he tried to hide it, knowing that he had said the right thing to get my attention. I knew there was a pretty big age gap between us and secretly wondered if that was his only hang up about being with me. I had spent plenty of time at work and in class trying to figure out whether I had misread everything between us. Was he really not interested in me? It sure didn't seem to be the problem when I sat on his lap and could feel the promise of a good time underneath me. A promise that quickly grew the longer I sat there.

"Fine. Talk." I sat up and turned toward him as I crossed my arms over my chest and glared at him. I was furious for him thinking that I was too immature but I didn't want to give him any more credibility by acting like a child right now and throwing a fit. I tried to relax my posture enough to show that I was still angry but not overly angry like a child who didn't get what they wanted. I needed him to take me seriously and treat me like an adult. I'd struggled all my life with everyone treating me like a child and now I was out on my own, an adult, and needed to be treated like one.

"Right here? Right now?" He quirked his brow as he looked over at the crime scene a short distance away from us and looked back at me. In that moment I felt like the child he thought I was. Someone so caught up and focused on their own hurt feelings that I didn't even pay attention to what was going on around me. I felt the blush creep up my neck as I relaxed my arms and turned away from him.

"Why don't we go back to my place? We can talk and then figure out the plan for where you're going to stay?" He offered as he stood up and looked down at me.

"Fine. But I don't plan to ever come back to this apartment so I want to pack up a few things first if that's okay?"

"That should be fine, I'll check in with the other officers and make sure there's nothing they need you to leave. How much stuff do you have?"

"Not much, I left most of my stuff at home and really just brought the essentials with me like clothes and stuff for the apartment." I shrugged as I looked around, comfortable with leaving more than half of the stuff here if it meant I never had to come back to this haunted apartment again.

"Go pack up your clothes and the stuff you need and I'll help you in a few minutes." He smiled and walked over to the other officers as I stood and reached beside the couch for my backpack. I started loading the books and stuff from the coffee table into my backpack when I remembered the note that I hadn't given to Max yet. I tucked it into my backpack along with the other stuff and made my way back to my dresser to pack up the little bit of clothes I had. A framed picture of me with my mom and dad before he got sick sat on my nightstand, my one personal item I had brought with me to make it feel more like home. I wrapped a thick sweater around it and placed it in the suitcase I had just brought back from Max's.

I sat on the edge of the bed with my suitcase almost ripping at the seams, over filled with clothes and my favorite blanket. My backpack sat on the bed beside me and for a moment I was depressed with just how little stuff I actually had in my life that meant anything to me. People always had stories about sentimental items and things that were given to them by a close relative but I had none of that. Max shook the officer's hand and walked toward me, eyeing the suitcase and backpack next to me.

"Is that all?" He looked around as if I had somewhere to hide additional luggage that he hadn't seen.

"Yup." I patted the suitcase and felt a sense of sadness wash over me as I had no idea where my life was going at this point. In just a few weeks everything went from calm and easy to chaotic and scary. I knew that Chet wasn't responsible for any of this after Max told me that he died shortly after our date, but it really felt like everything in my life was going well before I met him. I stood up and slung the backpack over my shoulder as he pulled the handle up on my rolling suitcase and followed him out of the apartment and away from the place I had hoped to call home.

<u>Fourteen</u>

Adam
7 Days Ago

Roses are red
Violets are blue
You don't see me
As I stand over you

My hand reaches out
To brush a strand of your hair
In the still of the night
You're completely unaware

I'll continue to watch you
Until you notice me
Things are more complicated
Than they really need to be

You've given me no choice
Than to go on this path
You think you've found new love
But I know it won't last

You can try to run
You can try to hide
I'll always be in the darkness
My time I'll gladly bide

Lurking in the shadows
Knowing your every step
I'll do whatever to make you mine
I'll go to any depth

Rest your pretty mind and
Cast away your fears
Pretend you're safe with the cop around
But remember, I'm always near

Fifteen

Max
7 Days Ago

My phone buzzed against my thigh, waking me up. Hannah and I had been up late the night before which led to me getting a late start Sunday morning. While I had hoped to talk to her and clear the air about what happened last time, she avoided me every time I brought it up. I was thankful to have her agree to stay with me and left it at that. I groaned as I rolled off of my stomach and fished my phone out of my pocket. Mindy's name flashed across the screen creating an irritation that I wasn't ready to deal with this early in the day. I silenced the call and rolled over, setting the phone on my night stand.

Thirty seconds later I watched the phone vibrate across my nightstand as Mindy called again. I could try to keep ignoring the calls and put my phone on silence but I worked with her long enough to know by the 3rd call she would give up and come over. Weighing my options, I ran my finger across the button to answer the call, given that it felt like the better option against having to see her.

"Yeah," I grunted into the phone without a single ounce of pleasantness.

"Nice to talk to you too." I could tell she was trying to test the waters by lightening the mood but I wasn't in the mood for it. I glanced over at the black folders sitting on my desk and clenched my jaw. I heard a deep breath on the other line and knew that she knew what my current temperament was.

"Okay, I get it, you're mad."

I rolled my eyes. I was about to hang up the call when she started to speak again and caught my attention.

"I know you have the files, and I know that you're pissed off that the cases were closed. I get it, I was furious as well. But Max, we have an update from the autopsy and they confirmed that it wasn't Elena's body."

I froze as I tried to process what she said. It wasn't Elena's body. That meant she might still be alive.

"Whose body was it?"

"They confirmed through dental records that it was another young girl, similar build and looks. Her family has been contacted and they are waiting for them to identify the body. There was a small tattoo on her ankle that they are hoping the family will recognize so they can confirm the identity."

"Did she know Elena? Was there any connection?"

"We don't know at this point. Just thought that I would tell you that it wasn't Elena which means her case is still open." I could hear the relief in her voice that matched my own.

"Thanks for the update." I was ready to hang up and be done with the call but something told me that I shouldn't be so hard on Mindy. If Elena was still alive, I needed all of the help I could get to try to find her.

"That also means I'm going to need the files back. Can I expect you to bring them by the office tomorrow or do you want me to come get them?"

"I can drop them off. I'll be out with Hannah tomorrow anyways, it's her last week of classes this week."

"How are things going with her staying with you? I heard about what happened yesterday, we're still trying to talk with the other neighbors to see if anyone heard or saw anything that can help us catch this bastard."

"Things are fine, she's trying to keep it together this week and focus on school but I really don't know how she does it. I don't think I would even know what day it was if I had been through everything she went through this past week."

"She's definitely had more than her fair share." Mindy let out a soft sigh and I could hear movement as she moved the phone to her other ear. "So, Jack said that he thinks we need to bring you back on the case. How do you feel about that? I know you're still looking after Hannah but we can see about getting another officer to take over."

"So they can have the same fate as the last one? I don't think so."

"I know, but we need you focused on this case if we have any hope of cracking it. You've seen how successful we've been without you." There was a pause as she waited for me to say something snarky. "Don't make me beg."

"I'll see what I can do. I really don't want to leave Hannah on her own but then again, I don't really trust anyone to keep her safe." I blew out a breath knowing this was going to bite me in the ass before I even said it.

"Well, there is one person."

"Who's that?"

"Trevor."

"You really think Trevor is the best person for this?" she asked cautiously. She had only met him a handful of times and he hit on her each time.

"We're basically the same person, so yeah, I trust him."

"If you think it will work." Her voice trailed off with doubt.

"Trust me, he's not going to hit on her." Annoyance flowed through me as I pictured the idea of him flirting with Hannah. What got me even worse was the idea of Hannah welcoming it.

"The only girls Trevor avoids hitting on are the girls you-" I could hear the palm of her hand smack her head on the other line. "Max, you fell for this girl? Already?"

"It's not like that."

"Except that it is. I can hear it in your voice."

I rolled my eyes as I got out of bed and adjusted my T-shirt. She was right and we both knew it. The problem was that I was still refusing to believe it myself.

"I gotta go. I'll be in touch tomorrow and let you know what time I'll be in the office. Thanks for the update on Elena, keep me posted if anything else comes up."

"Will do." She sighed as she hung up. My shoulders felt tense and while I would love to blame it on sleeping wrong or the built up stress from Elena, I knew that it was the tension between Hannah and I that was causing it.

I put my phone in my pocket and walked down the hall into the living room to find Hannah sitting on the floor at the coffee table with books spread out around her. Her brown hair was pulled up into a messy pile on top of her head with a few pencils holding it all together. She tapped the pen in her hand against her knee as she focused on the page in front of her, frustration etched on her face. I leaned against the wall and took her in as I tried to figure out how to start our day that would be better than how we ended our night.

She looked up, surprise written on her face as she noticed me standing there. She pulled the white cord that hung by her neck causing two earbuds to fall into her lap.

"Sorry if I woke you up, I was trying to be quiet." She reached down and turned the music off on her phone before unplugging the earbuds and wrapping them up into a neat ball before tossing them into her backpack.

"You didn't wake me, I got a call from Mindy with an update on Elena's case."

"I thought it was closed?" She moved her books from the coffee table back into her backpack except for one which she held on her lap after she climbed up and got comfortable on the couch.

"It was, but they confirmed the body wasn't Elena's. They are waiting on a positive ID from the family but they are pretty sure they know who it is."

"So what does that mean now? Do they know where she might be?" There was a hopefulness to her voice and I wanted to be as hopeful as she was that we would find my sister alive.

"Starting tomorrow I'll be going back to the office and working on the case." I waited for her response to this news before going on. Her face dropped and I waited for her to ask me not to go in, to stay with her and keep protecting her.

"I'm sure they'll be happy to have you back on the case. More heads are always better than one." She smiled and looked down at the book in her lap, her fingers slowly skimming the edge as she hesitated on opening it. It felt like now was the time to try to clear the air and talk about the other night. I needed things to be easier between us without all of this built up tension.

"Hannah, I really want to talk to you." I walked over, closing the distance between us as I sat on the other end of the couch and faced her. She folded her hands on top of the book and turned to look at me. Her eyes looked fiercely green and for a moment I thought I might get lost in their depths.

"Okay." She was short but the attitude that had been there the last few days had gone away. I held out hope that this would go well.

"I am so sorry for the other night. I didn't mean to hurt your feelings." My eyes searched hers, desperately looking for a sign of how she really felt about it. I might have stopped things between us the other night but now I felt like my heart was on the line and on the verge of being rejected.

"You didn't." She swallowed hard and I knew it was a lie.

"You know, this conversation will go so much better if we don't lie to each other." I tried to sound as playful as possible even though it was true.

"I'm not lying." A blush crept up her cheeks as she fidgeted in her seat. Lie number two. I raised an eyebrow in response which was immediately met with a blush that covered her neck and chest as her eyes darted away from mine.

"You know you're cute when you get caught lying."

I was taking a gamble and putting myself out there. If she felt the way I thought she felt about me then this should be easy and turn into a fun, flirty game. If I was misreading her then this would no doubt end with me being some weird, creepy, older guy preying on an innocent young girl. I prayed for the first option as I waited for her response. Part of me wanted her to want me as much as I wanted her, but I also knew that what we would both want out of this wasn't going to be the same and she would end up getting hurt. I hated myself for that but I found that I couldn't stop myself around Hannah. There was something that drew me to her and I felt like I needed her as much as I needed air to breathe.

"You don't know me well enough to know when I'm lying." She tilted her face slightly to look at me, still refusing to give me her full attention.

"I'm a detective, it's my job to read people." I grinned as I shifted in my seat and stared at her.

"Well then, you must not be very good at your job." Her tone was definitely flirty as she looked at me from over her shoulder.

"Alright, then let's make this fun, shall we? I will tell you everything that makes me believe you're lying and if I'm right, you have to scoot closer to me. If I'm wrong then you can move further away from me. Deal?" Excitement flooded through me as I thought about getting closer to her.

"Fine. I hope you like to lose. And I hope your neighbor has plenty of room for me in their apartment because that's how bad you're gonna lose." She smirked and my body immediately reacted to it. I was about to break every rule in the book, and for once, I didn't care. Maybe rules were meant to be broken.

"Alright, first sign that you're lying," I rubbed my hands together dramatically as if that would help.

"You swallowed hard when you said I didn't hurt your feelings."

She froze and I knew I had her as I watched her body get rigid.

"That wasn't a lie, you didn't hurt my feelings." She swallowed hard again and I had to fight to stifle a laugh.

"Your body is betraying you." I warned. She looked at me pointedly and scooted a fraction of an inch closer to me. My grin grew and spread across my face as I knew how hard this was really going to be.

"Sign two that you lied to me was the blush that crept up your face, not once, but twice."

"That wasn't a blush, it got hot in here." She folded her arms across her chest.

"Well, in that case, I could always open the window and let some fresh air in here if that's the problem?" I pointed to the window and raised my eyebrows in question. I watched as she shivered at the thought and chuckled.

"I'm fine now, thank you."

"Good, that's good. I would hate to point out how you shivered in response to the window being open, yet you still have that blush that creeps up your chest and throat, all the way to your cheeks." I pointed in her direction for her effect.

"I don't blush."

She was stubborn, I had to give her that.

"Oh really? Okay, so then what is this?" I lightly reached over and ran my finger along the trail of skin that was slightly pink, her body reacting to my touch. She rolled her eyes and scooted toward me.

"Third sign you're lying to me is the lack of eye contact. You'll look anywhere to avoid looking at me."

Her shoulders squared as she turned to look at me, a defiant look on her face as she refused to scoot any closer to me. There was a small gap between us which felt too big. I wanted her closer. I wanted to hold her and touch her and feel her body against mine.

"Well, that fixes one lie," I joked as I adjusted on the couch, closing some of the space between us. Her body reacted and I desperately wanted to reach out and touch her to see what else her body would do when I touched her.

"You think you know everything, don't you?" There was an edginess to her tone as she watched my body as if I might pounce on her.

"Not everything, but I do know a lot about people and body language. It helps to know when people are lying or when their body is saying something their mind won't allow them to." I let my gaze travel leisurely over her body, noticing everything her body was saying that she was trying so hard to fight. Like the way her knee was slightly angled toward me or her hand that had moved closer to mine on the couch. The way her breathing had changed the closer I got to her. Or the way her nipples hardened beneath the T-shirt she was wearing with the tight black yoga pants that I was eager to rip off of her.

"Okay, so what exactly is my body language saying?" She tilted her head to the side and her eyes tried to make eye contact as they fought the urge to roam my body. I could tell that she was as curious about this chemistry between us as I was but she was scared to explore it.

"Your body language is saying that it wants me. The way your legs are slightly spread toward me, eager for me to feel how turned on you are. Your breathing has gotten more rapid the closer we sit to each other. And you tilt your head in a way that leaves your neck exposed, an easy path for my tongue to run down it."

Her eyes grew hooded as she listened to the words I said, her attention focused on me instead of avoiding me. She looked up at me and our eyes locked on each other, desire evident on both of our faces. My hand fought the urge to reach out and pull her into me as she subtly licked her lips.

"Hannah, I wanted to be with you the other night, more than you could know. Which given that you were sitting on my dick, I'm sure you knew." I saw a blush creep up her face as she lowered her eyes, casting a quick glance at my crotch before looking at the floor.

"I only said no because I didn't feel right letting anything happen between us. I'm supposed to be protecting you, not hitting on you. And given how much you've been through recently, I didn't want you acting on impulse because you were upset. I needed to know that if we had met under any other circumstances, you would still want me. I couldn't risk taking advantage of you."

Her posture changed and became more relaxed as she stared down at her bare feet on the rug. Slowly I reached over and lifted her chin up so I could look at her.

"Don't think for a second that it was because I didn't want you or that I don't find you attractive. You're one of the sexiest girls I've met and it's taking a whole lot of self-control to keep my hands off of you." I let out a nervous laugh and waited for her to say something. Anything. Her silence was killing me as I laid it all out on the line.

"I think that even if I hadn't met you under the same circumstances, I would still be incredibly attracted to you." She scooted closer and I could feel the heat from her body close to mine. "So attracted that I would be lying if I said that I wasn't turned on sitting this close to you. You're not the only one fighting urges right now." She worked her bottom lip between her teeth and watched me.

I reached across and wrapped my hand around the back of her head as my lips gently kissed hers. Her hands wrapped around the back of my neck as she deepened the kiss, pulling me toward her until she was laying on her back, my body on top of hers. The kiss was hungry and greedy as we fought to catch our breath, lust too much for us to fight it. My hand roamed down her neck, across her shoulder, and over her breast as she arched her back in response. I could feel how ready her body was for me and worked quickly to strip her of her shirt. Her chest heaved as she worked to pull my shirt up and over my head, stopping to run her fingers down my stomach before reaching for the drawstring of my sweats.

It was so arousing to see that she wanted this as much as I did, my erection bulging beneath the thick fabric of the sweat pants. I wanted her naked beneath me, I wanted to lick every inch of her while memorizing every detail I could of her body. My hands trembled with desire as I reached down and pulled at the top of her yoga pants, pulling them down her long legs, along with her panties. Laying beneath me on the couch was the most beautiful girl wearing nothing but a black lacy bra. I took a step back and stared at her as I licked my lips and tried to adjust myself. Hannah's eyes grew wide as she took in my size, desire heavy in her eyes. I worked my pants and boxers down and let them fall to the floor as I stood naked in front of her.

She swallowed hard and licked her lips as she spread her legs in invitation. I wanted to be inside of her already but I was more focused on making sure I took care of her. Slowly I kneeled down on the floor and gently pushed her knees apart, my shoulders holding them in place as my mouth began devouring her. Within minutes I found the rhythm she liked and worked my tongue around her as she came undone, calling my name while wrapping her fingers in my hair. She looked absolutely stunning as she came and I knew it was a face I wanted to see over and over again. I slowly scooted her away from the edge of the couch and made my way inside of her, feeling her tighten around me as I chased my own sweet release.

Sixteen

Hannah
7 Days Ago

Sunday afternoon rolled by without us noticing as we had spent the majority of the morning making love. My body still felt the after effects of our love making marathon and I wasn't sure how I was going to sit all day the next day in class as the soreness was starting to build. To say that he was well endowed would be a huge understatement. Max had left twenty minutes ago to grab us lunch while I tried to get my attention back to studying with no luck. Frustrated, I tossed the highlighter to the floor beside me and laid my head back against the couch cushion, memories of Max taking his time with me overriding anything I had just read. There was a knock on the door and I stilled, unsure of whether or not I should open it. It wasn't my apartment and Max wasn't there to tell me what to do. I contemplated my decision as another knock came, louder this time.

I stood up and opened the door to a young kid holding a small bouquet of flowers between his gloved hands. He extended the bouquet to me, lifting it higher toward my hands when I didn't reach out to take it.

"I think you might have the wrong apartment." I looked questioningly at him and waited for him to confirm who the delivery was for, even though I didn't actually know any of Max's neighbors. It wasn't like I was going to be much help by saying, 'oh yeah, Ms. Jackson, she's two doors down.'

"Apartment 702. Says right here on the card." He plucked it from the pick that was holding it and flipped it around so I could see for myself. Printed in black ink was my name and Max's address. I reached out with a trembling hand and took the small vase, wondering who would be sending me flowers here. No one knew I was staying with him. I watched as he walked down the hallway and waited for the elevator before going back inside and closing the door. Just for safe measure I slid the deadbolt into place and locked the door.

I sat the vase down on the island and looked at the card that was still in my hand when I heard Max's key in the door. I walked over quickly and unlocked the deadbolt as Max smiled on the other side, a bag with take-out boxes filled to the top in one hand and a tray with two coffee cups in the other. His smiled faded as soon as he saw my expression and looked around the room. He came in and I closed and locked the door behind him.

"What's wrong?" He sat the bag of food down on the island next to the flowers and looked at them before looking up at me. For a quick second I prayed that it was some weird but romantic thing that Max did while he was out and that the flowers were from him. The voices in my head laughed hysterically as my hand started to sweat around the card I was still holding in between my fingers.

"Who are the flowers from?"

"I don't know. Someone just delivered them." I showed the card toward him as he walked over and took it from me.

"Did you open the card yet?" His eyes searched mine though I didn't know what he was looking for. I shook my head no and waited for him to open it for me. He flipped it over and read the name and address on the front before looking back at me.

"Does anyone know that you're staying here?"

I shook my head again and knew that was my confirmation that the flowers weren't some cute romantic gesture from Max.

"Do you want to open it? Or do you want me to?"

"Can you please?" My stomach churned as I waited for him to read it out loud. His finger ran under the seal on the back and pulled a thin card out. His brows furrowed as he read the card, my anxiety worsening as I waited. He looked over at me then down at the card again. A quick shake of his head before he began reading.

> *You don't know what you've done*
> *A fire you've done started*
> *Someday you'll have to make your peace*
> *With the recently departed*
>
> *I tried to warn you*
> *About playing by the rules*
> *A girl like you is never happy*
> *I refuse to be your fool*
>
> *Your time is coming*
> *The clock is ticking*
> *No one can save you*
> *Your blood will be dripping*

I felt the color drain from my face as his words filled the air around me, smothering me like a wet blanket. He flipped the card over and looked at the envelope it came in. I already knew that there wasn't any information about where it came from or who sent it. We both knew who it was, only we had no idea who it actually was. I ran my hands up and down my arms in an effort to get rid of the chill that covered my entire body.

"Are you okay?" He sat the card and envelope on the island and wrapped me in a hug. I felt safe with him and in that moment, I didn't want to be anywhere else other than in his arms. His apartment had felt like a safe place until now. Now everything in my life had been tainted by whoever it was that had become obsessed with me.

"Yeah, I'm fine," I lied. My stomach grumbled loudly and Max let out a soft chuckle.

"Why don't we sit down and eat before everything gets cold." He smiled warmly as he let go of me and walked over to the bag with our food. I stared at the flowers, a small bouquet of beautiful assorted flowers and felt sad that something so beautiful had been used for something so ugly. A hand reached out in front of me with a coffee cup and I snapped back to reality, smiling as I took the cup from Max. I grabbed his and took them over to the coffee table as he followed me with the food.

We sat and ate in silence with the tv on for background noise. I didn't want to talk about the flowers or the eerily creepy message that had been sent with them. I didn't want to talk about how someone found me at Max's apartment and how I no longer had a safe place to stay because this person always seemed to know where I was. I didn't want to talk about school and the stress of how I felt I was going to fail every class my first semester at NYU and lose my scholarship. I didn't want to talk, period.

After lunch we relaxed on the couch for a bit as I laid in his lap and he responded to several emails and text messages on his phone. I knew he was working on Elena's case and now the added details of mine. I wanted to force him to forget about everything and just be in the moment with me but I knew that wasn't possible. His high energy flowed through him and into me as I laid on him, making me feel more anxious than I already was. I needed to get up and do something to take my mind off of everything.

"I'm gonna go take a shower." I leaned up and kissed his cheek then made my way down the hall and into the bathroom. I stripped down and waited for the water to get hot before stepping in the walk-in shower. The water rained down on me peacefully as I laid my back against the cold tile wall and let myself cry. Slowly I slid down the tile until I was sitting on the floor with my knees pulled into my chest, warm water soothing my skin. I lowered my head and sobbed as I thought about everything that had happened over the past few weeks. Losing my dad had been one of the hardest and most trying times in my life, but this felt like it might be even worse. I felt helpless knowing that it wouldn't be long before whoever was stalking me would finally make their move. I heard a soft knock on the door before it slowly opened.

"Just checking on you, are you okay?" Max's voice was filled with concern but I couldn't catch my breath between sobs to answer him. The truth was that I wasn't okay; not even a little bit. I tried to catch my breath as I heard light footsteps approach the shower, the curtain pulled back as his eyes filled with sadness when they found me. He leaned in and turned the water off before reaching down and picking me up. I didn't care that I was naked or wet, I just let him carry me to his bed and wrap me in a blanket as he curled up next to me on the bed and held me. Slowly my breathing calmed and I felt my body relax against his as I drifted off to sleep.

I woke up a few hours later to an empty bed. It was embarrassing that Max had seen my meltdown and I felt even more like a child who had to be cared for. I got up and realized that my clean clothes were still in my suitcase in the living room. Reluctant to waltz in there naked, I decided to raid Max's closet and threw on a pair of sweatpants and a T-shirt that looked soft and worn out. I stopped to look in the mirror and noticed the puffiness in my eyes along with a small hickey on my neck. My hand reached up to touch it as I thought about Max's mouth on mine, kissing my neck as he thrust inside of me. The hickey was the result of his third orgasm. My hair was still wet in spots so I combed through it quickly and tossed it up in a messy bun on my head using a pen I found on his desk. I knew he wasn't expecting me to come out there dressed like a beauty queen but I didn't want to look like a complete slob either.

As I walked down the hall into the living room I heard him talking and stopped short when I saw Trevor sitting on the couch. Suddenly I felt very on display wearing Max's clothes and no underwear as they both looked at me, Max's face lit up with a smile.

"Hey Hannah," Trevor called over his shoulder as he turned his attention back to the tv.

"Hey." I looked at my suitcase in the corner and saw the clothes I was wearing earlier neatly folded on top leaving me no option to escape into the bathroom and put a bra on. Self-consciously I folded my arms across my chest and went and sat in my usual spot on the couch.

Spread out on the coffee table were sheets of paper with circles and arrows pointing in every direction. I leaned closer and found that it was all information related to my stalker and the little bit of information that Max had on Elena. I looked up at him as I leaned back on the couch and waited for him to tell me what was going on.

"We're trying to piece everything together." He nodded at the table as if that explained everything. I looked over at Trevor and he smiled though it didn't reach his eyes which made me wonder if he was called over to help solve this as a result of the card I got earlier. His eyes shifted and found the hickey on my neck, a smirk spreading across his face as he turned to look at Max with one eyebrow raised. I felt my cheeks flush, desperate to take the attention off of what had happened with Max and I earlier. I didn't bother looking to see what Max's reaction was, that would just make it worse. The fact that Trevor knew Max and I had done something was bad enough, I couldn't handle it if Max was going to gloat about it.

I slid off the couch onto my knees and leaned over the coffee table as I read the information they had linked to each bubble. There was a bubble for Elena, one for Amber, and the one in the middle was for me. My stomach soured as I acknowledged that they knew as well as I did that I was at the center of all of this. It seemed there was a connection between Elena missing and me, but I had yet to figure it out. I looked at my bubble and read each of the arrows with information on them. The notes I received. The cop that was murdered. My underwear drawer, which had been messed with not once, but twice. For all I knew this psychopath could be running around wearing a pair of them and I wouldn't even know it. I hadn't noticed that there was a new pair of underwear in my drawer with a note, would I really notice if a pair was missing?

I studied the information regarding the notes and each one had details about it being written in marker. I had never paid attention to that but then again, I hadn't paid much attention to the notes in general. Something was nagging at me just below the surface and I felt desperate to find it.

"Do you still have all of the notes that I've received?" I looked up at Max, hoping he still had them with him since he hadn't been in to the office.

"Yeah, let me go get them." He walked down the hall to the bedroom and came back with a Ziplock bag filled with the notes. He handed it to me and I laid each one out on the coffee table in the order in which I received them, including the one that came today.

Each note was a different size but each one was written on a page from a textbook. I didn't remember having any pages missing from my textbook other than the very first note but yet these still looked familiar. Each one had either a header or page number which seemed odd to me until I realized it was a clue. Instinctively I reached over and grabbed my backpack, flipping through the textbooks inside until I found my Introduction to Psychology book. Quickly I flipped the pages until I found the one that had been ripped. I placed the first note against it and found it matched perfectly.

I looked at the second note and saw a page number on the bottom. Going off of instincts I flipped through the same textbook until I found that page number. I studied the note and compared it to the same page of the textbook, the text the exact same. A shiver ran down my spine as I found the other note matched as well. I looked up at Max and Trevor as they leaned forward and studied me, waiting for me to confirm what I had found.

"All of these notes were written on pages torn out of this Intro to Psychology textbook," I held it up for them to see, "the only problem is that my book only has one page that is missing. That means these were torn out of someone else's book." There was a look of understanding followed by a look of confusion on their faces as they didn't make the same connection that I did.

"I had both Amber and Elena in the Intro to Psychology class." I let out a deep breath as my hand trembled holding the text book. Max leaned back in the recliner and closed his eyes as he ran a hand down his face.

"So you think the person that's stalking you also knew Amber and Elena?" Trevor asked as Max continued to rub his face.

"I do. That seems to be the strongest link, we were all in that class together and now one of us is missing, one is dead, and one is being stalked. I would say this is the path we need to look at."

Trevor and I talked amongst ourselves as Max called Mindy with the update. They decided it was best to keep working through the progress we were making which meant Mindy was on her way over to Max's apartment. I wasn't sure how I felt about meeting the woman who had decided that my best friend's case should be closed when the killer was still on the prowl.

I went through the notes I had collected for that class and didn't find anything that would be helpful, even though I had no idea what I was searching for. A handful of graded papers were sitting on the coffee table as I thumbed through papers from another binder when Max walked by and stopped abruptly in front of me.

"What class are those from?" He pointed to the stack of graded papers and looked across the coffee table as Mindy and Trevor shifted their attention to us.

"Um, I think these are all from the Intro class. Why?" I looked up at him as something crossed his face and he picked up the top paper and laid it next to one of the notes.

"The ink on this paper looks like the same on the notes- a fine point black marker. See?" He held up them up side by side for us to look. While they were both black markers, I didn't notice anything else that looked familiar.

"Let me see." Mindy extended her hand and Max passed them over to her. "It does look like the same type of pen but the curve and slant of the writing don't match. See how they slant their A in the note but it's not slanted here on the paper?" She leaned down and laid them on the coffee table to show us.

My mind was slowing down as it felt like we had spent hours going over the same thing, over and over again. I gently rubbed my temples as Mindy said goodbye and left. I was thankful for the break and hoped this meant that Trevor would leave as well so I could try to get some rest. A yawn took over and I fought the urge to curl up on the floor and sleep where I was. Max closed the door behind Mindy and slid the deadbolt into place before coming and sitting next to me on the couch.

"You ready for bed?" he asked as he laid his hand on my knee. I glanced over to see if Trevor had noticed but he was too consumed by something on his phone to pay attention as he rocked slowly in the recliner.

"Yeah, I have a long day tomorrow with classes so I better get to bed soon."

"How about you sleep in my bed with me tonight so I can make sure you're safe?"

I looked pointedly at him then looked at Trevor, pleading with my eyes for him to stop so Trevor wouldn't know we had hooked up. I saw the smirk on his face as he looked over at Trevor who still had his head down looking at his phone.

"Don't worry, I already know you guys are hooking up." He didn't bother looking up as he kept texting. I reached over and smacked Max's chest with my hand as he caught it and held onto it.

"You told him?" I whispered accusingly.

"He didn't have to. I could tell the moment I saw him. He's not all stiff and rigid like he was. Plus, there's the hickey on your neck." He looked up and smiled as he slid his phone into his pocket. I leaned back against the couch and closed my eyes while I prayed the couch would swallow me whole and spare me from this utter humiliation.

"It's not a big deal, is it?" Max leaned back against the couch next to me and spoke softly as I peered at him from the corner of my eye. I blew out a deep breath. It didn't really matter but I felt totally self-conscious that Trevor knew what had happened. Especially since Max and I hadn't even talked about it ourselves yet. Were we in a relationship? Was it just a one-night stand? I had no idea but the way he was looking at me and touching me made me feel like maybe it was more than that to him.

"I don't think it matters at this point." I sighed and stood up. "I'm heading to bed. And I'm taking your side because it's more comfortable." I raised my eyebrows and smirked at him as I started toward the hallway.

"Goodnight, Trevor," I called over my shoulder.

"Goodnight, Hannah. See you in the morning."

I stopped dead in my tracks and turned around, knowing there was something going on that I didn't know about.

"Why am I seeing you in the morning?"

"He's actually staying the night." Max swallowed hard and waited for my reaction before continuing. "Then he's going with you to all of your classes tomorrow." He smiled the cheesiest smile I had ever seen for half a second I couldn't be mad at him.

"Okay, walk me through it. Why is he going to my classes with me?"

"Hannah, whoever is stalking you found you here. They don't seem to care that you're staying with a cop so I don't trust them to not do something stupid. Trevor is staying here so he can help me protect you. And he's going with you to your classes to make sure you're safe." He let out a breath. "I can't take any chances Hannah. My sister is missing and that kills me. I can't stand the thought of something happening to you too."

"Fine." I sighed and looked over at Trevor who was watching the exchange between Max and I with the same interest someone does with watching a fight on Jerry Springer. "But we're stopping for donuts and coffee on the way in the morning." I turned and pointed to Trevor.

"You got it." He smiled and I saw Max relax as I walked down the hall and climbed into bed, leaving the day behind me as I drifted off to a place filled with memories of my dad.

Seventeen

Hannah
6 Days Ago

"That's your breakfast? A sugar filled glazed donut and vanilla latte?" Trevor eyed the donut in my hand as he flicked a packet of Splenda into his black coffee and put the lid back on.

"Hey, sugar keeps me going so I can make it through finals this week. I don't remember half of what I've studied and my only other option would be to start doing speed, and Lord knows, I can't afford a drug habit right now." I smiled as I took the latte from the barista and walked behind Trevor as we made our way out of the packed coffee shop. It was busy 24/7 with college students getting their fix for early morning classes or late-night cram sessions.

I slowly sipped my coffee in between bites as we walked across campus. It was another cold morning and I couldn't wait for the semester to be over. My bank account couldn't wait either given that I had taken this week off to focus on school. I took another big sip of coffee to try to warm myself up, pushing the impending financial crisis out of my head. I had plenty to worry about including new housing options on top of everything else. My recent phone call with my mom had ended with her asking if I needed to borrow money. That's when I knew I was in over my head- when my mom who is barely making ends meet, starts asking if I need money. My lungs filled with air as I took a deep breath and forced it out slowly and steadily.

"So, what's the deal with you and Max?" Trevor caught me mid sip, forcing me to turn away from him to keep from spraying coffee in his face. Of all of the things we could talk about to fill the silence, this was what he wanted to focus on?

"What do you mean?" I wiped my mouth with the back of my gloved hand and looked at him, hoping he would be clearer on what he was really asking before I embarrassed myself with divulging too much information. I had been obsessing over that same question.

"Are you guys just hooking up? Or are you wanting a relationship?" His eyes searched mine as if there was a secret answer that he was looking for that he didn't trust me to say out loud.

"We haven't really talked about it, things kind of just happened yesterday. I took a nap then next thing I know, you're living with us and asking about it as we walk to the final exam that I'm bound to fail." I veered off to the trash can and tossed in the dirty napkin from my donut and the empty coffee cup. When I looked back at Trevor, he was smiling but it wasn't a warm smile. I licked my lips as I tried to brace myself for a conversation I wasn't ready to have.

"You seem like a really nice girl, Hannah. I don't want you to get hurt, so you should probably talk to Max about what this is before things go any further. Just my advice- don't set your heart on a relationship. He's not that kind of guy." His words were direct and carried a punch that knocked the wind out me. I didn't know what to say to that so I walked past him through the double doors that he held open, and made my way to the lecture hall. I could hear his footsteps as he trailed beside me, a few steps back, and wondered why he felt the need to warn me about Max. More importantly, I wondered why he said that Max wasn't the kind of guy to be in a relationship. While I had secretly wondered about it myself, I wasn't ready to hear the actual truth.

The room was already filling up, the rows toward the front of the class already taken by a handful of students that I knew from their obsessive Q&A sessions at the end of every lecture. I made my way a few rows back from where they were sitting and took a seat at the end of the row so I didn't have to climb over anyone once I was finished. Trevor sat next to me and studied the room, his phone in hand as he sent text messages every few minutes. My guess was that they were to Max since my phone had been quiet the moment Trevor and I left, yet Trevor's phone hadn't stopped. I could tell that Max felt uneasy this morning about leaving and going back to work. He asked me about my schedule so many times that at one point I gave up and just text it to him so he would have it. It boggled my mind how he could be so concerned with me and where I was going or what I was doing, yet he didn't care enough to want to be in a relationship. Or was that just Trevor talking? I shook my head in frustration and tried to clear my head and focus.

My backpack was light today with only a few notebooks and pencils, which felt weird. I was so used to lugging everything around with me that I felt almost naked not having a heavy backpack full of books. I had purposely left them at Max's apartment to try to keep my nerves calm so I didn't freak out and try to cram a bunch of studying in while I waited for the final exam. As I tapped my pencil on the folding table of my chair, I instantly regretted not having my books so I could study. I watched as the room continued to fill with anxious bodies, all of us waiting on the professor, which according to Trevor's phone, was now 9 minutes late.

A few minutes later the doors at the front of the room flew open and Professor Wright walked in, offering a small wave as everyone watched him. Within minutes he had his briefcase open and was giving the directions for how to complete the final exam as he walked up each row and handed out a stack of tests to be passed down the row. By the time he got to me he was winded and his face was redder than usual. I reached for the stack of papers at the same time he lost his grip on them and they went flying around me. I bent down to pick them up and almost collided with his head, a nervous laugh escaping my throat.

"Sorry," I whispered as I grabbed what I could and sat up right.

"No big deal." He smiled and reached beneath the empty chair in front of me to grab the last few tests. As he turned to walk to the row behind me, I noticed something caught his step and looked down as he wiggled his foot, his black boot stuck in something on the floor. A quick shake of his leg and it was free, allowing him to continue on his was as he passed out the remaining tests. I took the test on top and passed the others to Trevor to pass to the rest of the row. My hands trembled as my anxiety spiked, worried about whether I was ready for this exam.

Professor Wright made his way back down to the front of the room and stood in front of his desk as he announced the start of the final exam which would have 10 minutes added to the end due to him being late. I was about to write my name on the top of it when I noticed Trevor looking at the exam with an odd look on his face. He leaned closer and reached across to rub his finger along the corner. A small red dot smeared into a bigger red blob, confusion on my face as I watched him. He looked at me and mouthed the words 'are you bleeding'?

I looked down at my hands and didn't see any cuts or scratches then pulled up the sleeves of my sweater, not finding anything either. I shook my head no and followed his eyes as they shifted toward Professor Wright who had his back turned to the class and was quickly wiping something off the sleeve of his black overcoat with a tissue from the box on the desk. He pulled his arm across him as he wiped along the back side of his forearm, up to his elbow, studying the fabric carefully. From where I was sitting I could see a tear in the coat as he pulled it tight against his arm as he worked to clean it.

Looking satisfied he took the tissue he was using and wadded it up, tossing it in the trash can before turning around and checking on the class. Trevor and I exchanged a look as we watched the tissue covered in bright red fall into the wastebasket. As I looked down at my test with the red stain staring back at me, I wondered what had happened that made him so frenzied when he came in. He was usually calm and collected, today it looked like he had gotten into some sort of altercation before class. I lowered my head, closed my eyes, and said a quick prayer before starting the final.

An hour later I walked up to his desk and extended a shaky hand as I handed in the exam that would determine my fate in the class. He looked up and smiled warmly as he took the test from me, quickly flipping through the pages to make sure I had completed all of them.

"Have a good break, Hannah."

"Thank you." My voice was soft to keep from disrupting the rest of the class as they continued working on their test but I still couldn't stop thinking about the blood on his jacket earlier.

"Um, Professor, are you okay today?"

I really hoped I wasn't overstepping but his behavior had me concerned.

"Yeah, I'm okay. Why do you ask?" He tilted his head to the side as he sat my exam face down in the pile on his desk.

"I noticed that you were bleeding earlier. Some of it had gotten on my test." I smiled nervously and watched as a faint blush crept up his face.

"Oh, yeah, that. I'm so embarrassed. I was trying to help a kid chase down their dog that got away and as I reached for the leash, the dog ran away and I fell into a chain link fence. Turns out I'm not as graceful as I thought." He chuckled softly, the corners of his eyes wrinkling in response.

"Well, I'm sorry that you have battle wounds, but I personally would have appreciated the gesture." I smiled at him as I saw Trevor waiting for me by the door. "Have a relaxing break, maybe I'll see you next semester." I shifted my backpack and returned his smile before heading off to meet Trevor.

We walked out into the cold air and I took a deep breath, thankful that one final was done. The day felt long and I was relieved to be done with 2/3 of my final exams by the time Trevor and I caught the train back to Max's apartment. My mind was tired and I didn't want to think about anything school related for the rest of the day. We lucked out and found 2 seats toward the back as people shuffled around us with each stop. We were two stops away when I noticed Trevor get up and looked down at me.

"You ready?" There was a different tone to his voice, like he was putting on a show for someone. Confused I looked around quickly and didn't notice anyone that looked suspicious.

"The stop is still two stops away," I said quiet enough for him to hear but not loud enough for anyone else to pay attention.

"We have a stop to make along the way." He spoke sternly as he side-eyed a guy sitting across from us, a few seats down. The guy was wearing a hoodie pulled low over his face, making it hard to see him.

"Okay." I stood up and let Trevor take my hand as we waited for the door to open. As people started to push around me, I felt Trevor's strong hand guide me out and to the side, away from everyone. He pulled me close to him and from the angle we were at, it looked like we were in an intimate embrace. I stilled as I smelled the musky scent of his aftershave and noticed the stubble on his jawline. My body was tense, though I tried to look relaxed, as I waited for whatever it was he was doing. He lowered his head and tilted it toward me as he shielded my face with his.

"What's going on?" I whispered as I watched him intently watching someone close to us. He glanced at me before raising his arm and leaned against the metal beam above my head. It was freezing on the platform as the train whirled past us, the crowd thinning out with it.

"Stay still and try not to move."

I froze in place, nervously waiting to know what had him so spooked.

"The guy in the hoodie followed us from campus and he was taking pictures of you on his cell phone while we were on the train."

His words shot a chill through me as I thought about someone watching me and taking pictures of me without me having any clue. I was thankful that he was there. Obviously, I sucked at protecting myself, case in point. His body relaxed against me as his hand wrapped around my waist and pulled me closer to him. I sucked in a deep breath as I tried to remember that he was doing something other than hitting on me.

"I want to see how he reacts to seeing you with another guy."

"He's still there?" I felt stupid for asking. Why else would we still be in this intimate embrace if he wasn't.

"He's leaning against the other wall, on his cell phone. We'll leave in a few, if he follows then I know he's following you."

"Just tell me what you need me to do," I whispered even though no one else was close enough to hear me.

"I'm going to pretend to kiss you, then we'll hug and you'll walk away. Go to the 7th street station and take the train the rest of the way. From there go straight to Max's apartment, don't make any other stops along the way."

I looked up at him with fear in my eyes, there was no way he would be putting me out there as bait. Was there?

"I'll be right behind you. If this is the guy Hannah, we need to catch him and this may be the best way to do it."

I sucked in a deep breath and tried to reassure myself that I could do this. All I had to do was walk to Max's apartment. And survive.

"Okay." I let out the breath I had been holding as I turned into Trevor and wrapped my arms around him. I twisted our bodies slightly to make it a clear view where the guy in the hoodie stood. If we were going to put on a show, might as well go all in. We needed this to work. I leaned forward and tilted my head, resting my lips gently on Trevor's. I could feel his body's initial reaction to it and wrapped my hands behind his head to keep him from pulling back. His body gave in and I felt as he pushed me against the column and kissed me deeper, knowing we were both putting on the best show we could. As he pulled away, I wrapped him in a hug and leaned close to his ear.

"Make it count," I whispered as I pulled away and let my hand linger in his, looking adoringly over my shoulder like I imagined lovers did. Or at least that's what I'd seen in the movies.

I turned around and let Trevor drift out of sight as I wrapped my coat tighter around me and adjusted my backpack on my back. I took the stairs quickly and tried to use my peripheral vision to see if I could see anyone next to me wearing a hoodie. Who was I kidding? It was winter in New York. Everyone was wearing hoodies or overcoats which made it feel like an uncomfortable Where's Waldo puzzle. Except that Waldo was a mysterious stalker who liked to kill people in their downtime.

The streets were busy as I tried to stay focused on getting to the next station and not on who was around me. I pulled the zipper up higher on my coat and tried to tuck my head inside as I pulled the drawstring on the hood tighter around my head. If I could try to conserve as much heat as possible, maybe it wouldn't feel so bone chilling cold.

I was a few streets over when the crowd started to thin out, people going their separate ways. A tingle shot through me as I thought about whether the guy in the hoodie was near.

Would he make his move out in the open like this? I tried to calm the fears that coursed through my mind as I reassured myself that Trevor was close by. I had no idea where, but I prayed he still had eyes on me.

The crosswalk sign lit up, encouraging me to go about my way when I felt someone next to me slightly bump my shoulder. I rubbed my hands together as I tried to get my mind to tell my feet to keep moving. From the corner of my eye I saw a black hoodie and my stomach dropped. Was it the same guy in the same black hoodie that Trevor was worried about or was it some weird coincidence that someone else in a black hoodie would bump into me? My mind tried to focus as I moved one foot in front of the other, crossing the street and continuing down the stairs to the train. My legs trembled as I swiped my metro card and pushed through the turnstile heading to the platform to wait for the next train.

The cold chill made my skin feel on high alert as I found a solid concrete wall to stand in front of, helping to ease my anxiety. I slowly looked around for a sign of Trevor or the guy in the hoodie and didn't find either. My stomach sank at the thought of going to the apartment by myself and turned sour at the thought that something could have happened to Trevor. I listened as the train approached and looked around once more before making my way through the crowd of people pushing their way around me. I held onto the handrail above me as the train pulled forward, still no sign of Trevor.

Eighteen

Max
6 Days Ago

"What do you mean you LOST her?" I barked into my cell phone.

"I'm sorry, Max. I thought this guy was following her and I needed to see if it was the guy who's been stalking her. I planned to meet up with her at the 7th street station but she walked faster than I anticipated and somehow got lost in the crowd." Trevor blew out a loud breath and I could hear the frustration in his voice.

"Have you checked my apartment?"

"Yeah, she's not there."

"How long ago did this happen?"

"If she got on the train that she should have gotten on, then she should have made it to your apartment twenty minutes ago. Easily."

"Did you follow the guy in the hoodie?" I tapped my foot impatiently as I tried to think of what the next step should be. I needed to find Hannah and I needed to find her now.

"I watched him walk up next to her at a crosswalk but he didn't make contact with her. They stood next to each other then went separate ways when they crossed. She was my priority, not him."

"So you're telling me that you lost her for nothing?"

"I feel bad enough already, just tell me where to look for her and I'll go there."

"Check her apartment, that's the only other place I can think of. I'll try calling her." I hung up the phone and paced behind my desk as I dialed her number and waited for her to answer. After the eighth ring I got her voicemail. I could feel my blood pressure rise as I hit redial and continued to pace along to the ringing tone in my ear. No answer. I looked at my watch and grunted knowing that she should have easily made it back to my apartment by now.

I ran a hand through my hair as I tried to think of other places she could have gone but I couldn't imagine that she would purposely tell Trevor that she was going directly to my apartment then go somewhere else. That wasn't like Hannah. Something was wrong.

Irritated, I hung up the phone and slammed it down on my desk. Mindy looked at me out of the corner of her eye with an eyebrow raised at the loud distraction. Staying in the office wasn't going to do any good if I couldn't concentrate and I definitely wasn't going to be able to until I knew where Hannah was. I grabbed my leather jacket off the back of my chair and flung it on, grabbing my cell phone and pressing send again as I held the phone to my ear and made my way to the 7th street station.

I walked the entire platform looking for any clues as I waited for the next train that would take me to the station that Hannah should have gotten off at to go to my apartment. I was out of ideas so I decided to retrace her steps and see if anything gave me a sign of where she could be. Trevor had called to confirm that she wasn't at her apartment and that the crime scene had already been cleared. While that was good news that Hannah could go home, I was reluctant to tell her because I wasn't ready for her to leave.

The train was nearly empty which gave me the opportunity to sit and think for a minute as I waited for my stop. There had to be something that Trevor and I were missing. Something that would lead Hannah astray. The train slowed to a jerky stop, forcing me to keep going. I walked the path that I imagined Hannah would have taken and looked down each dark alley for any signs she might have been taken down one. As morbid as it seemed, the detective in me knew it was a possibility.

As I got closer to my apartment, I felt tense and couldn't shake the feeling that I was missing something. Where could she be? Her apartment wasn't far from mine and there wasn't much in between other than apartments and a few restaurants and shops. Then it hit me, the only other place she could be that we hadn't thought of was the coffee shop that she went to all the time to meet up with her group from school. I turned on my heel and jogged down the block, hopeful that I would be right.

The coffee shop was packed 24/7 with a constant line out the door and today it was no exception. I pushed my way inside and ignored the looks and snide comments from those that thought I was trying to cut in line. Quickly my eyes scanned the room searching for Hannah, praying that my instincts were right and that she would be here.

I had almost given up when I looked around the entire room with no sign of her before spotting a table at the very back by the bathroom. Sitting by herself at the table, Hannah looked out the window and cried as she clutched her jacket tight around her. I let out a deep breath as I pushed through the overly crowded tables and made my way to her.

"Hannah, what are you doing here?" I kneeled beside her, her green eyes filled with tears as her fingers trembled above her lip as she tried to wipe them away.

"Are you okay?"

She nodded yes and then looked out the window again. I followed her eyes as she stared vacantly at the people passing by.

"What's going on? You were supposed to meet Trevor back at my apartment." My voice was gentle as I struggled to figure out what had happened and why she was so upset. She wiped her eyes with the back of her hand and reached into the napkin dispenser for another napkin to blow her nose. She took a rugged deep breath and turned to look at me. I smiled warmly as I pulled the chair out next to me and sat beside her.

"While I was on the train, I reached into my pocket and found a note." She sucked in a few breaths, the effects of crying making it hard for her to get her words out easily.

"There was a note in your pocket?" I was confused and prayed that it wasn't like the notes she had been receiving from the stalker. Maybe it was a note from Amber that she forgot was in there and seeing it made her want to come back to where they used to hang out. She nodded yes and reached down into her pocket to pull out the note.

"It wasn't there before I went to class and I haven't taken my coat off all day so I don't know how it got there. But it was there." She looked out the window while I read the note.

If you want to know who killed your friend
Go to the spot you used to meet
Don't talk to the cop
Or I'll hang the pig by his feet

Real classy. I shook my head and fought the urge to crumple the note, knowing that it would have to be added to the other notes that were being collected as evidence. So that's why she didn't tell us she was coming here and wasn't answering her phone.

"What happened when you got here?" I asked quietly while my blood felt like it was boiling. She continued to stare out the window as she started talking.

"I got here and didn't know what I was looking for. I scanned the entire room, looking for something- anything that would tell me what the note was about. All of the tables were empty except for this one. Sitting across from it was a guy wearing a hoodie." She looked directly at me. "The guy that Trevor was worried about."

A chill ran through me as I thought about her alone by herself with this psychopath.

"What did he say?" I asked through gritted teeth, furious that Trevor had put her in this position to begin with.

"That I was being followed. Not by him, by someone else and that he wanted to warn me."

I studied her face to look for a reaction to this but she was emotionless as she kept talking as if she was reciting the weather forecast for the next week.

"He didn't have any information, other than that. But Max, he knew Elena." Her eyes met mine and I froze.

"What do you mean that he knew Elena? What did he say?" My heartbeat was racing as I waited for her to tell me everything this guy knew about my sister.

"They had just started dating a few weeks before she went missing. She was supposed to meet him that night but she never showed up." I watched as she swallowed hard as she looked down and folded her hands in her lap.

"The night she went missing."

I leaned back against the cold metal of the chair and closed my eyes as I rubbed my temples. My head felt like it was going to explode.

"Did he say anything more? Did you get his name? Is he still here?" My questions came out as rapid fire as I searched the room for a guy who I had no idea what he looked like.

"He didn't say anything more than that. I didn't get his name, he was in a hurry to leave. He seemed scared and anxious, but I don't know why."

"So why would he leave you a note to come here then not tell you anything other than someone was following you and that he knew Elena?" The frustration was getting to me and came out in my tone, causing Hannah to flinch at the anger in my voice.

"He didn't leave me the note. I don't know who did. He risked talking to me to tell me to be careful. He kept looking over his shoulder like someone was watching him." She took a deep breath before continuing. "Can't say that I remember what it feels like to NOT feel like someone is watching me."

I smiled as I reached over and patted her hand. There was part of me that was relieved that she was okay but a bigger part of me that was disappointed that there was yet another dead end. I would give anything to find the sick bastard and put an end to all of this, to bring Elena home safe and keep Hannah out of harm's way.

"I'm sorry, Hannah, I know how hard things have been for you." I blew out a breath and instantly kicked myself for saying it. How could I possibly know just how hard things have been for her? I wasn't the one who was living this nightmare that she was stuck in and I hated that I sounded so insincere. "Well, I don't actually know because I'm not the one who's going through everything, but I can imagine." I ran a hand down the scruff on my face and looked around the coffee shop. Someone had left her a note to meet them here so there was a slight chance they had shown up though the likelihood of them showing their face now was pretty slim. Based on the last few notes, whoever was watching her was also now watching me and knew that I was in law enforcement. It got under my skin as I sat there next to her, feeling like we were being hunted. "I don't think that whoever wrote that note is going to show up." I nodded at the paper sitting between us on the table.

"Yeah, me neither." She took a deep breath and swiped it off the table before stuffing it back in her coat pocket.

"You want to get out of here? Head home?"

"I don't even have a home anymore, but yeah, let's get going. This place just reminds me of Amber and I can't handle it anymore." She stood up and pulled her backpack from beside her and slid it onto her back. It broke my heart that she felt she didn't have anywhere to call home and part of me wanted to tell her that she could actually go back to her apartment whenever she was ready.

"Actually-" My throat was instantly dry as I choked on the words that fought to get out. Her eyes watched me with concern as my coughing fit continued.

"Are you okay?" She gently touched my arm as I turned away to avoid coughing in her face. I knew I needed to tell her she could be free of staying with me but my body seemed to be standing in the way of being able to do so.

"Yeah, dry throat," I croaked in between coughs.

"Want me to grab you some water?" She offered as she glanced up at the line that wound out the door and around the corner. I shook my head no as I headed into the men's bathroom and turned on the faucet. I leaned forward and cupped my hand under the water as I took big gulps of water, hoping to stop the cough.

I came out of the bathroom to find Hannah exactly where I left her, her arms folded across her chest as she looked at me with concern.

"Are you sure you're okay?"

"Yeah, I'm fine. Let's get going." I placed my hand on her lower back as I guided her out of the packed coffee shop, the weight of my decision not to tell her about her apartment sitting heavily on my shoulders.

Nineteen

Hannah
4 Days Ago

"Do you want the last slice of pizza?" I called down the hall to Max who was in the bedroom trying to find a file for Elena's case. He had spent the majority of the day on the phone with Mindy or screening calls from his mom and sisters. It was over two weeks since Elena had gone missing and each day that passed seemed to increase the number of times per day that his mom called for an update. I could see the toll it was taking on him to not have an answer for his family each time they called.

"Nope, go for it!" he yelled back, rummaging through the mess he had made earlier. An anonymous tip had come in yesterday that someone had spotted Elena working at a night club that was known for human trafficking and Max had been obsessed with trying to get a lead that actually went somewhere. His team had immediately investigated the tip and scanned all of the surveillance video from the club and the neighboring businesses which all confirmed there was no sign of Elena. But the fact that someone had called in about her had everyone feeling anxious.

Max had been pretty restless last night and the few times that I had woken up he was in the living room plotting out the timeline and every tip they had received. Trevor had been around and was trying to be helpful but at one point he took a step back and warned me to let Max do his thing. Apparently when he got this fixated on something, there was no stopping him. The tension in the apartment was thick and we still had yet to talk about what was going on between us. It didn't take much for me to see that Trevor was right about Max not being a relationship type of guy, he was showing me that on his own. He didn't touch me or even spend time with me the last few days as things got more intense with the case.

Today was my last day of finals and I was desperate to try to make something feel like it was normal again so I suggested that we order a pizza and veg out. So far, I had eaten by myself while watching reruns of *The Big Bang Theory* while Max shuffled about distracted. While it wasn't my ideal way to spend time together, I gave in and realized that Trevor was right, I needed to let Max do whatever Max was going to do. I celebrated the small victory of getting him to agree to take a plate of pizza with him to the bedroom. Whether he ate it or not, I had no clue.

I was starting to feel restless as the night continued on and I had nothing else to distract myself from my own thoughts. Max's anxiety was like a wet blanket that was smothering the apartment which made the idea of going back to my own apartment seem very appealing. A room haunted by dead bodies or a place that wasn't home and filled with tension? Hmm, tough decision.

I shifted on the couch and grabbed the remote as I flipped through the channels on tv before giving up and putting it back on the same channel. My mind was busy and I needed a distraction. I could try to call my mom but it was already getting late and she was either working a night shift or sleeping before her early morning shift. Instinctively I opened my text messages and started typing a message to Amber when grief flooded through me and I remembered that I couldn't talk to her either. I closed my eyes and took a few deep breaths, working to calm myself as I heard Max's footsteps coming down the hallway.

"Hey, you okay?" He paused at the couch and looked down at me as I slowly opened my eyes and smiled.

"I'm feeling restless and anxious." I sat up straight and turned to look at him. He had a pile of papers in his hands and looked ready to do more work. My heart sank a little, desperate for any human interaction that would get me out of this funk. As if sensing my predicament, he sat the papers down on the coffee table and grabbed his coat off the back of the chair where he had tossed it earlier.

"Get your jacket." He nodded to the corner of the living room where my few personal belongings had started to accumulate.

"Why? Where are we going?" I asked as I reached over and grabbed my jacket.

"Out for some fresh air. I think we both need a break from this apartment." He sighed as he slid into his jacket and waited for me to zip mine up.

"Do I need to change?" I looked down at my worn-out jeans and the faded Yankees T-shirt I was wearing. I didn't know where he planned to go but I wanted to make sure I was warm enough and dressed okay.

"Nope, you're fine." He smiled as he walked to the front door and held it open for me.

We walked in silence for a few blocks before heading into a cozy diner that was tucked away on a side street. It was nice and warm inside with classic memorabilia adorned along the walls and a jukebox sitting in the corner by the waitress podium. A Beach Boy's song played softly throughout the room as a waitress wearing a poodle skirt and roller skates headed our way with a handful of menus.

"Just two?" she asked as she slowed down and grabbed onto the side of the podium to stop herself.

"Yes, please." Max smiled at me as we followed her to a booth in the back of the diner and watched as she skated off, nearly colliding with another waitress on roller skates. I stifled a giggle as I pictured how many times a day they must run into each other and envisioned it turning into a roller derby type atmosphere during their busy hours.

"What's so funny?" Max smirked as his eyes glistened, waiting for my response.

"I was just picturing this turning into roller derby when it gets really busy." I giggled as his gaze shifted to watch as another waitress almost ran into a table before catching herself and stopping.

"Yeah, I'm wondering if the skates are something new. None of them seem well coordinated to handle the skates." He chuckled as he looked down at the menu. I left mine sitting to the side of me since I was still full from the pizza I had pretty much singlehandedly eaten by myself not that long ago.

"I figured maybe we could get dessert? They have the best milkshakes and their peach cobbler is ridiculously good." He peered over his menu and smiled. There was something about the way that he smiled at me, so flirty, that just sent chills throughout my body. We hadn't talked much about the other night when we had slept together and so much had been happening since then that kept it from happening again. While I technically slept in his bed every night, we weren't anywhere near sleeping together. I remembered Trevor's advice the other day about not getting too close, Max doesn't do commitment. Maybe that was all that it was. A quick hookup and nothing else.

Part of me wanted to believe that there was something more between us. That he felt the chemistry as much as I did. That he was constantly as turned on by me as I was by him. Maybe it was all in my head. I shook my head to try to get rid of the thought as I felt his eyes land on mine.

"Everything okay?" His eyebrow arched.

"Yeah, I was just thinking."

"I can tell. Want to talk about it?" He sat his menu down and leaned back against the booth, watching me.

"Na, it was just silly thoughts." I lied as I tried to lift my menu higher to hide the heat from the blush that I felt creeping up my chest.

"What do you know? I happen to like silly." He reached forward and gently lowered my menu, his gaze quickly finding the blush that I knew he was looking for. I watched as he subtly licked his lips before looking back up at me, a smug look on his face. Just as he was about to say something else a woman came flying toward our table, almost slamming into it before bracing herself against the wall next to us.

"Sorry about that," she muttered as she blew a stray piece of curly red hair out of her face and pulled a pen out of the pocket of the apron tied around her waist. "I'm Wanda, what can I get you guys to drink?" She looked back and forth between us as her pen hovered over a folded-up piece of paper that had scribbled writing covering the majority of it. Max nodded towards me as he pretended to cough to hide the laugh that threatened to burst through. I chewed my bottom lip as I avoided looking at him, knowing that if I did I would lose it and be in hysterics.

"Hi," I cleared my throat to get rid of the laugh that still lingered, "I'll have the cherry cheesecake milkshake please. And a side of fries." I smiled as she jotted my order down and looked to Max.

"I'll have the same." He smiled but looked away as quickly as he could as she tucked the pen back into the apron pocket and used the table to turn herself around. She had to be in her fifties or sixties and it was apparent that she was not good at roller skating.

"Be out with those shortly," she huffed as she pushed off the table and rolled away.

Max and I looked at each other and erupted in laughter as she left. I couldn't remember the last time that I had laughed that hard but the more he laughed, the harder I laughed. Then the inevitable happened and I laughed so hard that I snorted, which of course made Max laugh even harder.

A few minutes later our laughter started to subside and we caught our breath. It was the distraction that I had been needing. For a moment I stopped to think about how much my life had changed in just a few weeks and panic started to course through me as I realized that I no longer had a normal. There wasn't the safety or familiarity of anything that was normal. The only constant in my life right now was Max and I wasn't sure how much longer I would have him. The easy answer was as long as someone was still stalking me and killing people, then Max would still be there. But what happened when it was all over? Where would we stand at that point?

The mood shifted between us as the waitress came rolling back to our table with two glasses of ice water. She sat them down in front of us and tossed a few straws next to them on the table.

"There's an issue with the machine for the milkshakes but they're working on getting it fixed. Might be a little bit of a wait. Did you want me to cancel them and get you something else?"

Max looked at me and raised his eyebrows for my input. I shrugged and waited for him to take the lead.

"We're not in a hurry." He looked to me as he said it and I nodded my head in agreement, "We'll go ahead and wait for them to fix it."

"Okie dokie." She smiled and rolled off again, leaving us to the awkward silence that had started to fill the space between us before she got there.

"What's on your mind?" Max peeled back the wrapper and stuck the straw in his water, twirling it around as he waited for my answer. I watched the ice cubes as they were shuffled about in the water, dancing around each other helplessly, and realized that it was symbolic of my own life.

"I don't have a normal," I blurted out as he watched me closely, still stirring the cubes around in his water with the straw.

"Care to elaborate?" His voice was gentle though I could hear a playfulness to it.

"In general. In life. I don't have anything that's normal. I don't have anything that is comforting. When things start to feel chaotic, I don't have anything to cling to, to try to ground myself. Everything is so out of the norm for me right now that it's actually become the norm to not have a norm. Does that even make sense?" My voice was rising with my anxiety and I quickly scanned the diner to make sure I hadn't caused a scene.

"It makes sense, I totally get it. Different situation, but I've been in your place before where your whole world feels like it's been shifted and nothing is the same." A sadness washed across his face as he looked down and let go of the straw.

"When I really look back, things haven't been normal since before my dad got sick. When he got sick, everything changed and nothing ever went back to normal. Then he died. Then I left for college. And now everything else that happened. I don't even know what normal is anymore."

"How old were you when he got sick?"

"It was my junior year in high school. I quit hanging out with my friends and quit softball so I could help my mom take care of him. I skipped most school functions so I could help out and be there for him. I promised myself that I would make my senior year the year that I did all of the things you're supposed to do and make it the best year ever. But then he got worse and I hardly did anything but go to class then go home to help out with my dad. I worked a part time job to try to help with the bills so that gave me even less time for school or friends." I let out a ragged breath as I thought back to how sick he really was. "By the time prom and graduation rolled around, we didn't know how much longer we would have with him so I missed both. I got my diploma but I didn't walk with my friends or hear the motivational speeches that are supposed to prepare you for the real world. He died a week after that." A tear slid down my face and I quickly tried to wipe it away with the back of my hand before he noticed.

"That's really tough, I'm so sorry Hannah."

"It's okay, it's life. Like you said, you know what it feels like to have your world shifted." I smiled and hoped that it would leave an opening for him to elaborate on his comment earlier and share something personal about himself after I just unloaded my life story on him.

"Yeah, life definitely isn't fair sometimes." He shifted uncomfortably in his seat and I could tell that whatever it was, he didn't want to talk about it. There was something in me that wanted to know. If there wasn't that much time left to spend with him, I wanted to make the most of what I had left. For once I wanted to be able to say that I actually tried to make something work, that I wasn't always a victim to the success of my relationships with others.

"So what happened?" I probed.

He sighed and looked at me like he was debating whether or not to tell me. He knocked his knuckles against the table as he looked away, working his jaw the way he does when something stresses him.

"Love happened." His eyes met mine and I saw a pain hidden behind the amber color of his eyes beneath the fluorescent lights. I waited for him to continue but when he looked away, I knew I would have to keep pushing. Just as I was about to ask him about it the waitress appeared at our table with a plate of mozzarella sticks and a bowl of marinara sauce.

"These are on the house since it's taking so long to get that machine fixed." She sat the plate down between us and rubbed her hands down the front of her apron. "My shift is over but another waitress will be by soon with those shakes. Just wave her down if you need anything before then." She smiled and rolled away.

I reached down and picked up a mozzarella stick, breaking it in half to let the steam out as I played around with ideas of how to get him to talk.

"So what happened with love?" I asked softly as I pretended to be distracted by the oozing cheese as I held it above my mouth and took a bite. It was piping hot and I immediately regretted not thinking this through before I tried to pretend to be cool.

"I was engaged. She left me on our wedding day. Stood me up at the altar. Had her sister tell me that she couldn't marry me because she was in love with someone else." He paused and looked up at me. "She was in love with my cousin and was pregnant with his child."

I felt the mozzarella stick fall from my fingers as it landed on the table in front of me, my mouth hanging open as I stared at Max.

"What?!" It was a stupid answer but all that I could manage to get out. Things like this didn't happen in real life. These were the kinds of things you saw on soap operas where people were paid to be terrible human beings.

"Are you serious?" I asked without realizing how rude it might come across.

"Unfortunately." He ran a hand through his hair and tilted his head to look at me. "That's why I don't do relationships anymore."

His words felt like they reached across the table and slapped me, the sting of them as I realized that this was the conversation that we needed to have but had been avoiding. I watched as he nervously ran his finger along the rim of glass, watching me as he waited for my response.

"I get it, it's hard to trust people when you've been hurt."
I tried to keep my answer simple and generic. Keep all
emotion out of it. Don't confess any secret feelings of hope
for a happily ever after with him.

"Look, Hannah-" he started and I knew where he was going
with it. My palms started sweating as I shifted in my seat
and looked down to avoid looking at him.

"I get it, Max. We don't have to talk about what happened.
It was a one-time thing," I snapped as I picked up another
mozzarella stick and shoved it in my mouth. I was far
from hungry but felt desperate to be unable to talk to him.
Maybe he would get the hint and do the same. While I had
really needed a distraction, now I was anxious to have any
conversation other than this one.

"Hannah, it wasn't like that." His voiced pleaded with me to
look at him so I did. Big mistake. His eyes were soft as they
searched my face and for a moment, I wanted to accept the
comfort they offered.

"Like what? A one-night stand?" I could feel myself getting
defensive and tried to keep it under control. He closed his
mouth and clenched his jaw as he leaned forward and played
with the empty straw wrapper.

"Because it's not like we've slept with each other since
then. We don't call each other boyfriend or girlfriend. We
don't say I love you." I was starting to ramble and knew I
needed to get to the point. "It's simple. We slept together
and that was it. You're protecting me until we find whoever
is responsible for everything, then we'll go our separate

ways. I don't have any other expectations. Trust me, Trevor warned me right away that you weren't a commitment type of guy. I got the message, loud and clear." I shoved the rest of the mozzarella stick in my mouth and looked away. My pulse was racing and my face was flushed as I prayed that I would be given one moment of peace and not choke on the damn mozzarella stick after having the guts to tell Max how I felt. Only I didn't really tell him how I felt. I told him what I thought he wanted to hear.

"Wait? When did Trevor tell you that I wasn't a commitment kind of guy?" He leaned forward and I could hear the change in his tone. I didn't want to get into the conversation that I had with Trevor, even though it was short, I didn't want Max to know that we had talked about him. It was a little too late now. I grabbed the glass of water in front of me and made myself busy as I sucked down as much water as I could to keep from having to talk to him.

Out of the corner of my eye I saw someone rolling toward us with a tray loaded with milkshakes and two baskets of fries.

"Hey guys, sorry about the wait." She placed the shakes on the table in front of us then sat the baskets of fries in between. She turned to look at Max as she sat his in front of him and I saw panic in his eyes.

"Max!" she exclaimed as she pulled the tray to the side and reached out to squeeze his shoulder. "Oh my God! I can't believe it's you!"

He looked like he had just seen a ghost as he pulled away from her touch and looked up at me.

"Hey Adrianna." There was no friendliness to his tone and the look he gave her made my blood run cold.

"How are you?" she asked cautiously while sneaking a peek of me out of the corner of her eye. I could tell she was trying to figure out if I was his girlfriend.

"You're really going to ask that?" He shot a look at her that made her straighten her posture as she licked her lips. "I see that you're still mad about the past but I really think we should sit down sometime and talk." She pulled her shoulders back and looked at him like a mother would a child that she was trying to teach a life lesson.

Max let out a laugh that sounded maniacal and I worried for a minute that he would turn into the guy from The Shining. I still couldn't get that movie out of my head. Everything felt like it was playing out in slow motion as I watched them, not knowing what was actually happening.

"Mad that you left me on our wedding day or mad that you got pregnant by my cousin- which one am I supposed to be over by now?"

My stomach sank as I realized who this woman was. I looked up and took in her features as I tried to picture how anyone could do to Max what she did. She was stunningly beautiful with black hair that was pulled up into a messy bun with a few side swept bangs. Her olive colored skin was flawless which allowed her to be beautiful without wearing much makeup. The red lipstick went perfectly with her uniform and she looked like the classic pinup models you saw in hotrod magazines.

She had the perfect shape with big boobs, small waist, and wide hips with a well-rounded ass. Instantly I knew that I would never be the type of girl that would be with a guy like Max. She was the type of girl that ended up with guys like him. The beautifully attractive always found each other.

My stomach churned as I continued to sit there uncomfortably as they talked, obviously for the first time since they were supposed to get married. I had no idea how long ago it was but Max seemed to be pretty hung up on it still which made sense why he didn't want a relationship. I thought about how to escape and leave without them knowing but as soon as I scooted toward the edge of the booth to get up, she took a step toward me and blocked me. I watched as she coyly looked down and smirked. I didn't like her for what she did to Max, but now I hated her for being such a bitch.

"Max, it was in the past. Can't we be adults and sit down and talk?" She reached over and ran her hand across his fingers on the table. "We have a lot to catch up on."

I wanted to throw up from the over the top show she was putting on. This wasn't my business and I had no intention of siting through anymore.

"I'm going to go and let you guys catch up." I shot him a look that told him I was done and grabbed my phone from the table. I scooted to the edge of the booth where she was standing and raised an eyebrow at her while giving her my best 'don't fuck with me' face. She chuckled as she rolled to the side enough so I could get out.

"Hannah, I'll walk you home." Max scooted to get up when I looked over my shoulder and gave him a cold stare.

"Don't bother." I walked outside and welcomed the bitter cold as I shivered from the flood of emotions that were racing through me.

<u>Twenty</u>

Max

3 Days Ago

Last night definitely didn't go as planned when I offered to take Hannah out for a much-needed distraction. The thought of us together in a relationship had been constantly nagging at me since the moment we slept together. I had feelings for Hannah, whether I wanted to or not, but I had no idea what to do with them. Honestly, I wished I could just go back to sleeping with random women and not having to try to figure out this whole relationship thing.

I was relieved when I got home that Hannah was there, laying on the couch. She pretended to be asleep when I came in twenty minutes after she got there, but I figured if she wanted space, I needed to give it to her. I knew she was mad and I couldn't blame her. We literally went from having a conversation about our relationship and her feeling like I didn't want to be with her to running into my ex fiancé and having so much tension in the room it could have smothered someone.

The walk from the diner back to my apartment was short and I desperately tried to get away from Adriana so I could catch up with Hannah. The last thing I had wanted was for her to walk the streets by herself at night when there's a psycho out there watching her. My focus was on Hannah regardless of how hard Adrianna tried to break it. I knew the moment she saw Hannah that she was jealous. The side-eyed looks she gave her didn't get past me either. She was the same jealous, insecure person she was when I was with her. Every attempt I made to get up to go after Hannah was met with a stronger attempt from Adrianna to get me to stay.

The over the top flirting that went ignored. The running her hand up my arm while pushing her leg against my side so I could tell she wasn't wearing panties. The not so quiet whisper of how she wasn't wearing panties. And when all of that went unnoticed, she resorted to fake crying and went on to tell me how her life fell apart in the three years since I last saw her.

She carried on about how my cousin left her and she lost the baby shortly after. No one loved her and she was seen as a cheater so people didn't respect her anymore. She lost her plush job and had to take this job waiting tables just to get by. The more she went on and complained about the petty things in her life that were a direct result of the poor decisions she made, the more I wanted to be with Hannah.

I tried to sleep but knowing that she was sleeping on the couch instead of in my bed really got under my skin. Maybe it was because I felt like I was supposed to protect her and couldn't if she wasn't next to me? Or maybe it was because I felt like I didn't want to be apart from her. Around 2:30 this morning I gave up and made my way to the living room so I could at least be in the same room as her. At some point I must have fallen asleep because I barely heard it when she slid the deadbolt and opened the door, looking over her shoulder as she tried to sneak out with her suitcase handle in one hand and her backpack slowly sliding down her back.

"Where are you going?" My voice was groggy as I rubbed my eyes and sat up straight in the chair.

"I am going to go look for a hotel to stay in for a few days while I look for an apartment." Her head was down while one foot lingered outside the door. I could tell she wanted to leave and never look back. But something held her there and I couldn't let this moment pass by.

"Hannah, can we please talk about last night?" I walked over and held the top of the door to try to keep her from closing it and walking out on me forever.

Her eyes looked away from mine as she fidgeted with the zipper of her coat while she thought about what I was asking of her.

"Please, Hannah. Just let me talk and explain what happened. If you're still wanting to leave after that I'll help you find somewhere to stay."

"Fine," she whispered as she tucked a strand of hair behind her ear and stepped back inside the apartment just enough for me to close the door.

"Do you want to sit?" I offered as I nodded toward the couch. Her standing there, ready to leave, was making me anxious and I felt like I was going to lose the nerve to tell her how I felt.

"I'm fine here."

One thing about her was when she was mad, she was really mad. I took a deep breath and swallowed hard as I rubbed my hands down the front of my sweats. I had six Italian sisters, I could handle this.

"Okay," another deep breath, "Hannah, I'm so sorry about last night. Nothing went how I had hoped it would and my only intention was to get you out of the apartment for a little bit and celebrate that you were done with finals." I let out the breath I had been holding as I rushed through the sentence. "Everything was a disaster and it was all my fault."

She stayed quiet while I talked, continuing to look anywhere but at me.

"Hannah, will you please talk to me? I know you're upset but this would be a whole lot easier if I knew why." I reached for her hand which was quickly pulled away so I couldn't touch her.

I blew out a frustrated breath as I ran my hands through my hair and shook my head. This woman just might be the death of me. I've never had to work this hard to get a girl to not be mad at me and I grew up in a house full of nothing but women!

"First of all, it would be a whole lot easier to talk to you if you were actually dressed." She looked at me then glanced at my bare chest before looking away. "Can you do something with that? Like, cover it up already." She pointed at my chest as a blush crept up her neck before she looked away.

"So my body bothers you now?" I asked with a smirk as I looked around for something to put on.

"Yes. Now cover your ridiculous abs and toned chest or I'm going to leave and we won't talk at all." She had turned fully around and was facing the wall while I had to hold in my laughter. I didn't dare tell her how adorable she was unless I wanted that wicked mean girl to come back. I found a shirt behind the couch and pulled it over my head as she was turning back around.

"Better?" I raised an eyebrow, challenging her to meet my eyes.

"Yes." She was still blushing and I was relieved that even when she was super pissed off at me, she still found me attractive.

"Now can we talk?"

"You know we don't have to do this, right?" she asked as if I was supposed to have some idea of what she was talking about.

"Do what?"

"Talk," she sighed, "I think we said everything we needed to say last night."

"I don't think we did."

"Max, you don't want a relationship, you made that clear. And then you ran into your ex-fiancé and I could see the tension between you two. That relationship isn't over and you deserve the chance to go after the person you love."

She didn't get it, she completely misread everything last night. I didn't want to be with Adrianna. Even if Hannah wasn't in the picture, I still wouldn't want to be with Adrianna. I learned the hard way the type of person that she is and that wasn't the kind of person that I wanted to be with.

"Hannah, I don't want to be with Adrianna. Not by any means. I could never forgive her for what she did to me and what she put me through. People like that don't ever change. And when I said I wasn't ready for a relationship, I meant right now. Or at least I thought I did? I really like you Hannah and I care about you. What does that mean in terms of a relationship? I have no idea. But you weren't just some random one-night stand for me. I've never felt that way about what happened between us." I took a step toward her and gently touched her arm. This time she didn't pull away.

"I think I still need to stay somewhere else for a few days. Clear my head." She refused to look at me as my hand fell from her arm. I sucked in a deep breath hoping it would replace some of the air that had just been knocked out of me. Even with everything I told her, she still wanted to leave.

"Okay," I sighed, "If you need space, I'll give it to you."

"Thank you. I'll let you know where I'll be staying as soon as I find something affordable." She turned toward the door and I knew I had to tell her that she could go back to her apartment.

"Your apartment is actually ready now if you wanted to go back there." I looked away to avoid having her see the guilt on my face for not telling her sooner.

"When did you find out that it was ready?" Her tone changed and I knew she was upset, again.

"A few days ago. Trevor went by to see if you were there when you didn't come back to my apartment and he told me the crime scene was cleared. Mindy called that night to confirm."

"So you've known for a few days that I could go back and you didn't tell me?"

I gulped as I looked down.

"I was trying to keep you safe."

"That wasn't your decision to make. I'm a grown woman, Max, I can make that decision for myself."

"Hannah, I'm sorry that I didn't tell you. But even if I had, would you really have gone back to stay there, given everything that's happened there? You said you didn't have anything that made you feel safe, yet you're walking away from it."

"I'm supposed to feel safe here?! With someone who's been lying to me and leading me on?!" Her voice rose and I knew I wasn't going to like what came next.

"I wasn't trying to lead you on."

"Well, you didn't do a good job of not leading me on, now did you?" Her eyebrows shot up in question as she waited for my answer.

I closed my eyes and pinched the bridge of my nose as I thought of what to say next. She was right, I hadn't been trying to not lead her on. We were both walking down the same path toward a relationship except at some point I took a detour and didn't tell her.

"Exactly my point," she snapped as she shifted the weight of her backpack and pulled up the handle of her suitcase, "I'm going to go back to the only place that I can call home right now because even with all of the death and unhappy memories of that place, it still feels better than being here with you. If you can't be honest with yourself, how can I ever expect you to be honest with me?"

She turned toward the door at the same time a loud knock came from the other side. She looked at me with confusion on her face, both knowing that it wasn't Trevor because he was out of town on business.

I walked over and opened the door to a woman covered in blood and bruises. My heart stopped and my stomach sank when I looked closer and recognized the battered face in front of me.

"Elena."

Twenty One

Hanna
3 Days Ago

I watched with my jaw hanging open as Max reached out and grabbed Elena before she fell to the floor. She looked weak and I barely recognized her as the girl from my class. Her black hair was matted to her head from the dried blood that looked to have been there for weeks. Her face and body were dirty and covered in cuts and bruises. The jeans she wore had tears in them with blood stains underneath. Whatever she had been through, it looked like she had just barely survived it.

I moved out of the way as Max brought her in and laid her on the couch. He was talking frantically to her, asking her to wake up and stay with him as he checked for a pulse while looking for the sources of injury. Adrenaline pushed through me as I watched, trying to figure out how to help.

"What can I do?" I asked as he spoke to her in Italian.

"Call 911, ask for an ambulance!" he called over his shoulder while keeping his attention on his sister.

I called and requested the ambulance and asked if they could get Mindy over here as well. Within minutes the apartment was filled with people shuffling about so I took it as my cue to leave. I walked the short distance to my apartment, constantly looking over my shoulder. It felt weird to be walking to my apartment and suddenly I realized just how scared I was to be by myself. And I was 100% by myself. Amber was dead. Max was busy with Elena. Trevor was out of town. There was no one left. No one to protect me. No one to keep me company.

As I took the few steps up to the entrance of my apartment building, I felt footsteps right behind me. I moved slightly to the right. They moved slightly to the right. I was almost in front of the elevators when I felt them stop directly behind me. My blood pressure skyrocketed as my heart beat wildly in my chest. Slowly I turned to look over my shoulder as the bell dinged to the elevator. Out of the corner of my eye I couldn't see anyone behind me. The doors to the elevator slowly opened with no one inside the cart. I was about to take a step when I saw a hand come out from behind me. I spun around as my hand flew to my chest in fear.

Standing at least three feet below me was a little boy, maybe four or five years old. There was a huge smirk on his face as he slyly waved, right before a frantic woman came barreling through the outside doors looking for him.

"Frankie! I told you not to run off like that!" she scolded as she reached down and grabbed his arm to pull him back to her, "I'm so sorry if he scared you, his older brother has been teaching him how to sneak up on people and he hasn't learned not to do it to strangers yet." She let out a heavy breath as she pulled him in front of her, tucked underneath her very swollen pregnant stomach. "As you can tell, I can't quite keep up with his speed these days." She laughed nervously.

"It's fine, really," I said as I took a step toward the elevator as the doors closed before I could get on. I pushed the button for the elevator to return as I watched the mom escort her son out of the building and hold his hand so he couldn't get away from her again.

I took a few deep breaths to try to calm myself as I waited for the elevator to return. In a way I was happy to have space from Max so I could clear my head, and so he could deal with things with Elena, but it also felt really unnerving being back at my apartment.

The bell dinged and this time a man and woman got out and walked past me as I took their place on the elevator. I waited anxiously for it to reach my floor as I played with keys in my pocket. Just a few more seconds and I would be back to the place that I swore I would never come back to.

The doors opened, forcing me to make a decision. Go back to the place that haunted me or make a run for it and never come back. I felt like I had been doing nothing but running for a long time and it was exhausting. If I wanted to be able to root myself then I had to start somewhere. Why not just make amends with my past, deal with my demons, and take control of my life? I pulled my shoulders back as I stepped off the elevator and walked down the hall.

The key shook against the lock as my hands trembled trying to unlock the door. I took a deep breath and tried to focus. It wasn't that hard. Just a key in a lock. No big deal. Except that the key was about to open a door that I didn't know what it held inside. I knew I wanted to move forward with my life but that meant I had to deal with things too. Was I strong enough?

"Need help?" A man's voice to my side startled me, forcing the key out of my hand and to the floor. I watched as Trevor bent down and picked up the key, unlocking the door for me.

"I thought you were out of town?" My mind felt like this was a dream, there was no way that Trevor was really there, helping me and keeping me from having to do this on my own.

"I was, I got back early." He shrugged as he held the door open for me to go inside. I pulled my suitcase and stepped inside, looking around unsure of what to expect.

The apartment was freshly cleaned, no sign of any of the recent tragedies that had taken place. The flooring had been replaced and new curtains were hung in front of the new window that had been updated from the makeshift one they had put up after Amber's death. The door closed behind me as Trevor stood next to me, taking it all in.

"You sure you want to stay here?" His voice was gentle and sincere with a hint of concern. I knew he had talked to Max.

"Yeah, it's better than the alternative right now." I tilted my head to look at him.

"I'm not the best at relationship advice and I shouldn't have said what I said about Max not being that type. Sorry I overstepped."

We stayed standing next to each other, staring at the couch as if we were glued to the floor and couldn't move. I was afraid that if I did, the conversation would stop and I wouldn't be able to say what I needed to say.

"You didn't overstep. You just told me the truth, and honestly, it helped. If you hadn't told me that he wasn't a relationship kind of guy, I would be sitting here, waiting for him to change his mind and want to be with me."

"What makes you think he doesn't want to be with you?"

"He told me at the diner that he doesn't do relationships. Then I saw how he was with his ex. I'll never be her so how could it ever work between us? It was bound to end, one way or another."

"You are nothing like Adrianna. Absolutely nothing about you is the same as her." The way he said it with such conviction made my heart hurt. I knew that I could never be her. And if I could never be her, then I could never have Max. I swallowed hard to try to force the lump in my throat back down.

"I know I'm not her. She's gorgeous and confident. And who knows, maybe she's actually nice?" I shrugged trying to get the weight of the world off my shoulders.

"Do you really think that you're not as good as her? Is that what this is about?" He folded his arms across his chest and turned to look at me. My palms started to sweat as I wanted to run and hide to avoid the intensity of the look he was giving me.

"I don't know," I muttered as I looked down and played with the handle of my suitcase.

"Hannah, you're 10 times the woman Adrianna is. Sure, she's good looking and men trip over their dicks trying to get to her, but you have more than that."

I had to bite the inside of my cheek to keep from laughing at the absurd and very detailed description he used to confirm that men wanted Adrianna.

"She's shallow and goes from guy to guy until she gets bored or she finds someone else who has something she wants. She's lucky that she's good looking because that's all she has going for her."

I breathed a sigh of relief and looked up at him. He was such a great person, it was no wonder that Max considered him a brother.

"Thank you, that's sweet of you to say."

"It's the truth. At one point, she even hit on me. But then again, who wouldn't?" He playfully nudged my shoulder with his.

"I'm sure Max took that well!" I joked then blushed when I remembered that Trevor and I had kissed the other day. I wondered if he had told Max about it. I knew I hadn't. Not that I purposely kept it from him, it just didn't cross my mind because it was so insignificant and I forgot about it.

"He was pretty pissed about it. With her. Not me." He rocked back on his heels and smiled. "I've always been the good friend that he can trust."

"Oh great, and here I am, the girl that kisses his best friend!" I palm smacked myself in the forehead and wished it would at least knock some sense into me.

"Na, he knew why we did it."

"He knows?!"

"Of course. Hannah, that was an innocent kiss but I still wouldn't keep that from him."

I lowered my head in shame and knew that I should have thought to tell Max about the kiss. What if he thought I was the same as Adrianna now? I kissed his best friend and didn't bother to tell him.

"It wasn't a big deal and he knew that Hannah. He wasn't upset about it. He didn't ask me questions about how it happened or who initiated it. He agreed that it worked for what we were trying to do."

I looked up at him cautiously.

"Give Max time, he's going through a lot right now and honestly, I don't think he even knows which way is up at this point. He may not be ready for a relationship, but he cares about you Hannah. I can see it in how he watches you and how protective he is over you."

"Did he send you here to talk to me?"

"Actually no. I called and he told me about Elena. I was headed over there to see her and try to help when he started freaking out that you had left. I told him to stay with Elena and I would come check on you. So, here I am." He held his arms out for proof.

"Have you heard any more on Elena? Is she okay?" For a moment I had gotten so consumed in my own world that I had completely forgotten about what had happened.

"I got a text from Max a few minutes ago. They are at the hospital. Her injuries were pretty bad and she's now in a coma. Max is staying there until they know more."

"Oh my god!" I covered my mouth with my hand as I took in the news. "Was she able to tell him anything about where she had been or who had taken her?"

"When I talked to him earlier, he told me that she had whispered 'five steps' but that she lost consciousness before she could finish. He's not sure what it means but I'm supposed to help him remember so we can look into it."

"That's weird. Maybe she was only 5 steps from home?" I pondered as my brain focused on trying to solve a riddle I knew nothing about.

"Could be. I'm planning to go back to his apartment later and go through the files to see if there's anything in the notes about it. Maybe there's an abandoned building close by that we didn't think of or maybe a house that we missed. Who knows, it's a pretty open clue, if it's even supposed to be a clue."

"Well, if you need help, just let me know."

"Thanks. You sure you're going to be okay here? I can stay if you want me to."

"Thank you, I appreciate the offer but I'll be okay. I would rather that you help Max with Elena. Will you keep me posted if they hear anything else about her?"

"Of course."

He smiled and gave me a hug before walking out the door and leaving me to the silence of the empty room.

Twenty Two

Adam

3 Days Ago

Roses are red
Violets are blue
It won't be too long now
Before I come for you

I have to be careful
And plan my next step
The last girl got away
Which means there's more to prep

I can't risk anyone seeing
What I'm about to do
I stood right next to you
And you didn't have a clue

Time will go quickly
Then we'll be together
Bound to each other for eternity
Like two birds of a feather

My fingers are itching
To reach out and touch you
I'll have to settle on pleasuring myself
No one else will do

You may not think you know me
You'd say we've never met
I've always been close by
Now I'm five steps ahead

Twenty Three
Max
3 Days Ago

"No, ma, they don't have any updates on her." I blew out a frustrated breath as I leaned back against the uncomfortable metal chair in the ER waiting room and listened as my mom continued to ask a million questions about Elena. They were all ready to get in the car and drive over the second they heard she was in the hospital, but luckily I was able to keep them at bay for now until she was awake. I just couldn't deal with that chaos on top of everything else right now.

"Look ma, I gotta go. I'll call as soon as I have any information, you don't have to come down here."

A man wearing scrubs and a lab coat came through the double doors wearing a look of defeat on his face. Panic filled me as I waited to see which family he was there to deliver bad news to. My mom was still mumbling in the background about lasagna or spaghetti and did I want my sister to bring me something to eat but I couldn't focus.

"Gotta go, love you, bye." I slid the button to end the call knowing that I would hear about it later. Mindy and Trevor were sitting a few seats over talking quietly when they saw the doctor approach and stopped.

"Sandoval family?" he called out as his tired eyes scanned the room.

I stood up and laced my fingers behind my head as I paced the short distance between the waiting room and the vending machines along the wall. Off in the distance a woman sobbed as the doctor assured her that they had done everything they could. My stomach was in a knot as I waited for someone to give us an update on Elena.

Before we got to the hospital she had lost consciousness right as she was trying to tell me something. Five steps was all that she was able to get out. Since then she had been slipping in and out of consciousness and at one point they thought she had slipped into a coma. Things have been unstable and unpredictable since then. We were waiting for them to finish running tests and labs, and hopefully in that time, Elena would regain consciousness and stay awake. The last few hours felt like days that were starting to blur together and it wasn't even noon yet.

Trevor had gone by my apartment after checking in on Hannah and making sure she was situated in her apartment. It killed me that she left earlier in the middle of everything else, especially given how the conversation between us had ended. She wanted space and though I was reluctant to want to give it to her, I found that I didn't have a choice now that Elena was found. Still, it didn't keep her off my mind. Thoughts of her constantly floated through my mind as I pictured her curled up on the couch in her baggy sweater watching tv, or sitting on the floor with her hair a mess on her head while she pushed her reading glasses back up her nose. While she probably needed new glasses, it was so adorable that I couldn't imagine not watching her chase them around.

"I'm going to go grab some coffee, can I bring you guys a cup?" Mindy asked as she stood up and picked up her wallet from the seat next to her.

"That would be great, thank you." I smiled as she walked away and took her empty seat by Trevor. There was a small table that was pushed up against the wall that had scattered magazines on it before Trevor took it over and laid out the papers from the file he brought from my apartment with Elena's case. He was deep in thought as he read through some of the initial notes that were taken. I sat back and closed my eyes, taking a moment to relax while I could.

"Hey, do you know what happened to the other notes you had? The stuff you wrote down when you were at your mom's?"

I looked over at him and scanned the table for the piece of paper I had used that day.

"It should be in the file. It's smaller, it was from my notepad."

"I can't find it anywhere." Trevor moved stacks of paper around and lifted the pile to look underneath as he grumbled under his breath.

"It has to be in there somewhere. I'll help you look." I reached over to grab a stack of papers when a note caught my eye. Trevor's eyes followed mine as I picked it up and read it. There was a print out of Elena's phone records leading up to when she was taken and for a few days after she was taken. My blood started to boil as I gripped the paper tighter, my knuckles turning white.

"Here you go, one cream, two sugar." Mindy held out a to-go cup of coffee in front of me as I pulled back and looked up at her with fury in my eyes.

"A simple thank you would suffice," She muttered as she sat the cups of coffee down between Trevor and I, and took a seat across from us. She leaned back and crossed her legs as she took a slow sip out of her cup.

"Why the fuck didn't you tell me they were tracing Elena's phone after she went missing? You said they weren't able to track it." My words were heavy, anger laced through each one.

"Because they weren't able to trace it right away. By the time they tracked it, she wasn't there anymore." She let out a sigh as her shoulders slumped.

"How do you know she wasn't there? Did you look everywhere? Check for hidden places that she could have been kept?"

"Max, the day we got the trace on her phone was the day that we found her phone next to the other body. The forensic team scoured that place and didn't find any sign of her. You know as well as I do that she was likely moved long before they ever tracked her phone."

"You still should have told me. I should have been informed of every little detail. God damn it!" I slammed my fist on the table almost knocking over the cups of coffee. Mindy flinched in response.

"Max, you can be mad all you want. I know that this is your sister and I feel for you, I really do. But you DO NOT get to sit there and act like we didn't do our jobs. I have worked tirelessly on this case, Max. I've spent more nights at the office, sleeping at my desk because it's the middle of the night, only to wake up obsessed with solving this case. How dare you sit there and come after me for not doing something! You don't have any idea the number of hours we have spent working this case. If anyone's been more invested, it's me!" Mindy stood up and stalked off, the sound of her boots fading in the distance.

I felt like shit for what just happened. Everything was starting to take its toll on me and I was lashing out at everyone it seemed like. I worked the muscle in my jaw trying to relieve some tension as I looked over at Trevor who was watching me while sipping his coffee.

"I'll apologize when she cools down," I muttered.

"I didn't say anything."

"You didn't have to. I see the look in your eyes." I tried to watch my tone before Trevor and I got into it next.

"Things are tense, I get it. Let's focus on what we need to and worry about the rest later. Okay?"

That was why this guy was my best friend. We balanced each other out and as always, he was being my voice of reason and forcing me to be logical because that's what was needed right now.

"Alright. What do you got?" I picked up the cup of coffee and took a drink as I looked at the papers in front of us.

"Unfortunately, not much. I've gone through and looked at all of the places that she had gone before she went missing and looked at what is near them in a five-foot radius. I'm not coming up with anything." He let out a deep breath and tossed his empty cup into the trash can behind him.

"So then I focused on the coffee house that she was supposed to meet that date at. There's a ton of stuff in that area, but five feet doesn't get you anywhere that would make sense. I started looking at 5 blocks and 5 miles," he tossed the papers down and leaned back in defeat, "I don't know, I think we're jumping down a rabbit hole with this whole five-foot thing."

"Why are you so focused on five feet?" My curiosity was peaked as I tried to figure out his logic and where he got five feet from.

"You told me earlier that the only thing she was able to say was 'five feet'." He looked at me with confusion on his face and suddenly it clicked in my head. I had totally blocked out what Elena had said to me which was why I had told Trevor right away so he could remember.

"Shit! I totally forgot about that!" I leaned forward and pushed the papers around as I looked through what he had on top.

"I was trying to go back to your original notes about everywhere she had gone before she went missing but I can't find them."

"That's odd. I can always call my sisters and see if they remember. Did you look at houses by my parents? Maybe it was someone at one of the neighbors? A neighbor could be five feet away." My mind was racing as I tried to think about what neighbors we had talked to and which ones we hadn't.

"Did you talk to all of the neighbors?" Trevor asked as his excitement started to build with mine.

"No, the girls only talked to a few. But it should be easy to get a team out there to do a quick interview and see if anyone seems suspicious enough to justify doing a search of their property to see if that's where she was being held."

"Romano Family?" A nurse appeared in the hallway and my heart stopped. She didn't make any efforts to come into the waiting area which meant she wasn't planning to talk to us out here like they did everyone else. My pulse quickened as I looked at Trevor.

"Go on, I'll talk to Mindy and give her the update so we can get this going."

I nodded and walked off to join the nurse as I tried to brace myself for what she was about to tell me.

Twenty Four

Hannah

3 Days Ago

An old 90's hip hop song floated through the apartment as I finished wiping down the counters with disinfectant wipes. Even though I knew the apartment had been thoroughly clean, I couldn't stop myself from going through and cleaning everything again. I tried to convince myself that it was the best way to feel like I was making a fresh start when deep down I knew that it was really just a way to keep myself busy so I wouldn't be alone with my thoughts.

I had called my mom earlier and caught her in between jobs so we had a little bit of time to talk and catch up. It felt odd not knowing what to talk to her about since I couldn't exactly be honest and tell her everything that was really going on. So I did what I did best and pretended everything was fine while shifting the focus away from me. My mom hinted that she had made a new friend and after thirty minutes I got her to confess that it was a boyfriend. I was surprised that she hadn't mentioned it sooner, but then again who was I to talk, given the secrets I was keeping. There was a mix of emotions that came with the news but I was pleasantly surprised when happiness overrode the anger and resentment that I had expected to feel.

It was after seven when I finished cleaning the apartment and decided to quit for the day. Trevor hadn't given me any updates on Elena and I felt awkward texting Max for an update. My mind was foggy where Max was concerned and I didn't want to complicate things any more than they were. As much as I tried, I could not get my mind off of Max. The way he made me feel when we were together. The random jokes he would tell when I found myself getting a little bit too stressed out with studying. How he would pick some place for dinner and then order a handful of items, hoping that I would like them when I was too distracted to pick for myself.

I played around with the idea of Max not being interested in me because honestly, it felt a lot better than to try to trick myself into believing that he was interested. It was confusing to say the least and I started to wonder if my lack of experience with relationships had tainted my view of what a real relationship should look like. The only one that I ever really saw growing up was my parents and they had a really great relationship. I wouldn't say perfect, because obviously I saw them fight about plenty of things, but for the most part it was damn near perfect. My dad constantly went out of his way to make my mom happy and she did the same. They were always so wrapped up and focused on whether they were making each other happy that I don't think they ever stopped to make sure they were actually happy themselves. I didn't doubt that they were happy, not by any means. But I did use their relationship to compare what I had with Max and felt confused when I saw some of the same things from their relationship overlapping in ours. If we even had one. I needed another distraction but this time I knew it was going to take more than some fresh air and a milkshake that I didn't even get to drink.

My stomach growled at the same time a knock on my door alerted me to my food delivery. I was starving and didn't have the energy to go buy actual food. I tipped the kid the few bucks that I had on me and took the bag of Chinese food as he walked away. The smell filled the apartment, replacing the overwhelming disinfectant and cleaning products I had been using. I locked the door and slid the deadbolt in place before heading to the couch with my food.

I turned the tv up loud to continue watching the Friends marathon I had been watching. It was cheesy comedy and it made me feel less alone as the sound of laughter filled the room. There was only so much silence I could take before my mind started to get the better of me.

I stuffed the last bite of egg roll in my mouth and sat the empty cartons on the table, leaning back to allow my stomach the space it needed to expand with the massive amount of food I'd just shoved in. It was hot. It was delicious. And it was just the right amount to send me into a nice food induced sleep coma.

Three hours later I woke up to the tv still playing episodes of Friends as I looked around for my phone to check the time. It was almost eleven and I was feeling pretty disappointed that I didn't have an update from Trevor or Max on Elena. My heart sank when I acknowledged what it really meant. If I had any questions about where I stood with Max, this just confirmed it. Important enough to make a show out of trying to talk me out of leaving but not important enough to give me an update on something important in his life.

As weird as it may sound, the apartment felt different as it did earlier now that it was night. Earlier I was a little anxious being back in the apartment but I was able to work through it. There were frequent pep talks to myself about how I could do it, I was a strong woman. But now that it was night the anxiety was even stronger and I felt even more restless than I did before. It must all be in my head, my subconscious playing tricks on me. I had learned about the power of the brain in my psychology classes so it wasn't that far-fetched that it would be messing with me.

I sighed as I got up and took my empty containers to the trash. It felt good to move around even though I knew I should technically be trying to fall back asleep. Who was I kidding? I knew there wasn't any chance that I was actually going to get sleep tonight. I opened the fridge out of habit, looking for something to snack on. Knowing that it was empty I started to close it when I glanced down and saw the bottle of champagne that Amber had given me right after midterms. We had been spending most of our time together and she wanted to celebrate the end of the semester by popping open a bottle and letting go of all of our stress from finals.

Tears rolled down my face as my hand trembled and reached out for the bottle. I debated whether to leave it in there forever or to open it and drink it. What would Amber have wanted? That was a stupid question. If I knew her, she would be mad that I let a good bottle go to waste just because she wasn't here. Amber was always focused on celebrating life, not waiting to live it. I wiped the tears from my face with the back of my hand and pulled the bottle out.

A few minutes later I popped the cork, scaring the shit out of myself from the sound as liquid came fizzing out of the top. Thankfully I was smart enough to open it by the sink to avoid a complete mess. I cleaned up the small spill on the counter and wiped down the bottle before taking it with me to the couch. Who needed a glass when you were drinking for one?

The marathon on tv had ended and of course, there wasn't much else on regular tv at midnight on a Thursday night. I tossed the remote next to me, taking another drink from the bottle, and grabbed my phone. Facebook proved to be a combination of boring and depressing as all of my friends shared celebration photos of being done with the semester, their cute and cuddly Christmas photos with their boyfriends, or the random drunk picture from partying too hard. Irritated that I didn't have anything remotely happy to share, I closed the app and scrolled through my phone for something else to entertain myself with.

There weren't too many apps on my phone so I scrolled through them fairly quickly before landing on the dating app. My finger hovered over the option to delete the app when I remembered why I had it in the first place. Amber. She had encouraged me to get it so I could start meeting people and make new friends. When I questioned the ability to make friends through a dating app she assured me that there were a lot of really great guys on there and that I didn't have to sleep with all of them, I could have standards and just be friends with them if the chemistry wasn't there. She always knew how to make a joke out of things so I wouldn't take it too seriously.

I adjusted on the couch and pulled my legs up under me before taking another drink of champagne and setting the half empty bottle on the coffee table. I was already feeling buzzed and didn't want to end up drunk and alone in my apartment tonight. I opened the app and scrolled through the few notifications I had waiting for me since the last time I had used it, which had been right after Chet. There were a few guys who had waved and a handful of unread messages.

I went to the unread messages and clicked the oldest message first. It was from almost two weeks ago and didn't have a profile picture. The message was short and generic.

ShyGuy247: Hi, I would like to get to know you.

I pressed the delete button and went to the next message. This account had a profile picture of greased up abs and no head. Just abs that looked like they were taken from a Magic Mike movie poster. I didn't have to read the message to know what it was going to say but I read it anyways.

BigToni187: Hey mami, hit me up if you want a taste of big papi from NYC baby.

I forced myself to swallow hard as I felt the champagne trying to make its way back up. Yuck! Seriously, this is what guys thought girls wanted to hear? I moved along to the next message and noticed all of the remaining messages were from the same person. They didn't have a profile picture either and it kind of creeped me out that they had been consistently emailing me for almost two weeks with no response back.

I sat up straight and opened the first message.

5StepsAhead: I find that women who study psychology tend to be more educated and highly intelligent, would you agree?

While I had expected a typical email about how lonely they were or how pretty I was, I was surprised that they didn't comment on either of that. They had actually read through my profile and saw that I was going to school and studying psychology. Curiosity took over as I opened the next message.

5StepsAhead: One of the hardest things about online dating is finding people who aren't there for the right reasons. Men who just want a quick hookup. Women who are looking for free fancy dates. It's rare to find someone who is on here for the right reasons, which brings me to ask, what are you looking for?

I was strangely impressed with the conversation and found myself wanting to talk to whoever this person was and answer their questions. I found myself feeling giddy as I opened the next message that was sent a little over a week ago.

5StepsAhead: I hope that I'm not being a bother, I've seen that you haven't been active recently or read my other emails so I assume you've been busy with school. I find myself drawn to wanting to talk to you and hope that you don't find this creepy or odd. Just say the word and I'll stop messaging you, though I hope you might be interested in talking to me when you're not busy.

I chewed my lip nervously as I debated whether to respond. Before deciding too quickly, I decided to read the last message that was sent yesterday.

5StepsAhead: I wanted to make one final attempt to try to sway you to talk to me. I really hope that you'll give me a chance, I have a feeling we would have a lot to talk about and maybe even be friends if nothing else.

The last sentence stayed with me after I read it and Amber's words rang through my mind about using the app to make new friends. If for nothing else, I could always say that I did it for Amber. It's not like I was agreeing to go on a date with the guy, I could just send a few emails and see what happened. There was no harm in that.

Then why did I feel guilty about Max? It wasn't like we were dating, he had made that pretty clear. And I hadn't heard from him in over 12 hours so maybe I should consider meeting this guy. I started feeling nervous as I thought about what to write when a new message popped up in my inbox from him.

5StepsAhead: Either you're taking a break from cramming for a final tomorrow or you're up late celebrating that finals are over. For your sake, I hope it's the latter.

A smile crossed my face as I began to type.

Me: I actually had my last final yesterday and am trying to figure out how to spend all of my new found freedom and downtime. You're up late as well, should I ask the same?

5StepsAhead: Congratulations! Here's to hoping you find a productive, yet relaxing way to spend your time. My last class wrapped up this morning and I am up late because I just sent in the last items that were needed for me to finish the semester.

Me: Congratulations to you as well. How do you plan to spend your new free time?

5StepsAhead: Unfortunately I'm pretty tied up with a project that didn't quite go as planned so I'm having to take care of a few things before I'll be able to enjoy my time.

Me: That's too bad, I hope it gets resolved soon.

5StepsAhead: It will, I can see the end in sight. Should only take a few more days for things to calm down, then I can pick up where I left off.

Me: I'll send positive vibes your way.

5StepsAhead: Thanks, that's super nice of you.

Me: You're welcome.

I didn't know what else to say and the conversation felt like it hit a dead end. Maybe it wasn't going to be as exciting as I had imagined. A yawn forced its way out and I considered wrapping it up and attempting to get some sleep. Right as I was about to send a message to say goodnight, a new email popped up.

5StepsAhead: Do you think I could take you out for a cup of coffee sometime? Go celebrate the end of the semester?

My mind raced with what to say to that. Did I want to meet him? It was just coffee, there wasn't really any harm in that, was there? Although my last coffee date with Chet didn't end so well. I was so confused and didn't want to make the wrong decision. Part of me wanted to make Amber proud and go for it, but the other part of me felt like it was way too soon to start dating. But then again, he had only asked to meet for coffee and his email did say maybe we could be friends. I closed my eyes and tried to think past the fuzz the champagne had created in my head.

Me: I don't know, I don't even know your name...

A few seconds later a new message popped up.

5StepsAhead: It's Adam.

Me: I guess coffee would be a good way to celebrate. Did you have a day in mind?

5StepsAhead: I'm tied up with that problem that came up for a few days, can you do Sunday?

Me: Sure, Sunday is fine. Did you have a place in mind?

5StepsAhead: How about Java Jazz on Union and Second? Is that close to you? If not, we can find somewhere in the middle.

My stomach dropped when I saw the name of the coffee shop and wondered if this was all a sign from Amber to go for it. How else would one explain drinking the bottle of champagne that she left on the same night that I start talking to guy who wants to be friends AND who wants to meet at the coffee shop that Amber and I used to go to. I wasn't about to mess with fate.

Me: That works for me. Just let me know what time on Sunday and I can meet you there.

5StepsAhead: I look forward to meeting you. I'm going to call it a night. Goodnight, sweet dreams, Hannah.

Me: Goodnight, Adam.

I closed out the app and yawned again feeling a mixture of nervous and excited about Sunday. I tried to figure out why I was feeling nervous when everything seemed like it was working out the way it should but something still felt off to me. Then I realized that I had no idea what he looked like and we didn't bother to exchange phone numbers. I had to remind myself that it was just a quick cup of coffee in a crowded place, nothing could really go wrong there, could it?

Twenty Five

Adam
3 Days Ago

The one that got away.

We all have one. Someone that was vital to something that was important to us. Someone who could make things better for us. Someone that we wanted to spend our lives with.

How she got away- I had no clue. But thanks to her I had fresh cuts from the glass she tried to stab me with before breaking free and running away. This wasn't the first time she had attacked me. Just earlier that week she had ripped a hole in my jacket and cut my arm, making me late for class. She was a feisty one, and that's what I loved the most about her. Even if she wasn't THE one.

She had delusions of wanting to leave and claiming that she didn't want to be there. I tried to understand the pleas she tried to get out from behind the bandana I had to gag her with but they just didn't make sense to me. We were meant to be together. Why would she want to leave? Every time she denied our love, it made me even angrier.

I tried to show her how much I loved her but she couldn't be trusted. If I gave an inch, she took a foot. If I untied her from the chair, she swung it at me. If I undid the gag, she would scream at the top of her lungs. If I tried to touch her she would jerk away and give me the dirtiest looks.

The hospital had been more than frustrating, refusing to let me see her unless I confirmed my relationship to her. Just as I was about to proudly confess that she was my girlfriend, the stupid cop showed up and refused to leave her room. His timing was impeccable. A nurse asked about the cuts on my arm and face, making too many mental notes about what I looked like, before offering to have a doctor take a look. That was my cue to leave and now thanks to Elena's antics, I was forced to lay low for a few days.

It was hard to accept that I had to let Elena go but how do you keep someone who keeps fighting so hard to get away from you? It felt like she didn't appreciate any of the things I was trying to do for her.

I was pleasantly surprised when Hannah answered one of my emails tonight, I was beginning to get frustrated with her as well. I'd spent weeks trying to get to her but people kept getting in the way and leaving messes that I had to take care of. She was a beautiful, intelligent girl, and I took notice of her in class the very first day. She looked so nervous in her oversized NYU hoodie as she had to keep sliding her glasses back up her nose as she tried to take notes during the lecture. She was focused and over the course of the semester, I found she had a lot of little quirks that were sweet and innocent, just like I imagined she would be. Chewing on her pens. Pulling her brows together in a frown when she was reading something that was complicated. I could tell she was interested too with the attention she gave me and how much she soaked up the words that I said. It was such a turn on to see how she responded so easily to me.

She agreed to meet me for coffee on Sunday and I thought it was only fitting to meet at the coffee house that we had been going to together for months. Maybe we didn't actually get to sit down and drink coffee together, but I was always there, always watching, nonetheless. I just needed a few more days to let the wounds heal before I took Hannah as my own. I could tell that she wasn't going to fight me the way Elena had. She looked like the kind of girl that liked to be controlled and I was happy to be that guy for her.

We were going to be happy together. I just knew it.

Twenty Six

Max

2 Days Ago

Beep. Beep. Beep. The machines hooked up to Elena blended together to form a numbing orchestra of sadness as she lay lifeless in the bed with tubes down her throat to keep her alive. The night had been long but I refused to leave her side as she fought as hard as she could before they eventually had to intervene. Early this morning I had to finally convince my family to go home and get some rest and I would let them know as soon as she was awake.

I rubbed my eyes as the sun started to filter through the window into the dark room. My body was exhausted but I couldn't stand the idea of something happening to her while I was sleeping so I drank my weight in coffee and stayed up to watch over her. I checked my phone, hopeful for a call or text from Hannah, yet disappointed when there was nothing.

I wanted to reach out to her yesterday to see how she was doing, but when I wasn't overthinking my decision to give her space, I was busy with stuff with Elena. Trevor had stayed with me the majority of the day and eventually left around ten last night, stopping to check on Hannah's apartment on his way back to mine to look for the missing notes we still couldn't find. He agreed not to bother her, just make sure everything looked okay.

My stomach had been in knots since she left my apartment yesterday morning and it was killing me not being able to talk to her. I wanted to finish our conversation and make sure she knew how I really felt about her but I didn't get the chance before my world exploded around me. Hell, I wasn't sure if I even knew how I felt but I still found myself wanting to talk to her about feelings that I hadn't bothered to sort out. Being with Hannah felt so different than being with Adrianna. Adrianna was a constant battle, it always felt forced. When people say you have to work to make a relationship work- I honestly believed that with Adrianna. But with Hannah, it never felt like work. I wanted to make her happy. I wanted to be around her. I wanted to soak up every smile she offered and drown in the sound of her laughter.

A nurse came in and smiled as she checked the monitors and made some notes on her clipboard.

"Any changes?" I asked quietly even though I knew the answer.

"Nothing significant." She sighed as she continued to write before looking up at me. "But right now, we're happy that she's maintaining. Hopefully her body will be able to rest and heal a little bit. The more rest she gets, the stronger she will be, and the easier her recovery will be."

I let out a breath as I leaned back against the worn-out leather chair and closed my eyes. It was a waiting game and we knew that, but it didn't make it any easier. I felt helpless which was a feeling I despised. There weren't many things in life that had ever made me feel the way I felt when I looked down at my baby sister, hardly recognizable. I silently said another prayer for a full and quick recovery, desperate to be able to talk to her and find out who did this to her.

My phone buzzed on the table beside Elena's bed as a text message came through. I felt excited for a quick moment that it was Hannah, but that quickly disappeared when I saw Trevor's name on the screen.

Trevor: Give me a call when you have a chance. I think I've found something that might be helpful.

I could feel the energy flowing through me as I pressed send and waited for him to answer, my fingers drumming along the table beside me.

"Hey, I wasn't sure if you were awake yet."

"Yeah, I didn't sleep last night so I've been up for a while now." I chuckled and smiled when I heard the faint laughter on his end. I looked to the side to check on Elena, careful not to be too loud even though she wasn't awake. I was hopeful that she was just sleeping and that she would be waking up and giving us all hell again really soon.

"I found the notes that we were looking for, the ones you had originally taken at your mom's house."

"Where were they?" It had been eating away at me that they were the only ones that were missing and they should have been with everything else in her file.

"On the floor behind the desk. They must have fallen or slipped through the crack behind the desk."

"I did have things spread out across the desk the other day so that makes sense. What did you find?" Anxiety was starting to build as I waited for Trevor to just get to the point and tell me what he found.

"You're never going to believe this- do you remember the guy Elena was going to meet up with from the online dating site?"

"Yeah...." I held my breath and waited as I tried to remember everything I could about the conversation she had with the guy. Nothing really bothered me about their conversation other than he didn't have a profile picture and I wasn't sure if she even really knew the guy.

"Guess what his user name is for his profile?"

I racked my brain trying to remember what it could have been when all of a sudden it clicked and my stomach dropped. I looked down at Elena and let out a heavy breath.

"Five steps ahead."

"Bingo."

Twenty Seven

Hannah
2 Days Ago

I pulled my hair up into a messy bun on top of my head and stared at my features in the mirror. Maybe I needed a new look? I seemed to live life the easy way these days and never bothered to actually wear my hair down anymore, let alone take the time to dry and curl it. I used to love spending hours getting ready, even if I had no wear to go. I sighed when I realized just how bad of a funk I was really in. I had never drastically changed anything about my look and wondered if now was the time to just go for it. I closed my eyes and tried to imagine myself with jet black hair instead of the light golden brown that everyone always complimented. It had always suited me and my fair complexion but black would make my green eyes really stand out. I played around with the idea as I pulled on my hoodie and grabbed my cell phone and keys before heading out for a quick run.

I wasn't much of a runner and never had been but today I decided it was a great day to start. I needed something new in my life, something to change who I was and propel me in a new direction far from where life had currently taken me. I started increasing my pace as I walked toward the park, trying to get my heartbeat up before I attempted to run like

I knew what I was doing. It was early in the morning for me but the city never sleeps so there were already quite a few people out walking and running. I pulled to the side of the path and stopped to stretch as I looked around and found that not a single person had even noticed me. That's one thing I was learning to love about living in a big city- you could be as invisible as you wanted because the majority of the time no one noticed you anyways.

I took a deep breath as I stood up right and looked at the path directly in front of me. There were a few people walking ahead of me and a handful of people hanging out in the grassy area beside me but other than that it wasn't too populated. Giving it everything I had, I pushed off and started running, not giving a damn about my insecurities or what anyone around me might be thinking about me.

It took a few minutes for my body to adjust as I struggled to catch my breath and had to slow down a little. For being so young I was apparently out of shape and needed to start slower than I thought. I slowed my pace to a comfortable jog and smiled when my body found a rhythm.

The weather was perfect for my impromptu run with a rare sunny sky and no snow or wind. It was a few weeks away from Christmas and there was another major storm expected to hit in a few days. I focused my breathing on inhaling deeply and felt alive and invigorated each time the cold air filled my lungs.

I was totally in the zone, unaware of anyone around me as my footsteps pounded against the pavement, creating a peaceful tune. Out of the corner of my eye I saw someone jogging next to me and tried to quicken my pace to put some distance between us. I didn't want to be obvious or rude and look directly at the person beside me so I kept my eyes forward and focused on my breathing as I ran harder.

The only problem was that the faster I went, the faster they went. They were constantly in line with me, running right beside me. Not having much of a choice I slowed down and moved over to the side to let the people behind me keep running. I was bent over at the waist, trying to catch my breath, when I noticed they stopped and pulled over too.

"What the hell is your problem?" I demanded as I straightened up, still trying to catch my breath. I had heard from Amber plenty of times about the dangers of running by yourself in the park and right now I was seriously kicking myself for not being more prepared. Why hadn't I thought to bring mace or some sort of weapon with me? Maybe I wasn't ready to be on my own in the big city after all.

"You're still not a morning person, are you?" Trevor teased as he took in the sight of me struggling to catch my breath.

"What are you doing here?" I made my way over to an empty bench and sat down, feeling it shift as Trevor sat beside me.

"Like you, I was going for a run."

"Are you following me?" I was irritated and part of me felt angry and hostile that he had found a way to taint my attempt at something new in my life. In reality, I think I was angrier that he caught me attempting to run and not being very successful at it given that he wasn't winded at all and I was pretty sure I was going to need an oxygen mask soon.

"I should be asking you the same." He leaned back against the bench and lifted a bottle of water to his lips, taking a long drink while watching me.

"Why would I be following you?" I eyed his water as my throat burned and wished I would have thought to bring a bottle of water with me. It was obvious who was the experienced runner between the two of us, even if his lean and sculpted body didn't give it away.

"I come running here every morning, and this is the path that I start on. Today is the first time I've ever seen you here running." His eyes danced wildly as they looked into mine and I could tell he was enjoying this. "So why are you stalking me, Hannah?"

I tried desperately to fight the smile that pulled at my lips and looked away in frustration. Just when I thought there wasn't anyone as charming out there as Max, along comes his best friend.

"I wanted to do something different. I'm in a funk." I shrugged and looked off in the distance.

"I get it. I've done crazy things trying to get out of a funk before." His tone was sympathetic and for a moment I imagined this might be what it felt like to have a sibling. That special kind of love where someone genuinely cares for you without wanting anything in return.

"I don't want to sound bossy but can I give you a piece of advice?" He looked at me out of the corner of his eye, making me nervous about what I might be lectured on.

"Sure." The initial irritation and frustration had subsided and I was thankful to be able to sit and talk with him for a few minutes.

"This park isn't always the safest place for women to run by themselves, even during the day. You might want to look at getting some mace, or if you want, I can let you know when I'm coming and we can run together."

My heart melted at the offer to run with him knowing that he was just doing it to be nice. I'm sure he runs way faster than what I'm able to do so I didn't want to take him up on the offer and hinder his workout. But I still felt important and that was a big boost to my currently deflated ego.

"Thank you, I'll look into getting some mace." I smiled as I rolled my eyes, knowing I had already given myself the same lecture a few minutes ago when I thought he could be some sex crazed predator after an imposter runner in the park.

"Sounds good. Just don't try to use it on me, got it?" He joked and I found myself laughing along with him.

"I wouldn't dare! Plus I'm sure you could outrun me anyways and get away before I got you."

"I don't know, you're pretty fast. You really picked up speed when you were trying to get past me."

"I was mad and irritated that someone was in my space." I laughed and remembered how focused I was on running and not at all worried about who was beside me.

"Well, remind me not to get on your bad side again." He playfully nudged me with his elbow as an awkward silence fell between us, the elephant in the room finally making its appearance.

"So, how's Elena?" My voice was low as I stared at the family having a morning picnic on the grass across from us.

"She still hasn't woken up yet. It's just a waiting game at this point."

"I'm sorry." I desperately wanted to ask about Max and see how he was doing but I didn't. I hadn't heard from him once since I left and deep down, I knew that it was my cue to walk away. Keep it as a clean break, don't muddy the waters. Forget the fact that my heart felt shattered into a mess of tiny pieces from all of the recent loss. Just move on.

"Me too." He sighed heavily and I could tell this was hard for him too. "But we think we have a lead and are looking into the guy from that online dating app, the one she was meeting the night she disappeared."

There was hope in his voice which made me smile.

"That's good. Hopefully it points you guys in the right direction."

I remembered Max telling me that she had met someone from the same online dating site that I had met Chet on and felt guilty about my upcoming date. I chewed my lip nervously as I looked away, hoping Trevor wouldn't notice it.

"What's wrong?" He leaned forward and turned toward me, invading my personal space.

"It's nothing." I was pretty sure my lip was going to look like it had been inflated with Botox from the amount of swelling I could feel building from chewing on it so much.

"Hannah." The tone in his voice got my attention and I found myself turning to look at him.

"Really, it's nothing."

"If there's something that you remember or that you know about the online dating site that could help us- I need you to tell me. I know that you're mad at Max, and I get it, but this isn't about him right now. It's about Elena. She's like a sister to me, Hannah." He reached out and held my hands as he pleaded.

"No, it's nothing like that. I promise."

I took a shaky breath and tried to figure out how to get around telling him that I had a date. He let go of my hands and watched me cautiously as he tried to figure out what was wrong with me. I was a terrible liar and knew that I didn't have much of a chance getting away without telling him.

"Is there something going on with you? Something with the guy who's been stalking you?"

I felt my face flush and looked away, my foot tapping uncontrollably. This felt like it was quickly getting out of control but I couldn't tell him that I had a date with another guy when I just barely stopped talking to his best friend a day ago. If Max had any questions about how I felt about him, this would confirm every doubt that he ever had. Not even a week after we stopped talking and I was already meeting someone I didn't know from the same dating app that his sister used when she went missing. If he didn't care about me as a girlfriend, I knew that it would still piss him off nonetheless.

"Hannah, I swear- I'm about to lose my mind. Just tell me what's going on. If not, I'm two seconds away from throwing you over my shoulder and locking you in my apartment until you tell me."

I licked my lips while my heart beat wildly in my chest. I pulled at the hem of my pullover hoodie and looked down.

"I have a date on Sunday."

There. That was it. The secret was out. I saw the surprise in his eyes as he processed the words and struggled with why it was so hard for me to tell him.

"Okay." He nodded and looked off in the distance, still processing.

"I didn't want to tell you because I didn't want you to think that I was the kind of girl to run from guy to guy." I watched him as I tried to explain, nothing but silence on his end.

"Max meant a lot to me. I've been really hurt that I haven't heard from him since I left but I get it. There's a lot going on and it's easier if we just have a clean break from each other. Whatever we were- we just break it off and go our separate ways."

"Hannah, I'm not judging you for going on a date."

"Okay." I straightened my posture and leaned back against the bench unsure of what he was going to say, if anything at all.

"Just promise me that you'll be careful, okay?" There was something in his voice that pulled at my heart, a worry of some sort that he hadn't spoken.

"I will. I know you're overprotective because Elena met someone from the same dating site but I promise, I'm getting to know the guy first." I smiled to reassure him then questioned if it was him that I was trying to reassure, or myself. In all honesty, I didn't know anything about him other than his name was Adam and he went to school. A shiver ran up my spine and I wondered if I was crazy for going on the date after all.

"That's not what I'm worried about." He looked at me and his eyes were soft as if they pitied me.

"I'm worried about you, Hannah."

"Why?"

"Because I think you're reaching a breaking point. You've been through a lot in a short period of time and you haven't really processed any of it. I've seen it too many times where people get pushed too far and they become so desperate to escape that they become reckless."

"So because I'm meeting someone for coffee, I'm being reckless?" I could feel myself becoming defensive as I thought about his words. I knew that I was in a rut but I wouldn't call it a downward spiral like he was insinuating.

"That's not what I meant, Hannah. You mentioned that you went running today because you're in a rut and needed something new. You're meeting someone you don't know for coffee when someone has been actively stalking you and you're not at all worried about it. So yeah, it makes me worried about you. You're not acting like yourself."

"Maybe I'm tired of being myself. Had that ever occurred to you? Maybe I'm tired of being the girl that is so boring and predictable that no one notices her. Maybe I want to actually live life for once and feel the thrill of doing something new!" I was practically shouting and knew that I had reached a new breaking point. But not the one he talked about.

"Look, I appreciate you wanting to look out for me but I'm good. And if you don't mind, I need to get going. I have places to go and things to do."

I didn't wait for him to say anything as I jogged off and made my way to the nearest store to grab some scissors and hair color before going back to my apartment.

Twenty Eight

Max
2 Days Ago

The battery icon on my laptop turned red as I continued my search through the online dating site, trying to figure out who 5StepsAhead was. I had created a fake dating profile and used a photo of Mindy- with her permission, to try to lure the guy in to talk to me. Unfortunately he was either smarter than I thought or dumber than I gave him credit for.

The notifications showed that he had opened and read the emails I had sent to him but there was no response. I tried one last time and had to put a lot of thought into how a woman would talk to a guy on an online dating site. I was clueless but knew that I had to get it right and make it seem like Mindy was really interested in him or it would fall through.

After several attempts with no luck, Mindy literally stepped in and took over my laptop, emailing the guy to tell him how impressed she was with the new book he was reading, and how he couldn't possibly be THAT smart AND good looking! I rolled my eyes as she walked Trevor and I through each response before he ended their conversation by telling her that he enjoyed their conversation but he wasn't looking for anything. After probing a little bit more he admitted that he had a date on Sunday and was interested in where it would go so he wasn't interested in meeting anyone else at this time.

It had now become my newest obsession to find out who he was meeting before Sunday, and if possible, where they were meeting. Trevor had been working with one of his friends who was an IT genius to try to get him to hack in and find out the location of this guy but that was proving to be impossible as well.

It was almost four in the afternoon and my body was feeling the impact of sitting at a makeshift table in the uncomfortable chair I had been in since last night. I sighed as I pushed the tray away and plugged in the laptop, allowing it to charge while I took a break. Mindy, Trevor and I had been working non-stop since this morning and I needed to stretch and get some blood flowing through my body. I was desperate for some fresh air and a view of anything other than the yellow tinted cream colored walls I had been staring at.

"Want to go downstairs and grab something to eat?" Trevor offered as if sensing my irritability.

I looked over at Elena, the urge to say yes overruled by the guilt of leaving her in case she woke up.

"I'll stay with Elena," Mindy offered, taking my seat by her bed. "Go get something to eat, stretch your legs, and get some fresh air. I'll call you if anything changes."

"Thanks, I appreciate it."

I knew that I could take my mom or sisters up on the offer to come and sit with Elena but I couldn't afford the distraction right now. My dad was doing a great job of keeping them distracted and had insisted that they spend time cleaning the house to get ready for Elena to come home. My mom was desperate to have her back home and didn't bother to object as she worked to deep clean the entire house. My dad was a smart man, I had to give him that.

Trevor and I took the stairs instead of waiting for the elevator. It felt good to be up and moving, my body sore from being sedentary for so long.

"Anything you feel like?" Trevor asked as we walked outside and headed toward the food trucks that were lined up.

"Burger sounds good, you?"

"I can do a burger." He smiled and something felt odd about it. It was the kind of smile he had when he knew something that he didn't want me to know.

"You seem off, what's up?" I asked as we got in line and waited.

"Nothing." He avoided eye contact and I knew it wasn't nothing. It was something. And it was something that I needed to know.
"Is it about Elena or Hannah?" I raised my eyebrow and waited for him to come clean.

"Hannah."

I watched as he kept his attention on the line in front of us instead of looking at me.

"What's going on with Hannah?" This time I put my hand on his shoulder and turned him so he had no choice but to look at me. He blew out a breath before sighing and making eye contact.

"I'm worried about her."

"Why? Has she received more notes? Did something happen at her apartment?" The worst thoughts I could think were flooding my brain, guilt for being with Elena instead of watching over Hannah taking over. I clenched my fist at my side while I waited for the bad news.

"No, she's fine. I think, I mean I don't know for sure."

"What does that mean? Why are you worried about her?" We moved forward and I waited anxiously for him to get on with it and tell me.

"I ran into her this morning while running."

"Hannah was running? I didn't know she runs." I shook my head at the thought and realized I didn't know as much about her personal life as I thought I did.

"She doesn't. She decided to start this morning because she's trying something new."

"Okay..." I was unsure of where he was going with this.

"She got really defensive, Max. About a lot of things. I think she's being reckless as a way to try to cope with everything that has happened."

"I don't know that running is really a cry for help," I offered, looking at the menu as we were next in line. I felt relieved that it wasn't as big of a deal as he had made it out to be.

"She has a date on Sunday. With some guy she met on that online dating site."

My head jerked toward him. There was no way that Hannah was going on a date with someone she didn't know. She wasn't that kind of girl, she had told me herself when she talked to me about her date with Chet. Was she just telling Trevor that to see if it would hurt me?

"Are you sure?" I asked between clenched teeth. "Maybe she just said that so you would tell me and I would get jealous?"

"That's the thing- I had to pry it out of her. She didn't just voluntarily tell me that she was going on a date. She wouldn't have told me if I hadn't pried it out of her."

I felt like the wind had been knocked out of me as I approached the order window with a sudden lack of appetite.

"What can I get you?" The guy asked from the window as he impatiently waited for my order.

"Burger and fries," I muttered as I processed what Trevor had just told me.

"Everything on it okay?"

"Yeah, whatever." I waved absently as I walked off in a daze, leaving Trevor to place his order. I sat down on the metal bench and hung my head as I thought about Hannah going on a date with another man. The thought of it made me physically sick. If she was ready and willing to date someone else that quickly then that had to mean that she wasn't that interested in what we had to begin with. Feelings of being with Adrianna filled my mind and I found myself comparing the two to each other. Both were beautiful and both had stolen my heart before giving theirs to someone else.

Twenty Nine

Hannah

1 Day Ago

It felt weird looking at myself in the mirror and seeing short, jet-black hair. Yesterday was the first day that I had decided to focus on being the new Hannah, the one who was adventurous and free spirited. After my conversation with Trevor I had never felt more excited to walk away from the old Hannah and find out who the new Hannah was.

He had said he was concerned about my reckless behavior but I didn't feel it was reckless at all. If I wanted to change who I was then that was all the approval that I needed. I had lived my life for so long being worried about what everyone else thought and seeking other's approval, never bothering to worry about my own.

A quick trip to the store and I had everything I needed to update my look. Gone was the predictable Hannah with the normal hair color. Here to stay was the new Hannah with a cute short bob of black hair that really made my eyes stand out. A couple of YouTube videos and half a bottle of champagne later and I was a new woman!

I had spent the morning getting groceries and picked up a few new outfits to try on for my date tomorrow. I liked the idea of spending the day playing around with my hair and makeup while trying on different outfits, especially since I had nothing else to do with myself on a Saturday. Lately my weekends had been consumed with studying but now that all of that was over, I could finally let loose and enjoy my downtime.

By noon my stomach was growling so I threw together a quick sandwich and sat down to eat while checking my email. There was a new one from Adam, asking me to meet him tomorrow at 11:00 in the morning at Java Jazz. I ate my sandwich while I thought about my response and played around with the idea of cancelling. It irked me that I was being so predictable so I confirmed I would meet him there at 11 and pressed send. There was no backing out now.

I went back to trying on outfits and seeing how they looked with my new hair and makeup, completely oblivious to the time. A knock on my door caught my attention and butterflies filled my belly as I wondered if it was Max. I sat the short dress down on the bed and walked over to the door, waiting to see if they were going to knock again before opening it. Really I was just trying to get the courage to open it in case it was Max. A few seconds later and there was another knock. Instead of peeking through the peephole like a normal person, I latched on to the excitement of not knowing who it was and opened the door.

"Wow." His voice was low as he leaned against the doorway and shoved his hands into his pockets.

"Wow what?" I asked as I pulled the door in, blocking him from coming in.

"You look different." His eyes studied my hair and face before traveling down my body and forcing the heat up my skin as I blushed.

"That was the goal." I nervously ran a hand through my newly short hair and looked at him. "What do you want, Max?"

"Can we talk for a few?" He stood upright and looked past me into the apartment.

"I think we've said all we've needed to the other day." I leaned against the door to make the opening even smaller.

"You might have, but I definitely wasn't finished." He stepped closer and I felt the buzz of his body next to mine.

"I don't think there's anything else we need to talk about." I protested as I tried to keep my position.

"Well then, you can just listen." He smiled coyly as he stepped further into my space and stepped inside. His body gently grazed mine as I felt his hand slide across my waist as he passed by.

I closed my eyes and shut the door. My nerves were on edge as I tried to figure out what he wanted and why he was there. I had wanted to talk to him days ago but now that he was here, I couldn't remember what I wanted to talk about. I turned to face Max and found him looking at the dress on the bed next to the other outfits that I had picked out for my date tomorrow. His brow was furrowed as he looked at each one, all skimpy outfits compared to what I usually wear. On the floor by the bed were a few pairs of thin heeled, strappy high heels to go with the outfits. He bent down and picked one up, holding it in the air by the stem of the shoe.

"Is this for your date tomorrow?" He eyed me cautiously as his jaw clenched. I licked my lips and swallowed hard.

"How did you hear about that?" I asked, knowing that he had talked to Trevor.

"Let's just say that I know things."

"You talked to Trevor."

"I did, he's worried about you. Told me that you weren't acting like yourself. I decided to come see for myself." He sat the shoe down where he found it and looked back at me. I felt nervous and uncomfortable as he looked me over, taking the few steps across the room to close the gap between us as he ran a hand through my hair. I closed my eyes and held my breath as I felt his touch that I had been desperate to feel for days.

"I can see what he means."

His words were simple but they felt like they cut through me with a knife. There was a condescending tone that started to eat away at me.

"Yeah, well, I wasn't looking for approval. Maybe you need to go." I squared my shoulders and stepped back.

"Is that what you want, Hannah?" His voice was low and raspy. My body felt alive next to his and I knew exactly what I wanted.

"Yes," I whispered, both of us knowing that I was lying.

"Look me in the eye and tell me, Hannah. Tell me that you want me to walk out that door and never come back. Say it and I'll do it." He watched me as he waited for my reaction.

My body turned slightly toward his as it felt the pull that I couldn't deny. I wanted to reach out and touch him. Kiss him. My fingers trembled by my side as they itched to grab him and pull him towards me. I looked up and licked my lips without thinking about it. No matter how hard I tried to control it, my body would always find a way to his.

"That's what I thought." He quickly reached out and grabbed me, pulling me in and wrapping his arms around me as his mouth crashed down over mine. I lifted my hands up and ran my fingers through his hair, clawing my way to bring him closer to me. He grasped down and lifted my butt as I wrapped my legs around him, feeling him walk over to the bed. The kiss broke for a quick second as he leaned over and pushed the outfits off the bed before laying me down on it.

There was a hunger in his eyes and I wanted him to devour me. I watched as he pulled his shirt over his head in one swift movement, revealing his rock hard abs and beautifully chiseled chest. He was seriously what girls dreamed of when they thought of the perfect man with the perfect body. His eyes looked me up and down as he unbuttoned his jeans and slid them down. Stepping out of them he leaned down on the bed, his erection trapped beneath his boxers, and pulled me closer to him.

"Were you planning to wear this on your date tomorrow?" he asked as his finger ran down the front of my lacy black button down tube top and hovered over the top of my denim skirt.

"Yes," I whispered as his hand slid down the front of my skirt and over my panties.

"Do you have any idea of what that does to me?" he grunted as his fingers pushed my panties to the side and slowly slipped a finger inside. I arched my back as I let out a moan as his finger easily glided back and forth. There was so much I needed to say to him but right now, I didn't want to talk, I just wanted him to keep touching me the way he was and help me get the release that I needed. I felt him pull the top of my tube top down with his teeth, freeing my breasts in the process. He groaned under his breath as he pulled a nipple into his mouth and sucked hard. My hands grabbed his hair and pulled him closer to me as my pelvis started to grind against his hand.

"I don't want anyone to see you like this, Hannah. Just me." He was breathless as he shot the words out in between the slow torture he was inflicting on my nipples as he went back and forth, sucking on both. His fingers dipped further inside causing me to want more. "Fuck, you're so wet, baby," he growled close to my ear.

"I want you, Max," I panted. "Now, Max, now!" I was getting closer, the friction on my clit the right pace to send me over the edge as I imagined his thick cock filling me again.

"Do you want me more than you want the guy you were planning to wear this for? Huh, Hannah? Do you?" There

was a possessiveness to his voice as he said it, turning me
on even further. I liked the jealousy in his voice.

"I want you more than anyone," I whimpered in his ear.
I was getting closer and needed him to get me there. I
adjusted my position beneath him to force his hand to rub
against my clit as his fingers moved inside me. The friction
felt wonderful as I rocked back and forth against his hand,
building the pressure I needed.

Suddenly he stopped and my eyes flashed open to look at him.

"Frustrating, isn't it?" He was propped up, hovering over
me as he watched for my reaction.

"It is." I blew out a frustrated breath, feeling my orgasm
slipping away as my chest heaved up and down.

"Now take your physical frustration and imagine what it
feels like to be me. To see the girl I'm crazy about wearing
this sexy fucking outfit to go on a date with another man
because she refuses to hear me when I tell her how crazy I
am about her. That's frustrating, Hannah."

My shoulders slumped as my body relaxed beneath him and
I took in his words. Suddenly I didn't have any desire to go
on the date tomorrow. I wanted this man right here in front
of me. The one who was making the effort to show me how
much he cared about me.

"I'm sorry." I let out a deep breath and looked him in the eyes.

"I'm gonna need more clarification. Is this just an apology so I'll finish getting you off?" He chuckled as he rolled over and laid next to me.

"No," I reached over and swatted at his chest, "I'm sorry for not listening when you were trying to talk to me and for making you jealous."

He grabbed my hand and laced his fingers between mine.

"You certainly know how to drive me crazy," he joked, a small laugh filling the room.

"Same here." I looked up and studied his face. "I wasn't trying to make you jealous, I was just trying to figure out how to move on with my life. How to get over you."

I lowered my eyes as he leaned in and kissed my forehead. While I wanted to go back to the hot, passionate road we were heading down just a few minutes ago, I was perfectly content just being in his arms. It felt right.

"Well, I'm happy to drive you crazy again...if you know what I mean?" His voice got lower as he rolled over on top of me and made his way planting kisses down my neck as his hands slid my skirt up to my hips. Firm hands grabbed my ass and my back arched, inviting him in to where I needed him.

There was an urgency to the way he moved as he freed himself from his boxers and slid my panties to the side before entering me. I gasped at the sudden contact and dug my nails in his back as he rocked back and forth inside me. There was no slow, gentle love making tonight. It was quick, and rough, and delicious as he took his time to give me my release before getting his.

An hour later I rolled over and felt his arms wrap tighter around me as he held onto me in his sleep. We had talked for a bit after we made love but eventually we both gave in and fell asleep, which was easy given neither of us had slept the night before. He had given me updates on Elena and where they were at with everything but it was quick and we didn't get into too much detail.

Around 11:30 we woke up to his phone ringing. I looked at him as I turned the light on, my stomach clenching as I waited for the bad news. No one ever called in the middle of the night with good news. He reached over and grabbed his cell phone, sliding the button to answer it.

"What's up?" he asked as he mouthed Trevor's name to let me know who was calling. I waited on pins and needles, waiting to find out what he was calling for.

"Are you serious?! Okay, I'll be right there." He hung up and quickly rolled out of bed, grabbing his clothes from the floor and getting dressed as he looked around for his shoes.

"What is it? What's happening?"

"Elena is awake." He smiled as he leaned in and gave me a kiss before rushing off to the door. He stopped to look at me before he opened the door.

"Go! Go!" I waved him off, excited for him that she was finally awake. "Update me later, just get over there and see your sister." I smiled and watched as the door closed behind him.

Thirty

Max

6 Hours Ago

The night had been long and the only way I was keeping track was with the hourly check-ins the nurses did on Elena. A new set of nurses came in as our regular nurses checked out for the day, confirming it was seven in the morning and the shift change was happening. I took a break to let Elena get situated with the new nurses and ran downstairs to get us breakfast. My family was already on their way down to the hospital so it was about to get even more crowded. The line at the food truck was moving quickly as I saw Trevor heading toward the entrance to the hospital. I waved and flagged him down before he went inside.

"Hey, how's Elena doing?" he asked as he clapped a hand on my shoulder.

"She's good. I'm hoping to talk with her this morning, she was still pretty out of it last night. But then again, my mom and sisters are coming so who knows how much talking we will get in." I chuckled as Trevor smiled, knowing that it was true. "Thankfully she stayed awake so that was a good sign that she should be on the road to recovery." I smiled as I took the cups of coffee from the girl in the food truck and handed them to Trevor as I waited for the last cup of coffee and our burritos.

By the time we got back up to Elena the nurses were leaving her room followed by a doctor. I was disappointed that we had missed the doctor but they hadn't told us that he was expected to go by for an update. I quickened my pace and caught up with him right as he made his way to the nurse's station.

"Hey, doc. I was wondering if you could give me an update on my sister, Elena Romano?" I stood back to give him some space so it didn't feel like I was being too aggressive. He peered over the thick bifocal lenses and looked me up and down before looking back at her file.

"Who did you say you were?" His voice was as raspy as someone who had smoked 10 cartons of cigarettes a day for the last forty years.

"Her brother. Max." I waited for him to acknowledge my relationship to her, surely the nurses had told him that I had been there with her since she was admitted.

"Your sister is doing well, considering everything she went through. We'll do some more tests and scans this morning to make sure there's nothing that we missed, but she should be able to be discharged by this evening or early tomorrow morning." He was vague and it was getting to me in the worst way.

"Is there any news on what had happened? Did you get the results back on her other tests?"

"Look, I have to get to the next patient in my rounds. If you want the full update, have your brother fill you in."

I stared at him confused.

"I'm sorry, who?"

"Your brother."

"I don't have a brother."

"Okay, then Elena's other brother. He was just here, I updated him on everything. Left maybe 10 minutes ago." He tapped his pen on the countertop and nodded toward the clock before grabbing another file and walking off.

Chills ran down my spine as I looked at Trevor and he looked at me. Who the fuck had been there, pretending to be Elena's brother? As if on cue, we both ran into Elena's room and pulled the curtain back. I was relieved to find it was just Elena in the room, no one else.

"What the hell?!" She held her hand to her chest as she looked at Trevor and I with fear in her eyes as we startled her.

"Was someone in here recently?" I asked as I looked around. Trevor pushed past me and checked the bathroom while I waited for an answer.

"Um, yeah. The doctor. The nurses. The person who brought me a tray of food." She nodded at the tray beside her. "You saw most of them before you left."

Trevor and I exchanged a look as I sat down next to her.

"Max, you're scaring me. What's going on?"

"I asked the doctor for an update before coming in here and he was really vague. When I asked for more information he told me that I needed to get the updates from Elena's brother. The one he had just talked to 10 minutes before I got there."

Her hand went to her mouth as the color drained from her face.

"He knows that I'm here," she whispered as her eyes filled with tears.

"Did anyone look or act suspicious that was in your room?"

"No, but I was really busy with talking to the nurses. The only person that came in that wasn't a nurse was the person who brought my tray, but they were still wearing scrubs so I figured they worked here. They were the only one who didn't talk to me."

"Have you checked your food tray?" Trevor asked right as the door opened and a bubbly woman came in holding a food tray in her hand.

Trevor and I watched as she approached the bed and noticed the food tray next to Elena. She looked down at the covered lid and stepped outside before coming back in.

"Can we help you?" I asked.

"I have a food tray to deliver but it looks like someone else already delivered one." She nodded toward Elena. "I thought maybe I had the wrong room but it says it's for 704 and this is 704." She shrugged as she held the food tray in front of her and waited.

"Well then, I guess she gets two today," I joked nervously, curious to see what was going on. "You can go ahead and set that one down over there if you don't mind?"

She smiled at me as she left it on the open counter space by the sink and walked out of the room. Elena looked confused as she looked back and forth between the two trays.

"Why would they bring me two food trays?" she asked innocently.

"My guess is that they didn't," I said as I looked at the food tray sitting next to her. I looked at Trevor, feeling nervous about seeing what was really under the lid. He gave a slight nod of agreement as I slowly reached down and lifted the lid.

Sitting on the plate was a bologna and cheese sandwich with a note attached to a toothpick stuck in the sandwich. I pulled the toothpick out and slid the paper down. I unfolded the paper which was a piece of paper torn out of a text book. As I unfolded it, I saw the familiar black ink from the marker used in the notes to Hannah. I cleared my throat as I read it out loud.

Roses are red
Violets are blue
You thought you could leave me
But I found you

I tried to build us a life
Where we could live together
You threw it all away
You severed the tether

I wanted to love you
And only make you happy
You wanted to defy me
Each time you attacked me

Everything I did
I did it for us
I say it was in the name of love
You say it was lust

I thought I was what you wanted
Everything you said you'd need
People tried to warn you not to talk to strangers
Their advice you did not heed

Maybe next time you'll learn your lesson
Of random strangers you shouldn't bed
Even though you got away I'll always be 5StepsAhead

My stomach soured as I read the note and saw the same patterns as the notes Hannah had been receiving. When I was done I looked at Elena who had tears running down her face.

"Elena, do you know who wrote this?" I asked as I held the note in the air. "Do you know who took you?"

She shook her head no as she violently sobbed. I went to her side and leaned next to the bed and held her as she cried. Her body felt small and fragile compared to mine as I focused on being gentle so I didn't hurt her.

"I don't know who it is. He never let me see his face, he always had it covered."

"Did you recognize his voice?"

"It always sounded familiar but I couldn't figure out why." She continued to sob as her breathing changed in response to her crying.

"Does this note mean anything to you?" I asked, feeling her cry against me again, unable to answer me.

"Leni, what is it about the note that keeps getting to you?" While I could imagine the whole thing would bother anyone because it was creepy as fuck, I knew my sister well enough to know that something in specific was triggering this reaction.

"It's okay, you can tell me. You're safe now," I whispered as I gently rubbed her back.

"The guy that I was meeting before he took me, his profile name was 5StepsAhead."

She cried even harder after she said it.

"Shh, it's okay. We're looking for him, not to worry." I tried to reassure her.

"What do you mean?" She wiped her tears away and looked up at me.

"When you first went missing, I went through stuff in your room and saw your conversation with him. Then when you came to my apartment the other day, you whispered 'five steps' before you passed out."

"I was so stupid to meet up with him. I didn't even know what he looked like." She let out a ragged breath.

"Can you walk me through what happened?" I asked, thankful for the natural progression into the conversation.

"I'll do my best, most of it is kind of fuzzy. There's a big chunk that is completely missing." She took a deep breath and then looked at Trevor and I.

"I was really upset about the fight that I had with mom, she was all over me about the guy I was seeing, even though she hadn't even met him. When this guy offered to meet up for coffee, I decided to go because I was so mad at mom and wanted to spite her. If she thought I was some cheap tramp who just went out with anyone then I would show her just how many guys I could date at once. I went to the Java Jazz coffee shop that he suggested and waited for him. I was pretty sure I had been stood up when this kid brought me a drink that I hadn't ordered. He said that he had been asked to bring it to me as an apology for making me wait, that the guy I was waiting for was on his way. I didn't think anything of it and it was delivered by someone wearing the same aprons they wear, so I drank it. Not even thirty minutes later I started to feel weird and got up to go home. I don't remember anything after that."

I swallowed hard as I stood watching her with my arms crossed against my chest, jaw clenched. It made sense now why she didn't know where she had been taken- she was drugged before he took her.

"Later, when I woke up, I was in this abandoned warehouse. I wasn't restrained at all, just left to sleep on the cold floor. That's when I called you. Not long after, I heard someone come in the room and that's when he found me on my cell and took it away from me. He was wearing a mask and said that he couldn't let me see him yet. That it wasn't time." She looked down at her hands before continuing.

"The first few days were the hardest because I didn't know what he wanted. He just kept mumbling about how he had to prepare, she was coming soon. One was for practice, the other was for keeps. He would bring in different things each time he came back and would be gone for long periods of time. The stuff he brought was weird- like canned goods, bottled water, and picture frames. But each frame was empty at first." A few deep breaths to steady herself then she continued with her story.

"I fought every chance I got that first week, or however long it was. It felt like forever. There weren't any windows so it was hard to tell if it was day or night. Shortly after he took me there, he tied me to a chair so I couldn't try to escape. He bound my hands and feet. Whenever he got close enough I would try to reach out and grab his knife or knock him down but he caught on quickly and would say, nope, she's not ready yet. Can't bring my love in until this one is in line. It was so weird and it felt really uncomfortable. I don't know who he was talking about but he constantly referred to them as his love."

I reached into my pocket and pulled out the pen and notepad that I always kept on me and jotted down the new information. Elena waited while I wrote and started again when I nodded for her to continue.

"Soon he started bringing pictures in and added them to the empty frames. It was all the same girl- long dark brown hair, really pretty girl. He would tell me how soon our family would be complete, we just had to wait until I was ready. So then it occurred to me that if I wanted to get past this guy, I had to play his game. Instead of constantly fighting him, I had to be interested in him. So I slowly started to act like I was interested in him. I stopped fighting whenever he would touch me and I acted like I liked it. He would tell me how I was doing such a great job and that he was staying five steps ahead. A few days before I escaped I thought I had a chance so I took it. Unfortunately, it wasn't a well thought out plan. He had brought in a new picture frame and I 'accidentally' broke it, keeping a piece of glass tucked inside my pants. As he was getting ready to go to class, he went to give me a goodbye hug- it had become our ritual- and I reached out and tried to stab him. The problem was that I missed and tore the arm of his jacket, cutting his arm in the process."

I shifted my position and looked up at Trevor who was listening with the same intensity as I had, and looked even more pissed off.

"When I cut him, that was when he finally went crazy. He kept screaming about why I didn't love him, why I didn't want to be with him. His anger turned to rage in a split second and that's when he attacked me. At one point I pretended to be unconscious so he would leave me alone. As part of my punishment he withheld food and water for several days, forcing me to eat moldy bologna sandwiches if I got hungry enough. I realized that if I wanted to live, I had to play the part again. He was starting to get obsessed with whoever this other girl was, adding several photos a day and building a shrine for her. I slowly started showing remorse for what I did and tried to play up the loving wife that he insisted I needed to be. The night I left we were having dinner, a celebration of my good behavior the past few days, so I was allowed to sit at the wooden patio table with him without having to be tied to the chair." Her shoulders rose and fell with the deep breath she took before she went on with the story.

"I had complete freedom of my hands and feet but I felt completely weak from not eating in days and was dehydrated. I think that was the only reason he didn't restrain me- he knew how weak I was already, I wasn't much of a threat. He poured us wine and went to check on something from his phone before joining me for dinner. As he sat down I reached over and smashed the wine bottle against the concrete wall and used the sharp point as my weapon. I held it out and swung at him every time he reached for me as I backed myself out the same path I had seen him coming and going. I tripped and started to fall when he reached out to grab me, my only opportunity to be free. I let myself fall as I felt him crush me as he fell on top of me, the sharp point of the wine bottle piercing his shoulder. I knew it wasn't enough to kill him but it was enough to immobilize him for a few. That's when I took off running and didn't stop."

She exhaled loudly as she shifted her position in the bed and laid back.

"Would you be able to describe the building you were in?" Trevor asked from the other side of me.

"I didn't see it until I left but then I was so focused on staying ahead of him that I didn't bother to look around or to look for any landmarks that would show where I was."

"I'm really proud of you, Leni." I smiled as I took in everything she had told me and wondered what additional information she might be able to give us about the guy if we asked the right questions.

We ate our breakfast and drank our coffee in silence as Trevor and I took in everything Leni had told us. A few minutes after she had finished telling us, my family came in her room, making the small space even tinier. I was thankful that for whatever reason, they were late today, and that I had a chance to talk to Elena before they got there. I don't know how much I would have been able to get from her with my mom sitting beside her, criticizing everything she did and asking her why she would meet up with a guy she didn't know. I knew my mom and sister well enough to know that not much was going to change from the fight they had before she went missing.

Once it was after 10, I texted Hannah to say good morning and see how she was doing. Since she wasn't an early riser I wanted to give her time to get up and get some coffee in her before I approached the topic of whether she was still planning on going on that date. After hearing what Leni told me, I would never feel comfortable with anyone doing online dating. It made my stomach hurt not knowing what Hannah's plans were.

Thirty One

Hannah
1 Hour Ago

I was pleasantly surprised to wake up to a text message from Max this morning. I sat up in bed to read it, soreness from the night before reminding me that he really was there and that it hadn't been just a dream. After the 3rd time our bodies were fully satisfied and depleted. I sent him a text back wishing him a good morning and stumbled out of bed to go make some coffee so I could get my day started. It was after 10 and I still hadn't decided whether to cancel my date or not but I knew I needed to make a decision quickly. It would be rude not to let someone know that I wasn't planning on showing up.

The coffee trickled down into the pot as the heavenly aroma filled the air. I took a cup with me over to the couch and sat down as I opened my laptop and waited for it to finish running some updates. I sipped my coffee while I waited, knowing that it would take a while for them to finish since my computer was so ancient. Ten minutes later the screen changed and a picture of me with my parents as my screensaver greeted me. I sat my cup down on the coffee table and picked up my cell phone to find a text message from Max, asking what my plans for the day were.

I chewed my bottom lip as I struggled with what to do, even though deep down I knew what I wanted to do. I wanted to cancel my date and spend the day talking to Max, or even better, be with him. But I felt guilty for not following through with my date because it might be what Amber had wanted. I took a deep breath and tried to clear my head. If I wanted to start a new life, I had to stop focusing on what Amber would want from me. She wasn't here to see it so it shouldn't matter as much as I was letting it.

I opened the dating site and went to my messages with Adam, clicking on the most recent email confirming our date at 11. It was 10:25 so there should still be plenty of time for him to see the message before getting there. I typed a quick message, apologizing for the last minute notice but I would be unable to meet him after all. I clicked the send button and leaned back against the couch, satisfied with my decision. A few seconds later a notification popped up with an error message. I clicked it open and it showed undeliverable due to a profile that no longer existed. Frowning, I closed out the notification and clicked on Adam's profile. Another error message- this user no longer exists.

Irritation lingered around for a few minutes when I realized that I was apparently the one who was going to be stood up since he had already deleted his account before we even met. Guess it was for the best anyways. I signed out of the site and closed my laptop, sitting it on the coffee table. I picked up my coffee cup and took a drink as I settled back against the couch and contemplated whether to call or text Max. I knew I should text since he might be busy with Elena and unable to talk, but the selfish side of me longed to hear his voice. As if reading my mind, a text came through from

Max, asking if I was okay since I hadn't texted him back yet. I smiled as my fingers moved across my phone to reply.

Me: Sorry, I had to take care of something. No plans today. You?

I watched as the dots danced across the screen as he was typing.

Max: No plans here, either. Spending time with Elena before she gets bombarded with questions from Mindy and the team. My family just left now so she'll get a small break before she has to tell the story again. They hope to discharge her this evening.

Me: That all sounds like great news. I'm happy to hear it.

Max: So, are you going?

My eyebrows pulled together as I read his message. Go where?

Me: Where am I supposed to be going?

Max: The date.

Oh. I rolled my eyes at my own forgetfulness as I totally spaced it out already and forgot that Max knew about the date.

Me: I cancelled it, but I'm pretty sure I would have been stood up anyways.

Max: Why do you say that?

Me: I emailed him to cancel and he had already deleted his profile.

Max: That's weird.

Me: Yeah, I guess. But at least I didn't have to be the one to cancel.

Max: True. Where were you supposed to meet? Please tell me he wasn't picking you up at your apartment.

Me: No, we were meeting at Java Jazz by my apartment.

Max: Was that your idea?

Me: Nope. It was his idea.

Max: Something doesn't feel right with this. Did you give him any of your personal information?

Me: I didn't give him any information about myself.

I thought back to our conversations just to make sure, nothing popped into my mind that I could remember that was personal other than I had just finished finals. We didn't even exchange phone numbers. Then it hit me that he had called me by my name yet I never told him what it was. A chill shot through me as I thought about how stupid I had been to agree to go on the date in the first place. My phone buzzed in my hand as Max's name showed on the caller ID.

"Hey."

"Hannah, does this guy know anything about you? Where you live? What you look like?" He sounded anxious which had me worried.

"We didn't talk about any of that, Max. I mean he knows what I look like because of my user profile picture, but he doesn't know where I live."

"Do you know what he looks like?"

"He doesn't have a profile picture." I sighed and knew what was coming.

"Hannah- " My name came out as a breath as I heard him sigh on the other line. "You agreed to meet a guy that you don't know, and don't even know what he looks like?"

"I know his name." I offered, hoping that it would give me a little more sympathy that I wasn't completely stupid.

"What's his name?"

"Adam."

"Adam what?"

I could hear the irritation in his voice and knew Detective Max was about to come through soon.

"I don't know, I didn't ask."

"Did you tell him your name?"

"No......" I stalled as I tried to think of how to tell him that he knew my name.

"But?"

"But he knew my name anyways."

"How did he know your name?"

"I don't know, Max! I drank half a bottle of champagne, I was exhausted and feeling sad- I didn't ask that many questions!"

"Okay, okay, I'm sorry."

I could hear voices in the background and he sounded distracted by whoever it was.

"You sound busy, I can let you go." I offered as I was ready to end this conversation.

"It's fine, it's the hospital police. They're here to talk about the security footage from this morning."

"Why? What happened?"

"A guy was here, asking about Elena. He pretended to be her brother to get information from the doctor about her." He pulled the phone away from his mouth as he spoke to someone else before coming back on the line. "Whoever it was got into Elena's room and left her a note inside of the food tray that looked like it was from the hospital. We're trying to see if we can get a good picture of who the guy is."

"Do you think it's the guy who took her?"

"I think it's a really good possibility. The note he left had some specific things that only she would know about from being held captive with him. But Hannah, the notes look identical to the ones you were getting. They are written on pages torn from a text book and are in black ink from a marker."

I shivered as my body was covered in goosebumps.

"Does she know who it is?" My voice was shaky with fear.

"She doesn't. She never saw his face, he wore a mask the entire time."

"Hannah, I have to ask- what was the profile name of the guy you were supposed to meet?" His voice was laced with tension that now matched my own.

"Five steps ahead," I whispered as I tried to connect the dots.

"Fuck!"

The boom in his voice startled me, causing me to jump in my seat. I got up and carried the coffee mug to the kitchen counter.

"Hannah, you're not safe there. I'm on my way to get you. Don't leave before I get there and keep your phone on. Don't hang up, whatever you do. Okay?!"

"Okay," I stammered as I tried to put the pieces together. Something was wrong. Very, very wrong.

Thirty Two

Adam
20 Minutes Ago

Do you know what the most frustrating thing in the world is? When someone agrees to do something then changes their mind at last minute. It was my BIGGEST pet peeve and made me see red every time it happened. Elena had said she would love me and promised to stay with me forever, then she attacked me and left. She was constantly just within my reach but her two little bodyguards at the hospital kept getting in my way. I wasn't so much concerned with having her back. Why beg someone to want to be with you? But regardless, she still needed to pay for what she did. And there was a hefty price tag on it.

For a little bit I had considered forgiving her debt because I was so excited about where things were going with Hannah. But then I found her flirting with the guy in the park, the same one who kept getting in my way with Elena. Shortly after that, I watched her try on and buy slutty clothes to go with the trampy new haircut and color. I was livid when she decided to change her hair without asking me first. She needed to follow the rules before she found herself in the same position as Amber and where Elena was headed.

I considered myself a very patient and disciplined man except for when you made me angry. And lately, I was angry a lot. So much so that I felt blinded by the anger. But everything would soon change, I could just feel it. All of my hard work and sacrifice would finally pay off.

Now we were in a moment of truth, a moment to determine Hannah's fate. She had spent the night with the cop, tsk tsk tsk. I could already tell that he had gotten in her head and would convince her not to meet me so I deleted my profile before she could try to cancel. She was confused, I could tell. But if she just let me between her legs as easily as she let him, she wouldn't be confused about anything. She would enjoy it, just like I did every time I pretended it was her hand working me over as I jerked myself off under the table in class.

I didn't have much time to waste thinking about all of the things she had already done. I had to get going if my plan was still going to work. It was almost 11, time for our date.

Thirty Three

Max

15 Minutes Ago

"He's going after Hannah- it's the same fucking guy!" I whispered loudly to Trevor as I tucked my gun in the back of my jeans. "Stay with Leni and don't let anyone in here. If they force her to be discharged, take her to your apartment and wait for me there."

I practically ran out of the room and down the hall while Hannah waited quietly on the other line. A few people yelled curse words at me as I flew by but I kept going. I had to get to her and I knew the clock was ticking.

"You still there?" I huffed into the phone as I ran out the front doors and into the crowded area by the food trucks as I darted in between people and made my way to the street. I could try to hail a cab and pray that there were no delays getting to Hannah's, or I could keep running the 5 blocks until I got to her. I checked my watch, ten minutes until eleven.

I wasn't sure if or when this guy was coming for her but something in my gut screamed for me to go get her. I shook my head and took off running down the street, deciding that I couldn't risk getting stuck sitting in a cab somewhere.

"I'm here. Are you okay?" Her voice was filled with concern.

"Yeah, I'm just running. Don't hang up, I'm coming to you." I panted as I kept running.

It felt like it was going to take hours to get to her at this rate, my body toying with the idea of giving up on me. I stopped for a quick second to catch my breath and looked down at my watch. Eleven on the dot. I could hear background noise at Hannah's and pushed the phone against my ear to try to hear what was happening.

"Wow, you got here quick," She said directly into the phone as I heard her turning the locks on the door. There was an easiness to her voice now, the sound of relief. My heart dropped as I heard the door open.

"Hannah! Don't open the door, it's not me!" I screamed into the phone, knowing it was too late. I started running, as fast as I could, as I kept the phone pressed against my ear. I heard a loud thump and stopped in my tracks. My pulse was racing as I waited to hear Hannah's voice again. There was movement on the other side and I prayed that maybe she just dropped her phone. A few seconds later I heard the door click shut and a male's voice came on the line.

"Wrong number."

Thirty Four

Hannah

Drip. Drip. Drip. The sound of leaking water filled the empty room that smelled of mildew from the dampness in the air. My head hung against my chest as I tried to lift it, the weight of it unbearable. Slowly I forced my head backwards and allowed a moment to rest as I blinked open my eyes and looked around. The room was dimly lit with concrete floors and windowless concrete walls with nothing around me other than the wooden chair I had been bound to with rope. I tried to pull at the restraints as the thick rope bit at my skin without giving.

I listened for the sound of the dripping water but couldn't hear it anymore. Did that mean that someone was there with me? My body trembled as I strained to hear any sounds that might tell me where I was or who was there. As I slowly tilted my head forward my eye caught a glimpse of something shimmering on the floor from the dim light that barely hung from the ceiling. I leaned forward as far as the rope would allow as I tried to see what it was. As my head dipped forward toward the ground, I heard the familiar dripping sound once more as I felt something wet trickle down my face. Beneath my chair was a puddle of blood. My blood.

My head was killing me and I assumed that it was from whatever injury I had that had caused so much bleeding. I didn't know how much time had passed by or where I had been taken. It was dark and the concrete made the entire room feel cold, sending a shiver through my body. My eyes adjusted to the darkness as I looked around.

A few minutes later I heard footsteps approaching and my body went rigid as I waited for whatever was about to happen. A man wearing the same mask as the person who was at my door stood in front of me and looked at me as they tilted their head. He reached out and touched the spot on my head where it was bleeding. I jerked back away from his touch, his fist clenching in response.

"You know, if you hadn't been such a naughty girl, this wouldn't have had to happen this way." His voice was quiet and almost sounded familiar though I didn't know why. I stayed silent as I watched him like a caged animal, focusing on every little move he made.

"I've been working hard to build us a nice home, would you like a tour?"

I didn't answer as there were no possible words that I could use to respond to that. Who the hell was this guy and why did he think he was building us a home?

"I'm going to untie you- you can be a good girl- can't you?" He tilted his head in question as he held a pocket knife in the air, waiting for my confirmation before cutting the rope. I felt the tension give as the first rope was cut, then the second. He bent down and cut the ropes around my feet, leaving me completely free. Part of me wanted to take off and run but from the way this guy was built, I knew he would catch me before I made it two steps. The last thing I wanted to do was provoke this guy.

He reached out his hand for me to take as I eyed it cautiously. I saw his jaw clench from under the mask and stuck my hand out for him to take it. As I looked around, I noticed the room was rather big with 5 different entry points. Each door lead to a hallway that went to God knew where. It felt like an impossible maze to try to figure out. I was ready to get this over with and took a step forward when he reached an arm in front of me to stop me.

"Not so fast. Close your eyes, it's a surprise." His voice had a sing song tone to it which made me feel even more uneasy as I closed my eyes and allowed him to lead me out of the room. I tried to count the steps I had taken before we got to the next place but lost track after he pushed me forward and I stumbled before his hand steadied me. A few minutes later we stopped and I listened as I heard his steps fade away from me.

"Okay, now you can look." His voice was cheerful, giving me the creeps, as he walked back toward me.

I let my eyes adjust to the lighting in the new room as I slowly looked around me. Off to the side was a wooden patio table that had been set with plates and wine glasses, a lit candle in the middle. I stared at it with curiosity as I tried to figure out what was behind it. It appeared to be some sort of shrine set up with picture frames of different shapes and sizes, similar to what you would see at a memorial site for someone who had died.

I felt his eyes on me as I looked at the picture frames before turning away.

"Don't be shy, you can go look at them. You'll like them, trust me."

I looked at him wearily as I slowly walked over to the area with the picture frames and found that there were upwards of 100 frames. Each one had a picture of me. My jaw dropped as I stared on in disbelief.

Me in class. Me at the library. Me at the coffee shop. Me with Amber. Me on my date with Chet. Me in my apartment watching tv. Me in the shower. My stomach churned as I kept looking at the series of photos until I got to the most recent ones.

Me with Max. At my apartment and his. Photos of me after Amber died. Photos of me at her funeral. Photos of me jogging with Trevor.

I lifted a trembling finger and held it to my lips as I looked at the photos of Max and I from last night. My black hair wound tightly in his hand as my head leaned back while I rode him. My bare breasts on full display. I felt like I was going to throw up. Whoever this person was, they had been obsessed with me for months. And I had been completely oblivious all along.

Thirty Five

Max

I was out of breath as I flew up the last few steps to
Hannah's apartment and burst through the door that was left
slightly open. My hands were steady as they held onto my
gun, my eyes quickly scanning the apartment for any sign of
Hannah. I cleared the apartment in seconds, confirming that
no one else was there.

"Son of a bitch!" I slammed my hand down on the counter
and closed my eyes. She was gone and I had no fucking
idea where she could be. My phone rang and for a second
I prayed that it was the asshole who took her, calling to
negotiate a deal. The problem was he didn't take her as
a hostage so he could get what he wanted. He took her
because she was what he wanted.

"Romano," I growled into the phone as I ran a hand down my
face and looked around for anything that looked out of place.

"Hey, it's Mindy. My phone died so I'm using the one in
Elena's room."

"What's up?" I felt irritated and frustrated, the last thing I
wanted to do was talk on the phone. I wanted to be chasing

this asshole down and get Hannah back but I had no fucking idea where to start.

"Trevor caught me up on everything. Where's Hannah?"

"Gone. I was too late." I quickly explained my phone call with Hannah as I was headed over and the moment when she opened the door. I also confirmed that it was the same guy who took Elena based on the notes and the consistent use of 'wrong number' when he hung up Elena's phone, Amber's phone, and now Hannah's.

"I started having them track Hannah's cell phone the second Trevor told me what was going on, just to be on the safe side. But..." Her voice trailed off and I knew what she was reluctant to say as I spotted Hannah's phone on the floor behind the door.

"But you can't because it hasn't left her apartment. I know, I'm looking at it." I let out a sigh as I walked over and picked it up.

"I'm sorry, Max. But we did find that the guy has a tattoo that Elena was able to describe for us."

"What kind of tattoo?"

"She said that it looked like a Y with a capital I in the middle of it. I did some searches on my phone and she confirmed the image. It's the Greek symbol for psychology, Psi."

Something about what she said clicked in my head and I closed my eyes to try to focus on why that sounded so familiar.

"Where was the tattoo?" I asked as a memory floated around in my head, just out of reach.

"His forearm. She saw it a couple of times when his sleeves were rolled up. It's the only thing we have so far that tells us who this guy is. We're going to go off of that lead and see where it gets us."

"Don't bother."

"Why not?" Her voice sounded worried.

"Because I know who it is." I grabbed Hannah's cell phone and made my way to my office in record time.

Thirty Six

Adam

My hand hurt and again and I was pissed that I was forced to have to do what I did. I wanted to spend the night with Hannah, getting her settled into our new home but then for whatever reason, she fought me on it. She ruined everything. She led me on. Led me to believe that she was the one I was destined to be with. The perfect woman who was content sitting in the shadows, not needing attention. The quiet one who never spoke up for herself, who was a natural submissive. The one who was going to save herself for me. For something special.

I don't know what happened to that Hannah. She started changing and I made every effort to rid her life of the negative impacts. Her blind date at the coffee house- he was just planning to sleep with her and forget about her. I saw him put the drug in her drink. Not going to lie, I was kind of disappointed in myself for not thinking about it first. But he had to go. I had to get rid of him so he couldn't corrupt Hannah.

And then her so called "best friend". Man, she was a piece of work. She never put any effort in with her school work and I could tell that Hannah carried her on all of the group projects. I knew she was the one who was encouraging

Hannah to date lots of guys and have fun and that just wasn't okay. So I got rid of that problem too.

But then Hannah got involved with the cop. Not just any cop. Turned out it was the brother of the girl who was going to be Hannah's new best friend. See, I wasn't a total monster. I knew that Hannah would be sad without a best friend to talk to and have girly moments with, so I had Elena lined up for her. She was another quiet girl in class, always focused on her studies and never paid attention to the boys in class.

Then I found that both Elena and Hannah were both on the same dating website and that made me furious. I started talking to Elena first, just to test the waters. I had been watching her for a while so I already knew how slutty she actually was. But it didn't matter to me, she wasn't Hannah. As long as Hannah wasn't sleeping around, everything would be okay.

Except I found that Hannah was fucking the cop. And not the sweet, romantic love making that I had pictured when I thought of her and I together. No, it was the dirty stuff that I watched on porn to jack off to at night before I started my collection of photos.

Things could have been easier. A lot less messy. No blood. No bodies to try to clean up. If only she would have listened.

Thirty Seven

Hannah

I opened my eyes to a pitch black room and wondered if I had actually even opened my eyes. One was swollen shut, dried blood pulling at the skin as I forced it open. Instinctively I tried to reach up to touch it but found that my hands were once again bound to a chair. The air was thick with a dampness that irritated my throat, making it hard to swallow. Or perhaps it was dry and raw from screaming for help earlier as I took a few blows to my head.

The room was quiet and I couldn't tell if I was alone or if someone was with me. It was too dark to see anything in the room which gave me intense anxiety. I took a deep breath and closed my eyes while I waited for whatever this was, to be over. A vision of my dad floated around in front of me and I relaxed at the thought that I would soon be with him.

Thirty Eight

Max

"Get me everything you can on this guy." I looked around the small office that Mindy and I shared as my team stared at me as I filled them in on what I knew. "I want it NOW!" I slammed my fist on the desk and watched as everyone scattered about.

It had been three hours since Hannah was taken and every minute that passed by felt like a dagger to my heart. Seeing what he did to Elena left me on edge every second that Hannah was with him. I walked over to the whiteboard and looked at the information that I had collected and taped to the board over the last hour. Elena had been discharged shortly after I left and insisted on coming to help out. She looked exhausted as she sat behind my desk, Trevor standing behind her.

"I still can't believe it's him," she said as she walked over to stand next to me and looked at his picture that I had printed from the school's webpage.

"Me neither. But it all makes sense now, in a way." I sighed and stared back at the picture of the guy that I had been in the same room with, never knowing he was the person responsible for everything with Elena and Hannah.

His picture reminded me of a high school yearbook picture as he smiled in front of a blue back drop, his brown hair and dark brown eyes complimented by the color. Professor Adam Wright had been teaching at NYU for three years and this semester Elena and Hannah had several classes together with him. The connection to everything had finally been pieced together but not before Amber lost her life and Elena barely escaped with hers. My throat felt dry as I tried to swallow and not think about what Hannah's fate would be.

I knew the moment Mindy described the tattoo on his forearm that it was him. Something drew me to his tattoo the day I went to class with Elena and saw it. There was something about him that day that I couldn't put my finger on. At first I just assumed that he was some stuffy pompous professor that was irritated that someone was in his lecture that wasn't enrolled but now I understood what the real issue was.

Looking back it felt like all of the clues were there all along, I just missed them. Maybe that was just how it was with this case, maybe it was a little more obscure than usual. Or maybe I was so distracted by Hannah that I had turned into a shitty detective and completely ignored the signs as they stared me in the face.

The notes that were written to Hannah had all come from a textbook, which she confirmed was one of her psychology textbooks. From a class that she had with Adam. The other notes were taken from the same textbook, just not from Hannah's. Hannah said from the very start that she had classes with Elena and Amber yet I didn't think of the fact that the notes could have been from one of their textbooks. One was missing and one was dead- that should've been on my radar. And the black ink used on each note was similar to that of the marker I saw him writing with during the few minutes I was in the class.

I was beyond frustrated and disgusted with myself for not catching these things earlier. My body was sore and achy, the tension starting to build. I went to my desk to grab a handful of Tylenol when I saw Elena walk closer to the board and study Hannah's picture. My heart hurt that I even had to put her picture up there. That she had gone from someone I had just seen and made love to 24 hours ago to someone that was missing and possibly dead. I shook my head as I forced myself to swallow the pills, trying to shake away the thought.

"Is this the girl that's missing? The one you're dating?" Elena pointed at Hannah and looked back at me. I watched as Trevor shrugged, knowing he had filled her in on my relationship with Hannah.

"Yeah, that's Hannah."

"She looks familiar." She turned back and stayed staring at the photo as she tilted her head.

"You guys had a couple of classes together, that's probably why you recognize her." I walked over and stood next to her, staring at Hannah's picture.

"No, that's not it..." She was lost deep in thought so I stayed quiet to let her think.

A few minutes passed by in total silence before Elena gasped and startled me.

"She's the girl!" She covered her mouth with her hands as her eyes went wide with fear.

"What girl?"

"The girl from the photos." She turned back to look at Hannah, the color draining from her face. "There were so many photos."

"What are you talking about? What photos?"

"He had this shrine with like a hundred picture frames, each one had a picture of her. He talked about her all the time, it was really creepy." She shivered at the memory.

"Why didn't you say something before when you knew it was Hannah?" My eyes searched hers wildly, wondering if having this information sooner would have made any difference in where we were with finding them.

"Because he never called her Hannah. I didn't know that was her name. He only ever called her his love."

I struggled to swallow the bile that threatened to make its way up from my stomach.

Thirty Nine

Adam

WHO THE FUCK DID SHE THINK SHE WAS? I WAS NOT SOMEONE TO FUCK WITH. YOU DON'T SAY NO TO ME! I AM THE FUCKING KING. THE ALPHA. THE OMEGA. I AM THE RULER OF MY WORLD.

I swung hard, feeling the energy flow through me the way it did every time I felt human bones splinter beneath my fist. The soft tissue tearing beneath the skin and turning a shade darker than my soul. The beautiful sound as they screamed out in pain. It was such a thrill and I loved the power and control I had over them when they watched me with fear in their eyes.

She quickly lost consciousness and I couldn't take it any longer. I stood in front of her and unzipped my pants while her head laid back against the chair, blood dripping down her face. I leaned forward and wiped the blood off as I pulled my dick out. I grabbed it with the hand covered in blood and watched it get harder with each stroke until it was covered in blood. I pumped harder and harder as I looked at her lifeless body in front of me, feeling the orgasm shoot out of me and all over her bloody clothes.

My body jerked as my dick fell limp in my hand. The fogginess that had taken over started to lift as I looked down and saw the blood stain on my hand and dick. I looked in front of me at Hannah and my heart sank, what had I done?

<u>Forty</u>

Hannah

"Good morning, Hannah. Do you want some breakfast?"

I woke up, unsure of where I was as I looked around. There was a small amount of light that filtered into the room from a skylight directly above me. It was different than the room I was originally held in when I first got here, but I still had no idea where I was. I looked to my right where the voice had come from and expected to see the guy in the mask. Instead my heart dropped when I realized who was there, talking to me.

"Professor Wright? What are you doing here?" I was confused and suddenly I wondered if I had been released and he had found me and taken me somewhere safe. He smiled as he poured orange juice into a glass and brought it over to me. I noticed a cut on his hand with a thin white towel wrapped around it.

"We can't stay here, we have to go!" Tension filled my voice as I looked around for any sign of the guy in the mask.

"We're not safe! I have to get to Max, he can help us!" I looked at him as a dark smile slowly spread across his face, sending chills through my body. As he stepped to the side I looked behind him and saw the picture frame with the photo of Max and I from the other night sitting on top of the wooden table. Slowly my eyes made their way up to his and the smile on his face started to fade.

"We won't be calling him. Not to worry, you're very safe where you are." He sat the juice down beside me when I refused to reach out and take the glass. "If you would've been a good girl when I tried to talk to you last night, you would know that."

He took a few steps away from me and lit a cigarette as he leaned up against the brick wall, his jeans soiled with blood stains. He was wearing a button down shirt like he wore to class and had the sleeves rolled up, showcasing the definition in his arms. My mind was still spinning as I tried to put everything together on how the man who I sat in front of every other day in class was the same man who had brought me here and attacked me last night. He watched me as he pulled a few drags from the cigarette.

I looked away and focused on the picture on the table. It was separated from the shrine and I blushed as I realized that it was the topless picture of me with Max. My cheeks heated as I remembered us being together and now how violated I felt that someone else had been watching. Just what else had he seen?

His eyes shifted to mine and he turned his head to look at the picture as he pushed off from the wall and stomped on the cigarette to put it out. He walked over and picked the picture up and looked at it as he ran a hand across his jaw like he was upset about something in the picture.

"Do you see this picture, Hannah?" He turned it toward me as he stepped closer, a look of anger in his eyes. I nodded my head yes, afraid to speak.

"Who is this girl?" His voice was steady with an icy edge to it as he grit his teeth. I looked at him but said nothing as my breathing quickened.

"I said, who is it?!" he shouted in my face, causing me to flinch. A brief flashback of last night floated through my mind as I remembered the back of his hand coming toward me and causing the same reaction before the sharp sting of the contact blinded me.

"It's me," I whispered.

"No Hannah, that's not you." He shook his head and walked off still holding onto the picture frame.

I let out a shaky breath as I quickly looked around and tried to find a door or a window, anything that could help me get the hell out of here. Nothing. A few minutes later I heard heavy footsteps as he made his way back into the room. The worry lines above his brow were thick as he walked over and stood right in front of me, holding a picture frame in each hand for me to look at.

"This- this isn't you, Hannah." He held up the picture of me with Max and shook it in the air. "THIS is you. This is the Hannah that I know." A small smile graced his lips as he looked adoringly at the picture. I leaned slightly forward, trying to get a better look at the picture without getting too close to him.

In the picture my hair was long and pulled over my shoulder, one hand twirling a piece of it around my finger while I looked down at my text book. In the background were tables and chairs from the cafe I used to go to with my study group. I don't remember much from this picture but I can tell that it was from the beginning of the semester by the way I'm dressed and how uncertain and nervous I looked in it. My eyes traveled away from the picture and to his face as I silently questioned how many other photos he had of me when I didn't know he was there. The thought sent chills through my body.

"Do you remember her?" He tilted his head to the side and looked at the picture as if that was going to give me some insight into what I should be saying.

"I do. I remember this timid looking girl who showed up for my class, looking scared and afraid as she picked a seat toward the back of the room. I could tell that you wanted to blend in and not be seen. But you were far too beautiful for that. So I moved you to the front, closer to me. And that was the best thing I ever did, Hannah. We got to know each other so well, don't you think?"

I didn't feel like I knew him at all. The professor I thought he was, was a completely different person than who was standing before me now. I swallowed hard, the bruises around my throat reminding me of what he was capable of.

"But this Hannah-" he held up the other photo, "I don't know who she is." He shook his head again and walked over to the tables and sat down the picture frames. He slowly made his way back to where I was as if he was stalking me. Waiting for me to try to make a run for it so he could have the thrill of a chase. I stayed put, barely moving with each shallow breath I took.

"So you tell me, who do you think she is?" His eyes danced wildly while waiting for my answer. A tear fell down my cheek as I chewed my lip nervously. I knew better than to speak. There was no right answer and being silent was as much of a wrong answer as trying to actually answer his question.

"You know what I think? I think she got mixed up with the wrong people and they led her down the wrong path. But it's okay. You know why?"

I shook my head no nervously.

"It's okay because you're young and naive. You don't know better. And thankfully for you, you have someone like me to help guide you." He smiled as he took a seat on the hard concrete floor across from where I was sitting. He crossed his legs and rested his hands in between and for a moment, I saw a vulnerable child in the way he looked.

"You see, Hannah, I've been taking care of things for you for a while now. Not with a thank you or even an acknowledgement on your part. But like I said, you're young and still learning. It takes some people longer than others." He winked and gave me a smile that under any other circumstances, would have been a welcomed gesture.

"When you first started coming to my classes wearing skirts and heels, I'll be honest- I thought you were trying to impress the other guys in class. But then you would put on your sexy reading glasses and participate in the lecture and I knew it was all for me. And I loved every fucking minute of it. I can't tell you how many times I would wait for you to cross or uncross your legs so I could try to get a glimpse of your panties. That was hot as hell! And then I realized that it wasn't just me who was attracted to you, you felt the same for me. Why else would you wear short skirts and silk blouses that showed how hard your nipples were when you took off you jacket? Girls your age don't dress that way for school. But I get it, you were trying to show me how mature you are so I wouldn't be worried about our age difference."

The way his eyes lit up as he talked about me made my stomach sour. I had to force myself to focus on a beam of light against the back wall to keep myself from throwing up. I hated the days that work had flowed into school and I had no choice but to run from one to the other, which meant I had to be dressed for work. Early on in the semester it was an almost daily thing but eventually I figured out a better system and Maggie worked to make sure I got out on time so I wasn't late for my evening classes. I never once paid attention that he was checking me out in class and waiting to see if I was wearing panties or not.

"You were a big tease but I'll admit, that was part of the excitement for me with this little game you started to play where you would show off for me, thinking that I wasn't paying attention. Hell, I have voyeuristic fantasies too so I get it. But then something changed and you started showing off for other guys. And that pissed me off. Then you would show up to class and you were all eyes on me again. The perfect little school girl, so eager for the professor to teach you what he knows. So the only thing I could put together was that Amber was the bad influence. She had to be dealt with." He shrugged his shoulders nonchalantly.

I closed my eyes at the memory of her, sadness overcoming me as I struggled to keep from crying.

"Then, on top of that, you started making bad decisions, Hannah. The online dating app. The date with that frat guy. None of those were you. You were better than that." He reached over and gently placed a hand on my arm, my body going rigid at the touch. A flash of anger quickly crossed his face but retreated as he pulled his hand away.

"I can't blame you for everything, like I said, you're young and don't know better. Like you didn't know that the frat guy had ulterior motives for your date. I was there that day, Hannah, at the coffee shop. I was so nervous and excited at the same time because I had planned to come over and talk to you. To ask you out on a date. You were warming up to me so much in class, I could just feel the chemistry between us. But then your date showed up and I watched as he slipped something in your drink before he gave it to you. I didn't want to have to step in, I wanted to see what you would do on your own. And I was so proud of you for walking away and going to the bathroom. You didn't let him win and get what he wanted." He took a moment to let out a sigh as he watched me until I made eye contact with him.

"You were better than that and I made him pay for what he tried to do. I saved you, Hannah, and I've been doing nothing but that ever since. I saved you from the frat guy. I saved you from Amber. I saved you from the rent a cop at your apartment who was busy watching porn on his phone than protecting you. Which was silly that he was supposed to protect you because in reality, I was already doing that!" He let out a laugh that quickly got louder and bordered on hysterical.

"And then you kept going downhill. You started flirting with the cop and I figured you did it to tease me, to make me jealous. I knew you were getting my notes, I saw each time you found them. But the cop, he was a bigger problem and not as easy to handle. I thought maybe you just wanted to test me, give me a real challenge so you could make sure I was capable of always taking care of you." His voice got quieter as his fists clenched near his sides.

"But then you fucked him. You cut your hair and changed the color so you could look like all of the other little whores that parade around this town, pretending their pussy is too good for me. You turned into someone I don't know Hannah and now I have to figure out what to do with you."

My hand trembled as I slowly reached up to wipe the tears away that were falling down my face. There was so much to process with everything he had just told me but if there was anything that was certain- it was that I was never leaving this room.

Forty One
Max

"Where are we with the information I asked for?" I shouted through my office knowing it would filter out into the surrounding offices to the team that was supposed to be finding out everything they could on this fucking asshole who took Hannah.

"We're working on it!" A voice shouted back, immediately getting under my skin.

"Work harder! I need something on this guy NOW!" My pulse beat in my ears as my blood pressure skyrocketed. I glanced down at my phone to see a text message from my sister of Elena sleeping. Even though I knew she wasn't at risk because this fuck face had Hannah, I still felt the need to know where she was at all times. That's the thing when someone you love goes missing- it changes something inside of you to never trust anyone or anything again. I slammed my cell phone down on my desk in frustration from our progress as Mindy eyed me from across the room.

"Breaking your phone isn't going to solve anything," she muttered from under her breath.

"Excuse me?" My emotions were on edge as I challenged her to say it to my face.

"Look, Max," she pushed away from her desk and stood to face me with arms crossed over her chest, "I know that this is frustrating and you feel helpless- but don't be a dick to everyone or you're going to find out just how helpless they can be. We're all working on this, as a team. Trust the process."

I looked at her as I worked my jaw back and forth, the anger compounding. It had already been 24 hours since she went missing and we all knew that the more time that went by, the less likely it was to have a positive outcome. I laced my fingers behind my head and turned to face the whiteboard that had been set up with Hannah's case. Every little thing we had was already a dead end.

A vibrating noise came from my desk and I walked over to see Hannah's phone ringing. My heart sank when I saw the words 'mom' on the caller ID. I wanted to answer and talk to her, to let her know that everything would be alright, but I couldn't do that because I didn't know if everything would actually be alright. I pressed the ignore button and turned my attention back to the whiteboard when I heard Trevor walk in and say hi to Mindy. There was no need to turn around and say hi, we both knew he wasn't there for a social call. He stood next to me and we both stared at the wall in silence. No one needed an explanation of why he was there, he had made it very clear that Hannah was now as much a part of his family as Elena, and he wasn't stopping until she was found.

A few minutes later an overweight college looking kid came flying into my office, huffing and puffing.

"We got a trace! We got a trace!" His face was red from running as he wiped the sweat from his brow with his arm.

Mindy came around from behind her desk and took the printout he held in his hand.

"Are you positive this is it?"

"Yeah, we searched every record we could find. He's not using burner phones so this is definitely his phone. It's linked to his name and the billing address matches his address." There was excitement in his eyes as he talked and looked around the room for someone to join in.

"Where does it show he's at?" I asked as I stepped closer and looked at the printout that Mindy held between us for me to look at.

"That's the problem, it's a very faint trace. It keeps pinging in an area full of abandoned warehouses so we don't have an exact location. But we have it pinned down to a five mile radius." He beamed with pride as Trevor and I glanced at each other.

"I want that location sent to me now, and get a team out there to secure every building. No one goes in or out of that area without being cleared by me first. Get the perimeter set up immediately, then we'll start moving in." I felt energized as I waited for the coordinates to be sent to my phone. Within seconds I had them as I grabbed my keys from the desk and took off with Trevor beside me.

Just as we were about to take the exit that would lead us to the location, a thought occurred to me and I veered off and took a detour. It wasn't the best decision but in the heat of the moment I felt like we could use all of the help we could get. I called my sister and had her wake Elena up, asking her to meet me outside in a few minutes. As I pulled up Elena was waiting outside with my other sister, Adelina. I kept my foot heavy on the brake as both girls climbed into the back seat as I waited impatiently for the click of their seatbelts before speeding off and making my way to the warehouses.

"What exactly is going on?" Adelina asked as she leaned forward between the front seats and looked back and forth between Trevor and I.

"They found a trace on a cell phone and we think we have the location."

"So, why do you need Leni if you already know where it's at?"

I loved that as the oldest of the girls she was just as protective as I was. She was always like their second mom, stepping in to steer them in the right direction when needed without overstepping her role as their older sister.

"Because they can't get an exact location. There are several warehouses and they can trace it within a five mile radius, but that's it. I'm hoping that something- anything- might look familiar to Leni and she might be able to point us in the right direction so we can narrow it down and find the warehouse she's actually in."

"I don't know how much help I'll be, I told you that I didn't really pay attention to much when I left. I just ran." Leni's voice was quiet in the backseat as Adelina leaned back and pulled her into her side to hug her.

"I know, Leni. It's okay if you don't remember anything. I just thought if there was the possibility that you did remember something once you were here, maybe it could help us." I smiled at her in the rear view mirror as I slowed the car and pulled to a stop in front of a gated in parking lot. I looked down at my phone and confirmed it was the right location as Trevor and I looked at each other. The gate had several locks on it, proving to be a challenge to actually get inside, let alone anywhere near the warehouses.

I sighed as I slowly crept forward, looking around for any signs of entry on any side of the massive property. This was an abandoned area right outside of town and these buildings all looked the same. I slowly went around the block and kept looking for another entrance. Just as I was about to keep driving forward I heard Elena gasp from the back seat and cover her mouth with her hands.

"What's wrong?" I slammed on the brake and whipped around to look at her.

"That building, across the street with the bell on top of it, I used to hear a bell in the mornings around sunrise."

I strained to lean forward and found the bell that she was talking about which gave me comfort that we were at least in the right area, even though I still had no idea what building Hannah was in. Then a thought occurred to me, how if everything was fenced in, did Elena get out?

"Leni, how did you get out of here if everything is fenced in? Did you jump the fence?"

"No, there wasn't a fence where I came out. It opened up into a field and that actually led to a main street a couple of blocks away. That's where I found someone to give me a ride to your apartment."

I looked around and leaned against the steering wheel, frustration getting the better of me. For miles and miles there was nothing but fence and no open field. And according to my phone's GPS, there wasn't a main street anywhere near here. I laid my head on the steering wheel and sighed as I realized we had been led down another rabbit hole.

Forty Two

Hannah

The room felt like what I would imagine a solitary confinement prison cell felt like. Solid concrete walls. Solid concrete floors. No windows, just a dingy light that hung from a rusted chain above me. The room was barely big enough for the wooden table and chair that he put in here before he locked the door and left.

My mind was still trying to process through everything that had happened and just how long he had actually been watching me for. I felt so stupid for not noticing anything. My mom always told me that I was way too trusting of people and that I had to learn not to walk with my head in the clouds. It appeared she was right.

I sat down at the table and looked at the handful of picture frames in front of me that had been left behind so I could figure out which girl I wanted to be. It was a timeline of when I first started at NYU until now. Even I was a little surprised by my own transformation. A quiet, meek, shy girl that was forced to adjust to life in the big city. I sighed as I picked up a recent photo of Max and I, thankful that this one had me fully clothed.

I tried to think back to who I was back then compared to who I was now. It didn't feel like I was that different, but deep down I knew that I was. And honestly, he was right. It was Amber that had changed me. She forced me to be confident and to go after what I wanted. She had warned me that nice girls like me would get swallowed up in this city if we didn't stand up for ourselves so I took her advice and slowly, I started to find out who I wanted to be.

So much of my adolescent years were focused on taking care of everyone else that I didn't really think about myself. I wasn't upset about the experiences I had missed because I felt needed by my family. And that was a good feeling. It made me feel like an adult.

But then when I got here and started college, I realized just how much of a kid I really was. I hadn't become an adult by any means. I was so naive that I didn't know what it meant to take care of myself on my own. Then Amber showed up and showed me how to be more responsible and how people my age should act.

Sure there were plenty of new experiences that I had in college when everyone else was having them in high school, but I found that unless you openly talked about it- no one knew you hadn't done it. Just like Max had no idea that I was still a virgin when we had sex. I had learned enough to know that if I had told him, he never would have gone through with it.

I didn't regret it, not even a little bit. I cared deeply for him and wanted him to be my first. The way he looked at me and how he treated me, it just felt right. And given that he never said anything about it, it didn't seem like he knew that I had no idea what I was doing. I was thankful that Amber had talked me into going on birth control right away, another way she taught me responsibility.

The pictures stared back at me as I leaned back in the chair and allowed myself a few moments to just let my mind wonder. It wasn't like I had anywhere to go or anything to do. Adam- it felt so weird to call him anything other than Professor Wright- had left and I had no idea where he went or when he was coming back.

I was still confident that I was not leaving the confinement of this room anytime soon, let alone leave this building. The only thing left to do if I wanted to stay alive was to figure out what game he was playing and how to play my hand.

Forty Three
Max

"There's no easy entry point. If I ram the gate like I want to, it'll be loud enough to give us away." I held my phone in front of me while I talked on speakerphone to Mindy. We had circled the property a few times, not finding any way in or out that wasn't locked and no sign of an empty field.

"Okay, I'll send the rest of the team further out and see if we can create a larger perimeter." Mindy sighed on the other end.

I drummed my fingers anxiously on the steering wheel while I waited for Mindy to confirm what our other options were after checking in with the team. Glancing in the rearview mirror I caught a glimpse of Elena asleep on Adelina's shoulder as she moved her fingers quickly across her phone before her eyes looked up and met mine.

"Just sending Gia an update so mom will stop calling Leni's phone every few minutes. She's super paranoid that she's going to go missing again, even though she knows that she's with us." She rolled her eyes and went back to texting.

"Hold on, we've got something." Mindy called out to someone else, bringing my attention back to her.

"What?"

"His phone is moving. Like he's actively moving right now. Son of a bitch!"

"Where?" I looked around and started the car, ready to go but no idea where.

"Let me zoom in really quick. He must have stepped into a good cell phone range and it finally picked up the exact location."

I chewed the inside of my cheek as I waited, each second feeling like an hour.

"Right there! He's 2 blocks over heading south on Broadbent."

I looked down at my phone and switched the screen to bring up the GPS location at the same time Trevor opened his and typed in the address. After zooming in a few times I found the street and realized it was 4 blocks away. I put the car in drive and sped off in the direction, determined to catch this prick.

"I'm on it-" I started before I was interrupted by Trevor.

"No one should approach him- I repeat NO ONE should approach him." He spoke loudly to make sure Mindy could hear him clearly from where he was sitting.

"And why the fuck not?" My nostrils flared as I turned to look at him, the car jolting to a stop. In the rear view mirror I saw Leni's eyes open as she sat up and looked around.

"Because, just because we know where he is, doesn't mean that we have any idea where Hannah is. What if he came by here to clean up another mess and he's keeping her somewhere else? We can't jump on this right away Max, you know better than that."

I slammed my hands on the steering wheel and looked out the window. He was right.

"Max, we'll follow him and I promise, we will NOT lose him. I'll keep you updated on where he is. Right now your only job is searching those buildings while he's gone and trying to find Hannah. If he has another place he's hiding, we'll find it."

I hung up the phone and continued driving, slowly, towards Broadbent. Adrenaline was coursing through me as I looked around, wondering if Hannah was even in one of these buildings or if he had purposely led us here to fuck with us.

As the car crept forward, I heard Elena shift in the backseat as she rolled down the back window.

"What are you doing?" I asked as I watched her in the mirror.

"I recognize that smell." She leaned her head out further, taking in a deep breath.

"What smell?" Trevor asked as he looked back at her.

"It's sweet, like a pastry."

I looked around and off in the distance I saw the sign for a local cereal manufacturer.

"There's a cereal plant up ahead." I nodded and pointed in the direction.

"Where do you recognize it from?" Trevor asked with curiosity.

"I smelled it when I ran, but I was pretty out of it and delirious so I thought I was just hallucinating that I was running to a happy place that smelled delicious."

I slowed the car to a stop at a light at Broadbent and leaned forward against the steering wheel. If Elena had smelled the cereal when she left then she had to be in this area since we didn't smell it until we got closer to Broadbent, which was also the street Mindy tracked Adam on. My gut told me that we were almost to wherever Hannah was being held but I still couldn't see an opening to any of the buildings.

Just as I was about to consider ramming one with my car, I pulled forward and sharply inhaled when off to my left was a hidden path that led back to a few abandoned warehouses. Along the unpaved road that led back to them was an empty field. I breathed a sigh of relief as I sped off toward the warehouses, praying that I wasn't too late.

Forty Four
Adam

I had no choice but to leave. To just walk away and hope that she would come back around and be the woman I needed her to be. Being in the same room with her, I could tell she was different. How could I have missed how far gone she really was over the last few weeks? I had been trying to work as quickly as I could to save her from that cop but things kept getting in the way, things I had to take care of. If only I could have gotten to her sooner…

I took my time walking the few blocks over to the gas station knowing that I was being watched. Honestly, I was surprised that no one had approached me yet, even as I lingered around inside the store, picking snacks that I had no intention of eating. But I knew their game and their angle was that no one would approach me until they knew where Hannah was. They would be careful and try to hide in the shadows, hoping I would screw up and somehow lead them back to her. The problem was that they would never find Hannah. That's what happens when you constantly stay five steps ahead.

Forty Five
Max

The car skid to a stop in front of four abandoned and run down warehouses, that honestly, didn't look like they were in any condition for anyone to enter. I put it in park and got out as I quickly looked around, trying to narrow down which one Hannah might be in. Each one looked identical which wasn't helpful at all.

I put Elena in charge of staying on the phone with Mindy so we knew where Adam was at all times, and apparently he was in no hurry whatsoever as he lingered on the chip aisle, contemplating which flavor of Pringles he wanted before putting them all back. It was odd behavior, to not be paranoid and looking over your shoulder when you're holding someone hostage which lead me to believe that he knew he was being watched and was putting on a show. That also meant that I had a short window to try to find Hannah before he got bored and came back.

The warehouses sat in a square with a small courtyard in between them, a dried up fountain in the center. I looked around and found the field that Elena had talked about and narrowed my choices down to the two buildings that were right next to it. She mentioned that she took off and immediately went into the field so it seemed unlikely that she would have been in one of the other buildings.

I ran a hand down the scruff of my face as I looked at the two buildings, trying to justify why I would pick one and not the other. If I screwed this up, it was someone else's life that was at stake. Trevor looked over and watched me before looking at the same buildings.

"What are you thinking?"

"I'm thinking it's one of these two." I pointed at the two buildings as Trevor nodded in agreement.

"How about I take that one and you take the other? We'll do a quick sweep and see what we can find."

I liked the idea of being able to cover more ground but it made me nervous having Elena and Adelina with us. I couldn't be focused inside the building while being worried about them out here by themselves and I felt a heavy burden allowing Trevor to go inside knowing that he was another innocent life I was putting at risk. It wasn't like he was law enforcement and this was just part of the job.

"I like that idea but I don't think we should leave them." I nodded subtly at the girls.

"We can split up." Elena offered, stepping forward. "I can come with you and Ade can go with Trevor. Then you won't have to worry about us and we'll have more eyes inside." She shrugged as she waited for my response. I blew out a heavy breath knowing that we didn't have any other options and we were wasting even more time standing out here talking about it when we could be inside looking for Hannah.

"Okay, that's fine with me."

Trevor and I exchanged a look and nodded before we walked in separate directions to the building we were going to check. Elena hung up with Mindy after giving her the update on what we were doing, and Mindy agreed to call the moment Adam started heading back this way so we weren't surprised.

I walked around the building and hoped that something would trigger a memory for Elena, confirming that we had the right one. She looked around but shook her head no in response to my raised eyebrows knowing what I was asking her. We made our way to the back side of the building that led directly out to the field and found a door. I pulled the handle, praying that he would be a complete idiot and it would be unlocked. I grunted as I kicked the door in frustration. It was a steel door with a handful of locks and chains wrapped around the handle. By the time I got someone out here to cut the locks and blow the door down, it would be too late.

"Max, look." Elena nodded to an area toward the end of the building that had boards nailed where a window would be. Hope pushed through me as I ran over and looked at the board. It was relatively thin, the wood starting to decay. I glanced beside me to make sure Elena was out of the way before leaning back and kicking the board, watching with satisfaction as it broke free leaving a small opening into the building. I pulled off my jacket and used it to sweep some of the debris out of the way before helping Elena in. I climbed in after her, giving it a second for my eyes to adjust to the darkness inside. It was eerily creepy as the cold cement sent a chill through my body. After a few seconds my eyes had adjusted to the darkness and I found Elena looking around.

"Anything look familiar?" I asked, hopeful that something would at least feel familiar. She shook her head no as we started walking down the narrow hallway that led to an open room shaped like a pentagon. Each wall had a hallway that led somewhere else making this the creepiest maze I had ever been in.

"I've been in this room," Elena whispered, walking ahead of me. "I barely saw it but I remember looking around to try to find a way out and feeling overwhelmed with so many options, not knowing where any of them actually went."

"Well, I guess we just pick one and start there."

We took a few steps and went down the next hallway that led to an empty room with a blanket and pillow. Off to the side was a memorial looking display with assorted picture frames. I was about to walk over to look at them when Elena grabbed my arm and pulled me back. Her face had gone pale in the dimness of the room, sadness filling her eyes.

"I don't think you want to go over there." She kept her voice low while her eyes pleaded with me.

"Why not?" I glanced back over my shoulder and looked at the set up. Chills ran up my spine as I thought about how much this reminded me of a sacrificial scene in a cheesy horror movie. "Let's just keep looking for Hannah." Her grip on my arm got tighter and part of me wanted to listen to her, to heed her advice, but the Italian part of me was too stubborn. I quickly slipped out of her grip and made my way over to the photos.

Sitting in front of me were pictures of random girls that I had never seen before. All of them in this room. All of them in pain. All of them terrified. My eyes scrolled through quickly, looking for the one of Hannah when I stumbled upon the one of Elena. My stomach dropped as I picked it up and looked at it, not fully prepared for what I was about to see.

In the picture her mouth was gagged with a bandana, hands bound behind her while she sat tied to a chair. I took a deep breath and shook my head, the chair catching my eye in the process. Not even 10 feet away from me sat the chair that my sister was bound to as she was tortured. I looked back down at the photo, at the look in my sister's eye, and that's all it took to get me running.

I heard Elena running behind me, sniffling as she cried, never slowing down as we ran into the next room. Then the next. Before I knew it we had made it through every room with no sign of Hannah. I stopped for a minute and bent over to catch my breath when I saw Elena pull out her phone and read a text message.

"Mindy sent a message 20 minutes ago but I just got it now."

"What's it say?" I was still out of breath while I waited for the update, hoping that they went ahead and just picked him up and took him in.

"He's here."

Forty Six

Hannah

Regret. Regret is what kills the living when we're forced to deal with the death of someone that we love. Regret that we didn't see them more often. Regret that we didn't talk about the things that were most important to us. Regret that we didn't say I love you as often as we should have. Regret that I never told my mother what was going on and now I would likely die without her even knowing that I was missing.

I stared at the beam of light on the wall above me, getting lost in my thoughts of all of the things I should have done differently. My mom was my best friend and I thought I could protect her by keeping this from her, but in reality I was hurting her more because she would never know what really happened. I took a deep breath and let it out as I felt my irritability rise each minute I was stuck in there.

It was hard to know just how long it had been because there were no clocks, no phones, no windows to know if it was day or night. Maybe this was all part of the plan. Maybe he was going to let me sit in here until I died and rotted. My body would be forced to shut down when it no longer had what it needed to survive, which honestly would be a better death compared to the brutal attack I had already been through.

I looked around for what felt like the millionth time, searching for any possible way out. There was a small vent above me that I could try to get to if I stood on the table and jumped, but given that I'm bigger than a rat, I wouldn't actually fit in the small pipe.

"Hannnnaaaahhhhh!"

My attention was immediately pulled to a faint voice calling my name. Calling like they were looking for me. I waited a few minutes and heard it again. I shook my head, convinced that I must be going crazy and hearing things when I heard it again.

"I'm in here!" I shouted back, desperate for whoever it was to hear me. My voice echoed off the concrete walls and I realized that the only way anyone would hear me was if my voice was loud enough to force through the vent and carry out into whatever room they were in.

This was it, my only option. I climbed up on the table and shouted as loud as I could, continuing to shout until my voice broke. My throat was dry but I kept forcing it, reaching on my tiptoes to try to get as close as I could get.

"I'm in here! Help me! Please! Help!" I screamed, praying they would come find me before it was too late. I startled as the door jerked open, Adam's eyes furious as he saw me on the table. His hand was trembling as I watched his body react to the anger. This was the same way he looked at me before he snapped last time.

"You should be careful who you ask for help." He taunted as he came over and kicked the table out from underneath me.

Forty Seven

Adam

Imagine my surprise when I got back and found Hannah acting like a lunatic, standing on the table, screaming out for someone to come help her. I'm not usually one to judge but in this case I would strongly recommend that she have a full psych evaluation to deal with her hallucinations.

I watched as she fell from the table, fear in her eyes as common sense came back to her. Maybe she wasn't as stupid as I thought. Maybe she was trainable. I smiled with satisfaction as she cowered beneath me, watching me like I owned her. Which I did.

The board in the back that was covering the window had been kicked in so I knew that one of the filthy pigs had been in here while I was gone. If they knew what was good for them, they would make sure they left. Putting your nose in other people's business wasn't something that I took lightly. It infuriated me. I looked at Hannah, so scared and desperate for love, and realized that maybe this was a good time to show her what I was capable of. To show her just how much I loved her by getting rid of those who didn't.

Forty Eight

Max

I slowly crept along the wall, reaching a hand behind me to guide Elena. We barely had a heads up that Adam was back before we heard the door open and found a place to hide. I sent Trevor a text as soon as we had the update and prayed that they would get out unnoticed. Granted none of us were getting out unnoticed since my fucking car was sitting outside in the parking lot, but at least he didn't know where we were inside. We had tried to call out to Hannah as loud as we could before he came in, and for a moment I could swear I heard her call out in response.

My nerves were on high alert as we slowly made our way down the hall, unsure of where he was. I quickly ran my hand over my back, making sure my gun was still there. Not that I've ever had an issue with not having my gun where I couldn't find it, I've just never needed it while playing a game of cat and mouse with a freaking psychopath.

I could hear faint voices and stopped, pulling Elena in behind me. My head strained to the right to try to hear better. If I could figure out exactly where they were, it would give me the advantage. My pulse was racing as I waited, desperate to hear Hannah's voice. A huge part of me now wished that I didn't have Elena with me, feeling like shit for putting her in danger, once again. I prayed that Mindy and her team were on their way, setting up a perimeter to make sure this asshole had nowhere to go if he decided to leave. One way or another, this was ending here and now. I took a deep breath and slowly inched along the wall in the direction of the voices.

It was a bold and risky move as we entered the open room, knowing that there was nowhere to hide. I had to make a quick decision about which hallway I thought led to where Adam and Hannah were. As I was about to decide, I found myself face to face with Adam as he walked into the room, dragging Hannah in by her hair.

My eyes went wide with terror as I looked at her and the bruises covering her body, dried blood in her hair. Her head was pulled down, preventing her from being able to see me. My heart sank and I wanted to rush over and grab her, get her away from him and the evil look on his face. I've met a lot of really bad people in my career but I've never been face to face with the devil. Until now.

I gently pulled Elena behind me as I reached back and drew my gun, pointing it directly at his head.

"Let her go!" I stared deep into his eyes, watching as they danced wildly with excitement. "Now!"

My voice echoed through the room, Hannah's body flinching at the sound. Adam watched me with wonder before titling his head back and laughing. It wasn't just any laugh, it was the blood curdling laugh you hear in your nightmares as you desperately try to wake up.

I kept my hand steady as I watched him, glancing down to check on Hannah. Her body looked limp and for a gut wrenching moment I feared I was too late. I had to remind myself that I had seen her move, she had responded to my voice. She wasn't dead.

"Do you really think that she wants you to save her?" He laughed harder and reached into his back pocket to pull out a knife. "She doesn't need saving from me," he paused for a moment as he held the knife in the air and watched Elena as she shifted behind me, "I'm saving her from YOU." He pointed the knife directly at me.

"And it looks like you brought back my other friend, sweet Elena." His voice was laced with sarcasm and disdain as he acknowledged her. I wanted to pull the trigger and be done with this psycho but I couldn't do anything until I was sure that Hannah was okay. Right now I couldn't risk her being that close to him with the knife. One quick movement and he could stab her as I pull the trigger.

I bit my lip as I watched, waiting for a fraction of second where Hannah was safe so I could make my move. There was no budging. As if sensing what I was thinking he pulled hard on her hair, forcing her closer to him. I watched as she started to fall before he yanked her up by her throat. Fury ran through me as I felt helpless, forced to do nothing but watch.

"Why does she need saving from me?" I asked through gritted teeth, hoping to get him talking so I could distract him away from her.

"Don't you see? You're the problem." He waved the knife in the air as he looked from her to me. "She was a sweet girl, the perfect woman to marry and keep as a wife until she met you. Then you had to stand in the way and poison her with your lies and lead her into temptation."

"I've never lied to Hannah. I care about her, just like you do. We both want to make sure she doesn't get hurt." I tried to remember everything I could from the hostage negotiation courses they required us to take but all I could really think was bullshit, bullshit, bullshit.

"So you've told Hannah everything? You told her about Antonio?"

Hannah looked up at me, Adam's hands still wound tightly in her hair. I had no clue how he knew about Antonio. I watched as Hannah looked at me, waiting for me to respond.

"So you haven't told her about Antonio..." He looked down at Hannah and forced her face up to his with the end of the knife pushing her chin toward him. "It seems that Mr. Righteous over here hasn't been all that honest with you, Hannah. It seems even he has some ugly skeletons lurking in his closet."

I waited for him to put the knife down, to move it anywhere other than underneath her chin. My blood pressure was soaring as I watched, helplessly.

"You see, Hannah, I did a little bit of research on him when I found out that he couldn't leave you alone. After some digging, it seems he has quite the temper." He slowly slid the knife down to her throat. "It seems that your little lover boy over here was once engaged, did you know that?" He looked at her and waited for her to shake her head yes. His eyes turned toward me and I could see the hatred in them as he continued.

"Did you know that his fiancé left him for his cousin?" He asked the question to Hannah while watching me the entire time. Hannah already knew this, it wasn't like he was telling her something she didn't know.

"And when he found out, he went a little crazy. Beat his cousin so bad it left him in a coma. Almost killed him. As for the fiancé, well, she sported a black eye for a few days that went well with the bruises around her throat." He gave me a look like he just played the winning hand in a poker game. I swallowed hard as I watched Hannah process the information. She knew about Adrianna leaving me for my cousin, but I had never told her the rest. Very few people knew the rest. It's why I didn't do relationships and never wanted another one.

I watched as Hannah's eyes grew wide before looking at me with horror. I swallowed hard to try to keep the bile down. This wasn't anything that I ever wanted her to find out, and definitely not like this.

"Is that the kind of guy that you want, Hannah?" He pressed the knife to her throat, pushing the tip harder against her skin until she shook her head no. My fingers itched to pull the trigger, this was pure hell.

"It looks like she's on the receiving end under your hand as well." I nodded to the bruises on her skin and winced at the black eye that I could see better now that her head wasn't being forced down.

"I didn't do this to Hannah!" His voice was high as if he was shocked that I would suggest such a thing.

"Hannah did this to herself. She was the one who couldn't listen or follow directions. Poor decisions have consequences, you know that." He looked at me sympathetically. "I love Hannah, I would never hurt her."

This guy was out of his fucking mind. I was debating on what to do next. Hannah was my biggest priority but I had yet to find a way to get her away from this guy while keeping both her and Elena safe. Off in the distance I saw a shadow move along the wall and held my breath as I waited to see who it was. As far as I knew, Adam was working alone, but I've also been wrong before. Now wasn't the time or place to be gambling on the unknown.

A few painstakingly long seconds passed by and I saw Trevor creep along the side of the wall that opened into the room behind Adam. His hands were steady as he kept his aim on Adam, acknowledging me with a nod. I turned my head slightly while keeping my eyes on Adam and whispered to Elena.

"Run, now. Go back the way we came and run fast. Do NOT come back here. GO!" I made sure she understood the tone of my voice as I saw Trevor move slightly to the side. His aim on Adam was better than mine and I was thankful that Adam hadn't noticed Trevor. With Elena out of harm's way it made it easier for us to try to get to Hannah.

Elena darted out behind me and took off running, just like I asked her to. Anger flashed across Adam's face and instinctively, he jolted forward to chase after her, letting go of Hannah. In an instant, Trevor ran across the room and grabbed Hannah, pushing her behind him as he turned and angled his body toward Adam. With his gun aimed at his chest while I kept mine at his head, we outnumbered him two to one and he just lost his only bargaining chip.

"So what's it gonna be? Are we doing this the hard way or the easy way?" I asked, taking a few steady steps toward him. While putting a bullet in his head would give me pure satisfaction, I was easily content with taking him in and seeing to it that he served a life sentence behind bars.

"You don't get it... you just don't understand what you've done." He ran his hands through his hair and pulled it as he looked back and forth between Trevor and I. I knew this look. I'd seen it too many times in my life to know that he was about to lose it and this wasn't going to end well for him.

"Why don't we go down to the station and you can fill us in?" I took another step forward as he started to pace back and forth.

"I can't go to the station. I can't go anywhere. You're screwing everything up. We're running out of time."

"Look, I have no idea what you're talking about, but you're really getting on my last nerve." Another step closer. My finger itched as I started to close the distance between us.

"No!" he shouted, startling all of us. Quickly he reached back and pulled out a gun from his jeans and pointed it back and forth between Trevor and I. Out of the corner of my eye I watched Trevor put one hand behind him as he tried to keep Hannah shielded, the other hand steady as he kept his aim.

"Hannah belongs with me. She always has, she always will. She's my soulmate and without her- neither of us deserve to live. She gets me, she's nice to me. She wrote a beautiful essay about what she went through when she lost her dad and it was like we went through the same thing when I lost my mom. Only, she loved her dad. I hated my mom. But when you kill someone, you have to feel somewhat bad about it. What kind of monster would you be if you didn't? I didn't want to hate my mom. I didn't want to kill her. But things happen and you have to move on. Hannah, she's just like how my mom was. So I'm gonna need you to get out of the way and release her before I have to kill you too."

The look on his face changed and I saw a side of him that I hadn't seen before. It was like something snapped and the nervous, anxious Adam that was rambling on a minute ago was replaced by a stone cold version who had absolutely no issue with killing Trevor and I to get to Hannah. I felt my hand start to sweat as I glanced at Trevor to make sure he was still shielding Hannah.

"Like I said, you need to get the FUCK away from her." Adam turned to face Trevor, gun tilted sideways as he took two aggressive steps toward him. I watched Trevor take a step backwards with Hannah right behind him. Everything felt like it happened in slow motion as I watched Hannah stumble to the side as Trevor took another step backwards with her, Adam leaning to the side and aiming his gun directly at her head. The gunshot echoed through the room as I heard the body drop to the floor, a pool of blood quickly forming around it.

Trevor turned around in time to catch Hannah, steadying her as I rushed over to Adam, kicking the gun away from his hand before reaching down to check for a pulse. I looked up to see Hannah cuddled into Trevor's side, eyes wide with terror. I shook my head to Trevor and stood up, walking as quickly as I could to get to Hannah. I pulled her into my arms and wrapped her in a hug, never wanting to let go of her again. Off in the distance I could hear Trevor on the phone, calling Mindy with the update and to confirm it was okay to send the team in.

I escorted Hannah outside, still tucked under my arm as we passed a slew of uniformed cops rushing to the scene. Outside the sky was overcast and gloomy as another winter storm was quickly approaching. My heart filled with joy when I found Elena and Adelina in the backseat of my car while Trevor leaned against the hood, waiting for Hannah and I to be done with questioning. Nothing felt better in my life than knowing the people who I loved and cared about were safe and that the psychopath who was responsible for everything was dead and rotting in hell.

Forty Nine

Hannah

"How do you feel?" Max asked as I slowly opened my eyes and looked around the room, remembering that I was in the hospital.

"A little sore," I croaked, my voice hoarse from screaming earlier. My hand reached up and touched my throat as I winced in pain from trying to talk.

Max gave me a sympathetic smile and handed me a Styrofoam cup filled with ice water. I took a long, slow drink, enjoying the comfort the ice created as the cold water made its way down my throat. I pulled back, indicating that I had enough as Max sat the cup down on the tray beside my bed. I glanced out the window and noticed the sun trying to push through the overcast sky.

It was early in the morning according to the clock on the wall but I had no idea what day it was. Being locked up in the warehouse with Adam felt like it was months when I knew that it was only maybe days at most. It's amazing how being held captive and tortured plays with your mind and creates delusions of reality. I took a deep breath and shook my head as I tried to get the image of Adam lying dead on the floor out of my mind. When I first heard the gunshot I didn't know where it came from and it felt like it took forever to know who had been shot. Trevor had pushed me back behind him when the body hit the floor and for a second my heart stopped beating, thinking that it was Max.

"I know that you can't really talk, which works out really well for me." Max scooted his chair closer to me and rubbed his hands down the front of his jeans nervously.

"I haven't been completely honest with you and I apologize for that. I didn't want to tell you about Adrianna before but now I think it's only fair for you to know why I didn't want to be in a relationship."

His shoulders rose and fell as he sucked in a breath and reached over to hold my hands.

"What Adam said, about me hurting Adrianna, that wasn't true. I never laid a hand on her, Hannah, I swear. I didn't tell you about what had happened because I didn't want to bring that part of my life out in the open again. I've worked really hard at pushing it away, and that's where it needed to stay."

I watched as he fidgeted in his chair, obviously uncomfortable with having to talk to me about this. My stomach dropped when Adam told me about Max attacking Adrianna and for a moment, I actually questioned whether it was true. Maybe Max really was a violent person and that's why he had pushed me away from the start.

"After things ended with me and Adrianna, I went my own way. I threw myself into work and I vowed to never see her or my cousin again. I was done with them. Then one day,

Adrianna showed up at my apartment with a black eye and marks around her throat where someone had tried to choke her. I wouldn't put it past her to do it to herself for attention but I could tell by where the marks were at on her throat that she wasn't physically able to do that."

He squeezed my hands tighter and I smiled, hoping to encourage him to keep telling me what had happened.

"She told me that Antonio had attacked her after she told him that she was pregnant with his baby. He didn't want to be a father and we all knew that. I was pissed that he had hurt her, so I went to his house and confronted him. Long story short, he denied it all and laughed when he thought I would believe Adrianna over him. She stood behind me, cowering while he made fun of her and called her a whore. And, I kinda lost it. I punched him so hard that he lost his balance and fell backwards into the solid wood coffee table. The impact of the fall caused brain damage and that's what put him in a coma. I was wrong for hitting him, but I never attacked either of them, Hannah. It's important to me that you know that. I would never hurt anyone like that."

His eyes started to fill with tears as I squeezed his hands before reaching up and wiping a tear from his face. It melted my heart to see him so open and vulnerable in front of me. I wanted to reach over and wrap my arms around him and never let go. This man had the biggest heart and would do anything for those he loved. I had no doubt in my mind that this now included me.

Fifty
Hannah

I sat by the window in my apartment and watched the snow fall outside as I waited for Max to get off of work. My work had closed early due to the weather and gave us the full day off for Christmas Eve, instead of the half-day they had originally promised. I wasn't sure what to do with my unexpected free time. It was the first time in my life that I was going to spend Christmas without my mom and that made my heart ache in ways I couldn't describe. I had made sure to send her gifts out yesterday, hoping they would make it in time for Christmas. Things had been crazy after I got out of the hospital and I totally spaced getting them shipped before the storm hit.

Max had been staying with me a few nights a week while I stayed with him the other nights. Neither of us wanted to be apart from each other but there still seemed to be some uncertainty in the air on whether we were ready to be exclusive. I knew I was but I didn't know where Max's head was at. Things had been busy on his side as well with his family and spending more time with them now that Elena was back. The whole situation was horrible and really shook all of us, but in the end it also brought Max's family closer together after they felt the impact of almost losing part of their family.

I tried hard not to be, but I was insanely jealous of Max's relationship with his family and how close they were. Sure, I was really close with my mom but I didn't make it up to see her that often anymore and we both seemed to fall into a new norm of it being okay. I missed her dearly but part of me knew that I still had to figure out who I was and what I wanted in life, which meant that I needed to give this a try, regardless of how much I wanted to call it quits and run back home to her.

My mood had been sour the last couple of days as I struggled to find things to put me in the holiday spirit and take my mind off of missing my mom and Amber. Max sent a text that he was on his way and that he had a surprise for me. I sat my phone down on the couch next to me and pulled the heavy knit blanket up over me as I laid my head on the pillow behind me and continued to watch the snow fall.

Twenty minutes later I heard a knock at the door and got up to let Max in. When I opened the door my jaw dropped as I saw my mom standing in front of me with her arms stretched wide and a suitcase by her feet. Right behind her was Max with a huge smile on his face.

"Merry Christmas!" She smiled and stepped forward, pulling me into a hug as the tears started to roll down my cheeks. I hugged her even tighter as I started to sob. Quickly she pulled back and held onto my arms as she looked at me, concern etched on her face.

"Han, what's wrong?"

"I missed you so much!" I started to cry even harder, unable to believe that my mom was in my apartment and that I wasn't going to spend Christmas without her.

She grabbed me and pulled me into another hug as we scooted to the side for Max to come in and sit her luggage down by the door. He gave us some space as he went to the kitchen and started a pot of coffee, smiling at me when I looked over at him.

"How did you get here?" I asked as I wiped my tears with the back of my hand and looked at my mom to make sure she was really there.

"The train," She teased then looked over at Max. I let out a laugh and walked with her over to the couch and sat down.

"Max actually reached out to me and asked if I could come in for Christmas. He said that my girl was having a hard time right now and could use some holiday cheer." She leaned back against the couch and gave Max a warm smile from across the room.

"Wait- how did you get in touch with my mom?" I leaned forward and waited for an answer.

"I had your phone and she had called the first day that you went missing. I kept her information in case I needed it." He swallowed hard and a silence fell over the room as the topic we all wanted to avoid talking about just came up.

I had called my mom from the hospital and told her everything that had happened over the last few months with Amber, Elena, Adam and the kidnapping. She was thankful that I was okay, but obviously disappointed that I hadn't told her what was going on sooner. In the end she was as supportive as she's always been and I regretted that I hadn't told her anything before then.

"So you brought my mom here for Christmas?"

"I knew how much it would mean to you and that you were feeling pretty down not spending it with her." He filled three cups of coffee and brought them over, sitting them on the coffee table between us as he stood next to me and placed a hand on my shoulder.

"I can't believe you did that." I looked up at him and ran my hand up his arm. My heart felt like it might combust with the amount of love I felt at that moment.

"I would do anything to make you happy, Hannah."

My mom's eyes filled with tears while she discreetly tried to wipe them away.

"I would do anything to make you happy too, Max." I smiled back at him warmly and watched as he looked to my mom before looking back at me.

Slowly he moved around to in front of me and got down on one knee. I let out a gasp as I watched him, nervous and uneasy as he cleared his throat before reaching into his pocket and pulling out a diamond ring.

"Max," I whispered. What was he doing? The man who swore he didn't want to get married was kneeling before me, holding the most beautiful symbol of love while my mom sat beside us, sniffling as she wiped the tears as they ran down her face.

"Hannah, I've made a lot of mistakes in my life. I've done a lot of things that I'm not proud of. I swore that I never wanted to be in another serious relationship, that marriage wasn't in the cards for me." He let out a shaky breath as his hand slightly trembled. "But when I thought I was going to lose you, when I saw what that monster did to you, I knew that I never wanted to live another day without you. I don't know what the future holds. I don't know what obstacles we'll face. But I know that I want to live each uncertain moment beside you. You've stolen a piece of me that I didn't know was still inside of me."

He reached up and held the ring up to me.

"Hannah, will you make me the happiest man in the world and be my wife?" His eyes looked at me with hope.

I covered my mouth with my hand as I looked back and forth between him and my mom, not believing what was happening.

"Max, are you sure?" There was so much doubt in me that this was what he really wanted. Were we ready for this?

"I've never been surer of anything in my life. Please don't leave me hanging down here forever." He let out a soft laugh as he shifted his weight.

I licked my lips as a huge smile spread across my face, leaning down and grabbing his face to plant a kiss on his lips.

"Yes, Max, I will marry you!" I squealed as I felt him stand up, wrapping me in his arms and swinging me around as I giggled.

"You had me worried there for a minute," he teased as he sat me down and slid the ring on my finger before bringing my hand to his mouth and kissing it.

"Well, I have to keep you on your toes." I winked playfully before sliding out of his arms to sit next to my mom, showing her the beautiful ring. My heart felt overwhelmingly full as I sat between the two people I loved most in the world, excited for what the future would bring.

****

Thank you so much for reading Five Steps Ahead! Get ready for Trevor's book, Ten Seconds Too Late (Dark Shadows Book 2) https://books2read.com/u/3JRgVB

Want something a little more flirty and less thrilling? Grab your free copy of my super steamy novella Finding Love In Apartment 2C https://BookHip.com/VSWBGAM

Acknowledgments

If you've finished reading the book and are still reading this, I can guarantee you that all of the stalking and killing is done. It's over. I promise. Really, it's done and over. Well, at least until the next book.

If you're STILL reading this then I know that you're looking for all of the good stuff with the warm fuzzies, so I'll get right to it!

Thank you so much to everyone who picked up a copy of this book and read it. Writing is my passion and that only gets stronger when I see how many people are enjoying reading my books. I appreciate you taking the time to sit down and read the stories that have floated around in my head until they made their way on paper. If I'm a new to you author, thank you for taking a chance on me and I hope you enjoyed the book. If I'm not new to you, thank you for coming back and reading another one of my books! I plan to keep them coming!

I want to give a HUGE, heartfelt thank you to my incredible beta reader team. Thank you so much for constantly letting me bounce ideas off of you and for giving me the feedback I asked for. From proofreading to helping with the plot, you guys really did a tremendous job!

Debi, you never let me down when you offer to read and proofread my books for me. Thank you so much for the time and effort you put forth with helping me make sure I have the right words and that the autocorrect demons didn't take over again. I enjoy your enthusiasm every time you finish a book and feel so proud to have you on my team.

Katie, thank you for letting me send you what feels like hundreds of pictures of random people while we try to figure out if they're the right fit for the characters. And thank you for also picking apart the characters when I ask you to so I can put them back together and make them better than before. I really appreciate your help with making this book the best it could be!

Azucena, our late night chats have covered many topics and I secretly hope that no one ever goes back and looks through our phone records to see what all of those texts were about! I love how invested you've become with my writing and how you help me flesh out ideas and come up with new ones. You're so much fun to bounce ideas around with and I really appreciate your help with fact checking things for me. You're the best!

Jennifer, you have no idea how much you helped me along the way with your feedback on the plot. Thank you for showing me where there were some weak spots, and for helping me to make them better. I appreciate your feedback as someone who is an avid reader in this genre. I want to make you proud and write the kind of books that you can't put down. Thank you for your enthusiasm as you jumped right in and read quickly, ready to give me feedback when I needed it.

Chelsea, I honestly love how I can send you a random text about the book we're working on, or another random book idea, and you're always on board to help me with it! You have been so instrumental to the success of this book and I appreciate you showing me the flaws with things as we went as well. I'm so excited to continue to work with you on the other books as well!

As always, I want to give a huge thank you to my very loving and supportive family. My parents and sister are always cheering me on along the way, and I love that they never stop believing in me. Thank you for pushing me forward and helping me get one step closer to reaching my goals and living my dreams.

My dear, sweet, husband. Thank you for staying married to me when I'm sure sometimes it feels like I'm a walking, talking book. I know that my passion is sometimes a lot to handle but I always love when we can sit down together and talk about the book and how to make it better. I love that you read the book with the intent of editing and get so caught up in what's happening in it that you have to go back to look at stuff again. I might just turn you into an avid romance reader by the time we're done! You have hands down been the absolute, most supportive person that I could have ever asked for. Your dedication to making my books a reality is never overlooked and I will forever be indebted to you for the amount of work you put into each one for me. I love you so much and I will go to my grave thanking you for everything you do for me.

To my sweet girls, I want this to be proof that you can do anything you set your mind to. Just because you reach one goal, doesn't mean that you should ever stop trying to reach the others. Push yourself as hard as you can and always remember that I will be right beside you to help you if you fall.

About the Author

Samantha lives in the southwest with her husband and two small children after abandoning her childhood dream of living in a cabin in Colorado when she found that she couldn't afford to live there and was deathly allergic to the woods. When she's not writing she's usually spouting off sarcastic remarks while drinking wine out of a coffee mug to look like a functional adult while chasing down her toddlers. She enjoys spending time with her family, watching reruns of FRIENDS, and the 24/7 flow of coffee that can be found in her veins. Be sure to follow her on social media for updates on what she's working on.

You can find her here:

Facebook: https://www.facebook.com/AuthorSamanthaBaca

Instagram: https://instagram.com/author_samantha_baca

Goodreads: http://www.goodreads.com/authorsamanthabaca

Facebook Reader Group:
https://www.facebook.com/groups/2945710968775398/

Webpage: https://authorsamanthabaca.wordpress.com

Newsletter: http://eepurl.com/g0NcSj

Other Books By Samantha Baca

The Haven Brook Series (Romantic Suspense)

'Til Death Do Us Part (Haven Brook Book 1)
https://books2read.com/u/m2RJNR

The Cradle Will Fall (Haven Brook Book 2)
https://books2read.com/u/b6O0QE

The Ties That Bind (Haven Brook Book 3)
https://books2read.com/u/mqgoz8

A Very Haven Christmas (Haven Brook Book 4- Novella)
https://books2read.com/u/mvqGjj

Three Strikes, You're Gone (Haven Brook Book 5)
https://books2read.com/u/mvqL2z

The Dark Shadows Series (Romantic Suspense)

Five Steps Ahead (Dark Shadows Book 1)
https://books2read.com/u/38Q0gO

Ten Seconds Too Late (Dark Shadows Book 2)
https://books2read.com/u/3JRgVB

Against The Clock (Dark Shadows Book 3)
https://books2read.com/u/m2YwoR

<u>The Stone Creek Series (Small Town)</u>
Chocolate Covered Mistletoe (Stone Creek Book 1)
https://books2read.com/u/3LRk9N

Candy Coated Promises (Stone Creek Book 2)
https://books2read.com/u/mldP5Y

Pumpkin Spiced Possibilities (Stone Creek Book 3)
https://books2read.com/u/bojdwV

<u>Standalone Books</u>
One Last Wish
https://books2read.com/u/mqg7D9

Finding Love In Apartment 2C (Novella)
https://books2read.com/u/bze9aZ

Cocky Counsel: A Hero Club Novel
https://books2read.com/u/31Kzkn

<u>Holiday Books</u>
Snow Place To Go
https://books2read.com/u/4A560N

A Christmas Wish
https://books2read.com/u/4EKXpE

359

FIVE STEPS AHEAD